LOVE ME,
LOVE ME NOT

S M KOZ

LOVE ME,
LOVE ME NOT

Swoon
READS

SWOON READS NEW YORK

A Swoon Reads Book

An imprint of Feiwel and Friends and Macmillan Publishing Group, LLC

LOVE ME, LOVE ME NOT. Copyright © 2018 by Shannon Kozlowicz.
All rights reserved. Printed in the United States of America. For information,
address Swoon Reads, 175 Fifth Avenue, New York, N.Y. 10010.

Our books may be purchased in bulk for promotional, educational,
or business use. Please contact your local bookseller or the Macmillan
Corporate and Premium Sales Department at (800) 221-7945 ext. 5442
or by e-mail at MacmillanSpecialMarkets@macmillan.com.

Library of Congress Cataloging-in-Publication Data is available.
ISBN 978-1-250-13783-8 (hardcover) / ISBN 978-1-250-13782-1 (ebook)

Book design by Brad Mead

First edition, 2018

10 9 8 7 6 5 4 3 2 1

swoonreads.com

To all the foster kids I've met along the way—
each of you has taught me more than you can imagine,
inspired me to be a better person, and impressed
me with your unending strength to accept your past,
live your present, and create an awesome future.

CHAPTER 1

"YOU NEED TO BE QUIET," I WHISPER, STEADYING CHASE'S ELBOW while he clears the windowsill with his leg.

"Dammit, Hales, you're pinching me!"

"Sorry," I murmur, loosening my grip and helping him land his other leg on the worn carpet that still looks a hundred times better than the carpet I'm used to. The fact that I actually have my own room is another bonus. Of course, the biggest bonus of all is that unfamiliar tightness in my stomach, telling me I can't eat another bite, despite desperately wanting to.

"Not bad," Chase says, casing my new bedroom. "The TV's kind of old, but I could get a few bucks for it."

"You're not stealing from my new foster mom," I say. "I've been here less than three hours, and I already kind of like her."

"You liked the last one, too."

"And you ruined that for me."

"I didn't ruin nothing," he says, pulling a plastic bag out of his pocket. "I got us a half zip."

I frown at what the bag contains. It's not for us—it's for him. "You're not smoking that here."

"Shit, Hales, what's up your ass tonight?"

"I've spent the last three nights in three different houses!" First was my mom's, then Mr. and Mrs. Garner's, and now Ms. Jacobson's.

He rolls his eyes and then plops himself on the bed. Before I can join him, his shirt is off and his pants are unzipped, making it clear what we'll be doing if I don't let him get blazed. My eyes drift up from the plaid boxers peeking out between his fly to his long, bony arms, and then to his face. He's got a sharp brow and jawline and sunken cheeks. It's from not eating enough, and I know I'd look the same if I glanced in a mirror. I suddenly feel guilty for not sneaking anything from dinner for him.

"Come on," he says, shimmying out of his jeans.

I sit on the edge of the bed and allow him to wrap his arms around me. I'm exhausted, but it feels nice to be close to him. Sighing, I lay my head on his chest like usual, clinging to something familiar when everything else has been turned upside down.

After not even a minute, he lifts my skirt and slides down my underwear. Stifling a yawn, I slip my fingers under the waistband of his boxers and ease them over his hips. When they're only at his knees, he flips himself on top of me. I focus on the strip of light under my door. Ms. Jacobson made it clear I could not have boys in my room. I waited to call Chase on her phone until I was pretty sure she had fallen asleep, though. As long as we're quiet, I doubt she'll ever find out.

"I need this right now," Chase says, his eyes closed, his hands roaming under my shirt and up my body.

"Hmmm . . . ," I murmur, as I continue to focus on the light in the hallway.

Without warning, he rocks into me hard and the headboard slams against the wall. "Chase!" I yell in a whisper, ignoring the pain.

"Baby . . . ," he moans.

I mimic his moaning and try to move things along quickly, but he becomes unusually slow and gentle. I grip his rear end harder and urge him to speed things up.

"You want it rough?" he asks, pinning my arms to the mattress.

Without waiting for an answer, he picks up his intensity. Moments later, the headboard bangs again, and I know I need to end this immediately. "Now," I say.

"Almost . . ."

"Come on, baby. Now," I urge.

Just then, I hear a click and the strip of light becomes a flood. Chase, naked, is still on top of me with my skirt around my waist. Ms. Jacobson is in the doorway holding her hand to her mouth.

For a brief moment, no one moves. Then Ms. Jacobson turns around. I push Chase off me, throw him a blanket, and yank down my skirt.

"I'm sorry," I yell to her back. "I didn't mean to! I promise I won't do it again!"

"I'm calling DSS," she replies, causing my shoulders to slump. The Department of Social Services. Sherry's going to kill me. "When I get back, he needs to be gone."

Chase is already dressed and halfway out the window. "Call

me when you get settled at your new place," he says with a wink and a gleam in his eyes. For him, this was an exciting night.

For me, it was another mistake.

A huge mistake.

Moments later, I hear the roar of his recently borrowed motorcycle grow loud and then fade away as he leaves me alone to deal with the mess.

* * * *

"Hailey Marie Brown, what am I going to do with you?" Sherry asks, shaking her head. She's my social worker and was not at all happy about being woken up in the middle of the night to remove me from another foster home.

I stare at the dotted yellow lines in the road so I don't have to see any more disappointment on her face as we travel through rural North Carolina. I've known Sherry for a couple years but haven't had to deal with this look from her until the past two days. She gave me what I wanted—a place to stay far away from my mom—but it seems all I can do is mess things up.

"Chase is a negative relationship. You need to start building positive relationships," she says.

"He's all I have," I mumble.

"You have me."

"It's not the same." Chase made me feel loved when no one else did. He came into my life when I needed him the most. I mean, when the options are a screaming, drunk mom threatening to lock you out of her house or a guy who welcomes you into his home and can't get enough of you, the choice is pretty easy. Sure, he's not perfect, but who is?

We're quiet the rest of the way to DSS. In fact, she doesn't say anything until she's given me one of their prefilled hygiene packs, I've washed my face and brushed my teeth, and I've settled onto a sofa in the children's playroom. She's lying on another sofa in the same room with her eyes closed. I think she's asleep until she asks, "Are you still taking your birth control?"

"No," I reply, wishing I had remembered to grab it from the trailer when I left. It was just so hectic with Sherry there and my mom screaming at her and me trying to throw a few things into a backpack.

"Did he use a condom?"

"No," I say again, readying myself for a lecture. Instead, I'm met by more silence.

"You should go home," I say. "I'll be fine here by myself."

"That's not how it works."

"Won't Jared miss you?" Jared is her boyfriend. I've only met him once but liked him immediately. He's a second-grade teacher and adores Sherry. I could tell by the way he constantly touched her arm or guided her through a door with his hand at her back. I can't imagine Chase ever treating me like that. The closest I've ever gotten is when he put his arm around my shoulders during a pep rally at school. Of course, that could have been to keep himself steady since he was also trashed that day.

"Jared knows this comes with the territory," Sherry says, and then rolls over to face the back of the sofa. I take the hint and close my eyes, praying tomorrow will be a better day.

CHAPTER 2

WAY EARLIER THAN I WANT TO GET UP, I FEEL THE CUSHION beneath my butt dip, followed by the sound of papers shuffling. "The good news is I've found you a new home," Sherry says.

"Great," I reply without opening my eyes. If this is anything like the other two foster homes, I'll be out before the day is over thanks to Chase.

"The bad news is it's not in your current school district. You'll be living in Pinehurst."

"Wait. What?" I ask, bolting upright. I can't go to a different school. I'm a senior. I'm almost done. I know all my teachers. I even have a few friends. And Chase is nearby.

"Sorry, but there were no more options in your district. You know it's hard to find placements for older teens."

"I can't go to a different school."

"You have no choice."

"There has to be another option."

"No, there's not. And, to be honest, I'm happy you'll be starting off fresh somewhere new. I think you'll like the family, and the best part is it's far from Chase."

I narrow my eyes at her. She's happy about the one thing that scares me the most. What if the placement turns out to be awful and I need him?

Holding up her hand, she says, "You can glare at me all you want, but he's ruined two placements for you already, has left you to take the blame for stolen property, and may have impregnated you or given you an STD. Putting on a condom is not rocket science, you know."

I flop back on the couch and cover my eyes with my hand.

"Oh, no, you don't. It's time to get up," Sherry says, pulling on my arms until I'm on my feet. "We'll make a stop at the health department, and then I'll take you to school. You'll meet the Campbells this afternoon."

"You just took me to the health department a couple days ago," I complain. That was the first thing she did after rescuing me from my mom.

"And you had unprotected sex last night," she says before turning around and heading back out the door, making it clear I have no choice but to follow.

The morning turns out to be as awful as expected. In addition to making me pee on a stick, the doctor at the health department made me get another full exam. There has to be a better way of getting checked out than being prodded with cold metal tools like I'm a beat-up old truck and the doctor's my mechanic. At least my tune-up turned out fine.

After that, we headed to school, where I'm currently sitting in the office biting my nails as Sherry talks to the young, bored-looking woman behind the desk.

This school is bigger and nicer than what I'm used to, which only makes me more nervous. More kids to make fun of me.

"Thanks for all your help," Sherry says to the woman before turning around to face me. "You're all set. I'll pick you up after school right out front."

"Great," I mumble, still chewing on my thumbnail.

The woman approaches me from behind the desk. "I'll take you to your classes today to make sure you learn your way around here."

With a final wave, Sherry leaves, and I feel like I've been abandoned in a foreign country.

It's already the middle of third period, so thankfully, the pristine halls are empty. We pass a few display cases overflowing with trophies, which is also different from my school. We had a few trophies in the office but not enough to fill multiple cases, each one dedicated to its own sport. I don't like sports at all, but football and wrestling seem to be big here.

As we walk, the office assistant points out a few things, but I barely hear her. I'm trying to peek through the small windows of the classroom doors to get a glimpse of my new classmates. Pinecrest has the reputation of having a lot of rich kids, which means I'll stick out even more than usual.

"Here we are," the woman says, stopping at door 216. "Geometry with Mr. Picciano."

Of course I would have to start with geometry. My least favorite subject. At my old school, I had As or Bs in all subjects except math. With math, I was lucky to pass each semester.

She opens the door, and I take a deep breath as my eyes tingle with the threat of tears. I cannot cry. Not here, not now.

She walks toward the teacher, and I immediately head to the back of the room, staring at the floor and praying I can hold back the tears for just a while longer.

Even though I'm looking down, I can tell all the other students are watching me in the hand-me-down and two-sizes-too-big jeans and wrinkled T-shirt Sherry found for me at DSS this morning. It's going to be just as bad as I expected here. At my old school, everyone knew my story starting in the first grade, so I was able to blend into the background as we got older. Here, being the new kid, I'll stick out like a sore thumb. Everyone will stare and talk.

I finally make it to an empty desk and slide in. They're still staring. I've never had dreams of being head cheerleader or president of my class. My dream has always been to go unnoticed. I realize it's not much of a dream, but it works for me. At least it did at my old school.

"Everyone, please welcome Hailey. She's new," the teacher says.

I feel my cheeks heating up. Why couldn't he ignore me and go back to the problem on the board?

Although I can't see who's saying it because my eyes are plastered to the top of my desk, I hear a number of different voices murmuring hi. Then there's some shuffling noises, and the teacher starts talking about isosceles triangles.

The tingling behind my eyes is even worse now. I shift my eyes up to the ceiling, trying to stop the tears, but it's no use. A couple roll down my cheeks, and my hand darts up to wipe them away. Luckily, everyone seems to be focused back on the teacher.

I try to follow the lesson, but it's useless. On a good day, I'd have trouble with math. On a day like this, there's no chance.

When the bell rings, I lower my head, letting my long hair provide a curtain between me and everyone else as I slowly gather my belongings and hope no one will remember I'm in the class. It works, and I slip in behind the last student to leave.

"Ready for lunch?" the office assistant from earlier asks as I exit the room.

I can't handle lunch. I'm not about to sit at a table all by myself. I'd rather forget about food and hide in the library. It's not like I'm not used to being hungry anyway. It was rare for my mom to keep anything other than beer in our fridge.

"I'm not hungry," I say. "Where's the library?"

"You have to eat. Plus, I need to make sure your meal-plan information transferred over here correctly."

She tugs on my arm and leads me back down the hallway toward the cafeteria. This time, though, the hallway is packed with students. They're rowdy—yelling, laughing, and a few guys throwing mini footballs—but no one seems to be paying attention to me. Maybe I will eventually be able to blend in here. Maybe it won't be so bad.

"What would you like for lunch?" the office assistant asks when we get to the cafeteria. The line extends out the door and down the hallway, but she just slips through the door and past the entire line of students being handed hamburgers, soup, and grilled cheese.

"I told you I'm not hungry."

"You've got to eat something. How about some fruit and a sweet tea?"

I don't reply, but she reaches between the students anyway to fill a foam cup with tea and then plucks an apple from a bowl. I reluctantly accept them when she hands them to me. She then steers me toward the front of the cafeteria line, which earns a scowl from some of the students. At least it seems more directed at her than me.

"Enter your number," she tells me, pointing to a small machine like the one I'm used to from my old school.

I do, and the machine beeps.

The cafeteria worker standing there swivels the machine around and squints his eyes to read the display. "There's an error. Did your parents say anything about needing to add more money to your plan?"

I shake my head, keeping my eyes down.

"I was worried about that," the assistant says in a lowered voice, but still loud enough for the crowd of students to hear. I feel their stares at my back and want to crawl into a hole. So much for being able to blend in.

"She gets free state-subsidized lunches. We'll work with DSS to get that straightened out. Until then, let her get whatever she wants."

"All right," he says, nodding. "Does she get breakfast, too?"

Now everyone within earshot knows exactly how poor I am.

The assistant looks back at me. "Breakfast?" she asks.

"I—I don't know," I whisper. Will my foster family feed me breakfast before school? Will I get to school in time for breakfast? How will I even get to school?

"Well, it's yours if you want it."

I nod, and then the assistant disappears, leaving me alone in the middle of the crowd. I stand at the junction of the food line and the tables, looking back and forth. Most of the tables are packed with a mixture of guys and girls, laughing. There are a few tables in the back that are empty, so I decide to go that way. I hide behind my hair again, so no one can make eye contact with me, and begin the hike, trying to melt into the floor.

About halfway to the table, my eyes land on a pair of Nikes right in front of me. I glance up and find a large frame walking backward as he yells something to his friends and gestures wildly with his hands.

I jump to the right, trying to get out of his way, but I'm not fast enough. His elbow smashes my face. My nose, actually. The jolt causes me to drop my cup. It goes flying in the air, sending sweet tea everywhere—onto the floor, onto the guy's pants, onto my borrowed shirt—as I stumble.

"Oh shit, I'm so sorry," he says, grabbing my shoulder to steady me. "I didn't see you."

"It's okay," I say quietly, trying to step away from him.

"No, it's not. Let me grab some napkins for you."

"Really, it's fine," I say, pulling back.

He takes the hint and lets go of my shoulder, but doesn't stop talking. "You're bleeding."

I wipe under my nose and sure enough, my fingers are covered in blood. My day is just getting better and better.

"I'll take you to the nurse."

I shake my head. So much for my stealthy walk to the empty table. Everyone in the cafeteria is now staring at me as blood drips from my nose onto the gray tile floor.

"Seriously, you need a nurse. Here," the guy says, handing me a stack of napkins. "Let's go." He steps to the side and holds out his hand like he wants me to lead the way.

I push the napkins under my nose but shake my head again. "I'm sure it'll stop soon."

"What if it's broken? You need to get it looked at."

Who is this guy? Is he always so pushy? I glance at his face for the first time and find myself staring into the most intense blue eyes I've ever seen. And they seem legitimately worried.

"I can make it there on my own," I mumble, and start to walk toward the exit. Okay, I have no idea where the nurse is, but he doesn't need to know that.

He follows me to the door like the stray cats I used to feed at home. "What's your name?" he asks.

I pause, surprised he'd even care. "Hailey," I say, then quickly lower my gaze and dart out of the cafeteria in search of the nearest bathroom, hoping he'll finally leave me alone.

CHAPTER 3

THE REST OF THE DAY IS A BIT SMOOTHER. MY NOSE STOPPED
bleeding after a few minutes, and I was able to reach my classes
early and take a seat in the back. Most of the other students were so
busy talking to their friends they didn't even notice the new girl in
stained clothes.

Eventually, the final bell of the day rings, and I let out a deep
breath, one that it feels like I've been holding for hours. The first
day in my new school is over, and it wasn't as bad as it could have
been. Yes, there was geometry and the lunch incident, but no one
teased me or called me names. I guess I should be thankful for
that. It could've been much, much worse.

I'm wondering what the Campbells, my new foster family, will
be like when I reach the front of the building where Sherry is supposed to pick me up. Most of the students are either in the student
parking lot or sports fields. Only a few of us are waiting for rides,
which is a good thing because Sherry pulls up in her standard
government-issued white sedan with yellow license plate. I groan.

I might as well have a big, blinking neon sign over my head reading FREAK! FREAK! Even though there are only a few students nearby, I dash to the car, jump in quickly, and yell at Sherry to go.

"What's the rush?" she asks, looking out my window.

I slink down. "They're going to think I'm a juvenile delinquent or something."

"No one will think that."

"Can we just go? Please?"

"No, I need to pick up someone else first."

This gets my attention. There's someone else in foster care at this school?

"Who?" I ask.

"Brittany. And there she is now."

The back door opens, and a girl about my age slides in. That's where the similarities end, though. She's got a nice olive complexion compared with my pale skin. Her eyes are a bright green and narrow, unlike my big brown ones. And her brightly dyed red hair is cut in a sharp line along her jaw and looks nothing like my drab brown strands that hang limp along my forehead and back. Basically, she looks like a rock star while I look like a kid who woke up with no home and no family this morning.

"I'm Brittany," she says in a much too upbeat tone.

"Hailey," I murmur, turning around and then staring straight ahead.

"You new to the system?"

I nod.

"I've been doing the foster-care thing for ten years, so let me know if you need anything."

I hear the click of her seat belt, and then Sherry puts the car in drive while Brittany continues her chattering.

"Why isn't Joelle picking me up?" she asks.

"She was called out on a case and asked me to do it instead. I'll drop off Hailey first, and then take you to your doctor's appointment."

"Can you tell Joelle I have fantastic news?"

"Sure," Sherry says, pulling away from the curb. "Care to share that fantastic news with us?"

I feel my seat jerk backward as Brittany grabs onto it and shoots her head between the two front seats. "We did it! My band got second place in the countywide competition last weekend! It's the best we've ever done!"

I guess my first impression about her being a rock star was correct.

"That's wonderful!" Sherry exclaims, adding to the enthusiasm in the car. "Y'all need to perform at one of our foster-care parties. Joelle has been bragging about you forever, and it's time we all see this talent firsthand."

"Well, we are an award-winning band now. . . ."

Sherry glances in the mirror again. "Meaning you want to be paid for the gig?"

I turn my head to watch Brittany. She flashes a bright smile. "I'm just saying we're booking up fast. I'm not sure we'll be able to fit it in."

Sherry shakes her head. "We'll pay you in pizza and soda. All you can eat and drink."

"You've got yourself a deal!" Brittany yells, and sits back in her seat with a satisfied grin.

"You would've agreed without the soda," Sherry says, turning onto a residential street in a swanky neighborhood.

"I would've agreed without the pizza, too," she says with a smirk. "So, Hales, what grade are you in?"

The nickname makes me cringe. I hate it. Only Chase calls me *Hales*, and that's because I don't have the guts to tell him I don't like it.

"Twelfth," I say, staring straight ahead again. "Please don't call me Hales."

"Are you against nicknames in general or just that one?" she asks, completely unfazed.

"That one."

"How about Lee, then?"

"That's a boy's name."

"What's your last name?"

"Brown."

"Hmmm . . . I've got nothing with that." She pauses. "Whoa, you're lucky, Hailey. Looks like you won the foster-kid lottery."

I ignore her and concentrate on the road names. I need to make sure I get the address of where I'm staying, so I can tell Chase.

After three more turns, we pull into a long circular driveway lined with tall trees. In front of us stands a two-story brick house with four fancy columns. A couple of rocking chairs and miniature trees planted in giant urns sit on the front porch.

"Can I come in?" Brittany asks.

"Why?" Sherry responds as she parks the car in a spot off the gravel driveway.

"This may be my only chance to see a house this nice."

I glance back at Brittany, who's sitting on the edge of her seat, craning to look at the mansion with eyes as round as full moons.

"We have to be quick," Sherry says.

Brittany flings open the door and sprints toward the front steps. I wring my hands in my lap.

Sherry rests her fingers over mine, slowing their motion. "Let's meet your new family," she says with a smile, but the wrinkles around her eyes give her away. I'm sure she's worried she'll be making a trip out here later tonight to pick me up after I somehow mess up this placement, too.

"Hi there! Please come in," says a middle-aged woman, opening the front door while we're still on the walkway leading to the porch. She looks like she just came out of a bank. Her dark, silky hair falls to her shoulders, where it meets what must be a super-expensive suit.

"Nice to see you again, Sherry. And . . . which one of you is Hailey?" she asks.

Brittany points to me and then enters the house. She lets out a low whistle. "Whoa, nice digs. Is that a real Monet?"

"You like art?" Mrs. Campbell asks.

"Depends on what it is. That," she says, pointing into the other room, "I like."

"Well, sorry to disappoint you," Mrs. Campbell replies. "It's a Meier. She was inspired by Monet but never made it big. It's still my favorite piece, though. Come on in, and I can show you more."

I stand awkwardly in the foyer as Brittany follows Mrs. Campbell like a puppy. Sherry swipes her phone a couple of times and says, "Brittany, we're going to be late for your appointment."

"Just give me a minute," she hollers from the other room.

I wrap my arms around my waist and chew on my lip, unsure of what to do. I don't know anything about art, but maybe I should have followed Brittany. Instead, I'm standing here like an idiot with my thrift-store clothes in their fancy house.

I'm about to go back outside where it might not feel quite so awkward when Mrs. Campbell returns. "Hailey, please come in. I'd love to show you around."

I take a step forward but don't say anything.

"This is your home. Gil and I want you to feel comfortable here. Do you have any bags?" she asks, looking around me.

"No." All I have is my backpack with some school books, the hygiene pack from Sherry, and a month's worth of birth control.

"That's fine," Mrs. Campbell replies with a wave of her hand. "You're what . . . a size two?"

I nod.

"We have some things you can wear for a few days until we have a chance to go shopping. Would you like to see your room now?"

I nod again.

"Can you find Brittany and tell her it's time to go? We're going to be late for an appointment," Sherry says.

"I bet she's in my gallery," Mrs. Campbell replies. "I'll send her your way. Come on in, Hailey." She gently touches my shoulder.

We walk along a hallway, passing what looks like an office or library covered in dark wood paneling and furniture straight out of a different century. Next, we pass a dining room with a table that could fit my entire geometry class. Finally, we enter a large airy space with a vaulted ceiling and an inside balcony for the second story. The furniture here is tan and comfy-looking. At the back of the room is a wall of windows that frame a brick patio and pine trees as far as I can see. This room feels much more casual than other parts of the house. Through the railings of the balcony, I catch Brittany's back as she studies the artwork.

"Your room is upstairs," Mrs. Campbell says, leading me through a huge kitchen with shiny appliances and dark cabinets to a staircase.

When we reach the top, I see Brittany again. She's staring at a painting of a woman's face in bright colors.

"Warhol?" she asks.

"Yes. My grandfather collected art as well. He purchased this just as Warhol was starting to make a name for himself. When Granddad died fifteen years ago, he left it to me."

"Wow," Brittany says with wide eyes as she momentarily looks at Mrs. Campbell before focusing on the next one. I wouldn't call it a painting—it looks more like shiny metal twisted into strange patterns. Kind of like a sculpture, but it's hanging in panels on the wall.

"Who's this?"

"DeRubeis."

"I like it."

"I do, too. He created a new style all his own. He's still early in his career, so I'm excited to see where he goes."

Brittany continues her tour down the landing, stopping at another painting. "You've got, like, your own mini art museum here."

Mrs. Campbell laughs. "Well, I am an art dealer. This is my personal gallery, but I have another gallery in town with pieces for sale."

My stomach drops a little as I take it all in. What if I break something? What if I trip and spill something on her art?

"Do you have any Wylands?" Brittany asks.

"My son does."

The word *son* makes my head snap to Mrs. Campbell. In the other two foster homes, I was the only kid. It never dawned on me I might have to share the house with another.

"I'd show you, but Sherry is in a hurry."

"We can be quick. Please," Brittany begs, clasping her hands together in front of her chest.

"Okay, okay, let's go. Hailey, your room is the first door over there," she says, pointing to a hallway on the right. "We're going this way."

I look back and forth. I want to go to my room, but I also want to meet her son. How old is he? If he owns artwork, he can't be too young.

I decide to follow Brittany and Mrs. Campbell. I catch up with them just as Mrs. Campbell knocks on the door. "Brad, honey, can I come in for a second?"

A muffled reply comes from inside. "It's open."

When the door swings inward, I find two guys about my age sitting on beanbag chairs with their backs to us, staring at a huge television. They're frantically pushing buttons on handheld controllers as cars race around buildings in some video game.

"Brad Campbell," Brittany says matter-of-factly.

He turns his head to her voice and stares. It's those blue eyes. Those vibrant blue eyes from the cafeteria.

"Hailey." Apparently he also remembers me and what happened. "And Brittany. What are you doing here?" He doesn't sound mean, just confused, as he glances between her and his mom.

"Dropping off your new sister," Brittany replies. That term causes my face to heat up. I'm not his sister. I'll only be here until I turn eighteen. Seven more months. Or until they kick me out.

Brad's eyes move over to me, and he smiles, revealing a dimple in his right cheek. I lower my gaze to the floor.

"I'm Brad," he says. "And this is my friend Adam."

"Yo," the other guy says, continuing to play the video game.

"Hailey," I say quietly.

"And there's the Wyland," Brittany says, moving closer to Brad's bed. Above his headboard is a simple painting of a whale's tail. It's actually kind of pretty—much nicer than what was on the landing.

"I love it," she replies. "It's not his usual style. Much more subdued."

"Okay, let's not keep Sherry waiting any longer," Mrs. Campbell says, ushering Brittany back into the hallway. "Brad, can you show Hailey to her room while I say good-bye?"

He answers by stopping the game, which makes Adam complain. "Dude! I was kicking your ass!"

"Because I stopped playing. That's the only way you can kick my ass."

I glance to Mrs. Campbell to see how she reacts to the cursing. Based on her appearance and the immaculate house, I expect her to object, but she doesn't seem to care.

Brittany peeks back around the doorframe. "See you Monday, Hailey. Meet me in the cafeteria before first period."

My eyebrows inch up a bit at her offer. We barely know each other, yet she's being super nice. I have no idea why she's doing it, but I do appreciate it. Maybe school won't be so bad after all.

Once she's gone, Adam grabs his phone out of his pocket and starts tapping on the screen. "How's your nose feeling?" Brad asks.

"It's fine."

"It's not broken?"

I shake my head.

"I'm really sorry about that."

"It was nothing."

There's an awkward silence, and I pray he'll let it go.

Luckily, he does. "So, what grade are you in?" he asks, standing up. He runs his hand though his hair, causing his bangs to flop back on his forehead and hang over his eyes a bit.

"I'm a senior."

"Us, too. You're new to our school, right?"

I nod. "Started today."

"Where you from?"

"Union Pines."

"We killed you in football last week."

I nod again because I don't know what else to do. When he doesn't say anything, I add, "I don't really keep up with football."

"Well, you'll have to start now that you're part of this family. High school, college, professional—it's all we talk about in the fall. And I'm sure my parents will drag you to my games."

"You're on the team?"

"Yeah."

"He *is* the team," Adam chimes in. "He's the quarterback."

That means nothing to me, so I just nod again.

"Anyway, welcome to your new home," Brad says, holding out his hand.

I stare at it. Does he want me to shake it? Like we're making some kind of business deal?

I reach out and lightly lay my palm in his, letting it hang limply as he uses a strong grasp.

"Thanks," I say, biting my lip.

"Sorry," he says, apparently feeling as awkward as me, as he drops my hand. "I'm not really sure how this is supposed to work."

Adams stifles a laugh as he gathers books and shoves them into a backpack.

"How'd it work for all the other foster kids?" I ask.

"You're the first."

"Really?"

"Yeah, my parents just got licensed last month. I guess we'll figure it out together."

"I'm outta here," Adam says. "Nice to meet you, Hailey. See you around school."

Brad and I head back through Mrs. Campbell's gallery and to my room. It's huge compared with what I'm used to. The walls are painted beige and are empty except for a mirror and a corkboard. The bed has a plain white headboard and a striped white-and-navy-blue comforter. There's a silver floor lamp in the corner, next to a white desk with an alarm clock. It's pretty but seems like something you'd find in a magazine, not somewhere you'd actually live.

The tiny room I shared with my mom had a lot more stuff—walls covered with pictures I tore out of magazines of all the exotic places I knew I'd never visit, a bookshelf filled with my projects from art classes over the last eleven years, and a closet overflowing with her work clothes. Although I don't miss her, it would be nice if I had something from home with me. Even just one of my pictures would make this place feel more like somewhere I belonged.

"I think there are some clothes in the closet," Brad says. "My mom is a neat freak so they're probably organized by size." He opens the door and then says, "Make that gender and size."

I guess she planned ahead, not knowing who they'd be taking in. That also explains the furniture and bedding—it could easily work for a girl or a guy.

"Well, you probably want to get settled, right?"

I don't have anything to get settled, but it will be nice to have a little alone time after this very long day. "Yeah."

"Dinner's at five tonight since there's a game. Every other night it's seven. Don't be late. It's one of my dad's . . ." He pauses, which draws my eyes back to his face.

"What?" I ask.

"Sorry, he's your dad, too. It's one of Dad's pet peeves."

"It's okay. He's not my dad. She's not my mom. They're your parents." I would never expect random strangers to call me their daughter. And I'm sure they wouldn't want me to call them Mom and Dad.

He shakes his head and waves me off as he steps back into the hallway. "I'm happy to share," he yells over his shoulder.

I lower myself to the bed and take a deep breath. It's been a crazy day. A crazy three days, actually. I should call Chase and tell him I'm at my new place. I look around the room but don't see a phone. I could go searching for one, but I don't want them to think I'm snooping around. They might assume I'm casing the joint or something and then have a reason to kick me out.

I can't move again.

The last three days have been an exhausting ride. One I'd love to jump off of, but I can't. The doors are locked tight with both Sherry and Chase grinning at me through the window. Of course, Sherry's grin is because she's trying to make things better. Chase . . . not so much.

I sigh as realization sets in. I probably shouldn't call Chase. Not yet. Maybe once I get settled, we can meet someplace away from the Campbells' house so he can't mess anything up.

I nibble on my nail and look out the window at the quiet street below. He's the last tie to my past. Am I really ready to say good-bye to him for a while? I don't feel ready. Of course that gnawing in my gut makes it clear I don't want to be kicked out of another place, either.

Maybe, sometimes, you have no choice but to do things before you're ready.

CHAPTER 4

AT PRECISELY ONE MINUTE TO FIVE, I HEAD DOWNSTAIRS TO the dining room, starving because I skipped lunch. I can't imagine what dinner will be like with four of us around that huge table. Maybe Brad's football skills will come in handy when his mom asks for a roll. He can chuck it from one end to the other.

When I enter the room, I'm surprised to find it empty. Just then, Brad comes tearing around the corner. He slams on the brakes when he sees me in the doorway.

"Dinner's in the kitchen. We only use this room for holidays and parties."

I nod and follow him to a table in a corner of the kitchen. His mom and dad are already sitting down with bowls of different food spread over the tabletop. My mouth starts watering at the sight and smell of everything, and then I start wondering how they could possibly eat this much. It'd take my mom and me a week. Maybe two.

"You must be Hailey," Mr. Campbell says, standing. He looks

like an older version of Brad, with the same sharp jaw and mostly the same hair color, but with a little gray peeking through. He's also got a dimple on his right cheek, just like his son. Unlike Brad, he wears black-rimmed glasses. They make him look distinguished, and I wonder what he does for a living.

"Sit down, please," he says, gesturing to the chair across from him.

"It's nice to meet you," Mr. Campbell continues. "Would you like chicken?" he asks, passing a bowl to me. I accept it and take a piece for myself before handing it to Brad, who piles three pieces on his plate.

"So," Mrs. Campbell says, "do you like being called Hailey? Or do you have a nickname you prefer?"

"Hailey, please."

She nods. "And what would you like to call us?" she asks.

"Umm . . . I don't know. What are my options?" Neither of my other foster homes gave me a choice. It was Mr. and Mrs. Garner and Ms. Jacobson.

"Mom and Dad. Mr. and Mrs. Campbell. Ms. Gigi and Mr. Gil. Aunt Gigi and Uncle Gil. Gigi and Gil. Whatever you feel comfortable with."

"Pain-in-the-ass number one and pain-in-the-ass number two?" Brad suggests. At first, I think he's serious, but then he shoots a smile at his parents, who shake their heads in return.

I think about my options. Mom and Dad would be weird. I already have a mom, even if she doesn't deserve the title. And no one, not even my mom, knows who my dad is. I used to dream about a guy showing up on our doorstep, telling me he was my dad, and sweeping me up and away from everything, but that never happened. It never does in the real world.

Calling them Mr. and Mrs. Campbell seems very stuffy, like I'm in school. It's fancy, like their house. It's going to be hard to feel at home here if we're that formal with one another.

"Maybe Gigi and Gil for now?" I say.

"That's fine."

"Not nearly as much fun as my option," Brad says, spearing a piece of broccoli with his fork.

Ignoring him, Gil says, "Now that that's settled, we have to deal with the . . . uncomfortable part of a new placement—the ground rules."

"Ground rules?"

"Just to make sure we all understand one another. They're the rules we set for Brad, and we'll also expect you to follow them while living with us."

I nod and accept a bowl of mashed potatoes from Brad.

"Rule number one: If you ever have a boy in your bedroom, you need to keep your door open." He pauses for a moment. "Actually, this rule should be modified a bit. Whenever you have a friend in your room, please keep the door open. That goes for both of you from now on."

Brad rolls his eyes. "Yes, because Adam and I are going to go at it with the door closed."

"The rules apply to both our children," Gigi says.

Brad shakes his head and turns to me. "This is their way of covering their bases because they don't know which way you lean romantically."

I cough as chicken gets stuck in my throat. I look at his parents, who wave off his comment. "We don't care either way," Gil says.

"We just want to keep you safe," Gigi adds. "That means no sex."

"Got it," I mutter, staring at my plate. Their rule is no different than in my other foster homes, but hearing them say it makes my stomach drop anyway. Even if I decide to stay away from Chase, that doesn't mean he'll decide to stay away from me.

"So, which way do you lean?" Brad asks.

"Bradley Nolan!" Gigi exclaims.

"Dude, she's my sister now. I should know these things."

"I have a boyfriend," I mutter.

"That's wonderful," Gigi says.

"Let me know if I ever need to kick his ass." Brad shovels seconds onto his plate. I can't believe he stays so fit with how much he's eating. It's easily three times the size of my meal, which explains why they make so much food for dinner.

"Rule number two: No drugs or alcohol," Gil says. "But if you ever are intoxicated, please call us to pick you up. Never get into a car with someone under the influence. We'll pick you up, no questions asked."

"It's true," Brad adds. "But then you'll feel like a complete failure the next day because you screwed up big-time and they won't even yell at you. They'll just look at you with disappointment as though you aren't disappointed enough in yourself. It sucks. Just don't do it."

"Sounds like you have personal experience with this," I point out, starting to enjoy his commentary.

"A little."

Gigi ignores our side conversation and says, "Rule number three: No stealing. If you need money for something, let us know. We're happy to work out a chore and allowance schedule or help you get a job, if you'd like to do that. We'll cover all your food, toiletries, and school expenses, including any clubs or sports you'd like to join. DSS will give you a small stipend for clothes twice a year, and we'll supplement that as needed. Other things like music or entertainment are on you."

I look to Brad, expecting his expert advice, but he's silent as he chugs a glass of milk, which makes me think this might be a rule that only applies to me. I can't blame them really; they don't know me. I obviously have no money. Of course they'd assume I'd steal from them.

I nod and slump against my chair, having lost my appetite. They've seemed like such great people, and I honestly thought they saw me differently, but it's clear that's not true.

"You okay?" Gil asks.

I nod again.

"Last rule," Gigi says. "We know we won't always see eye to eye on things, but we want you to feel comfortable coming to us when something's bothering you. We won't judge you. We want to help."

Won't judge me? It seems like they already did with rule number three. I don't want to get into that with them, so I just say, "Okay."

"Dinnertime's not an official rule?" Brad asks, looking at his dad.

"You're right! Rule number five: Dinner at five on game nights and at seven all other days. It's my favorite time of day. Don't be late."

"If you are, you'll face the wrath of Dad," Brad says.

I smile politely.

"You don't want to know what the wrath of Dad entails?" he asks. "I'll tell you anyway. If you're late, he'll force you to watch his god-awful Westerns from the fifties. It's so painful. They are horrible, horrible movies."

"Those are high-quality films!" Gil says, sounding hurt. "Much better than the CGI crap you call movies these days."

"High quality? They're in black and white and have no special effects!"

"Because the point of the movie is the plot. You don't need explosions if you have an actual plot."

"Sometimes I don't understand how I could be your son," Brad says, shaking his head and pushing his empty plate away from himself. "May I be excused? I need to finish some homework before the game."

"Yes, dear," Gigi says. "Are you finished, Hailey?"

I nod, and then Gigi takes my plate from me.

"I can wash the dishes," I quietly offer.

"Are you sure?"

I nod and clear the rest of the table.

"Okay, would you like this to be your chore?" Gigi asks.

"Um, sure. I usually did this at home."

"Perfect. How does forty dollars a week allowance sound?"

"For washing dishes?"

"And putting them away."

Forty dollars might as well be a thousand. I've never had an income, since I never had a car to get me to a job. And, despite doing all the housework, my mom never once gave me an allowance. Why would she want to waste her precious few dollars on her daughter when there was crack to buy?

"You don't have to pay me," I say, piling dishes in the sink. "I'm happy to do it since you're letting me stay here."

"Don't be silly. Brad gets an allowance for doing our landscaping; you should get one for whatever chore you choose. Dishes work for me, if that's what you want."

"Brad does chores?"

"Of course."

"And gets an allowance?"

"Yes, why?"

"I thought rule number three only applied to me."

Gigi steps next to me and wraps her arm around my shoulders. "Oh, honey, no. Like I said, the rules are for both of you. I'm sorry we weren't clear."

"It's okay," I say quietly as that heavy rock in the pit of my stomach disappears into thin air. It's a relief to know my initial impression of them being wonderful hasn't been ruined just yet.

I glance around the sink, eager to tackle the dishes now that I'm feeling better about the Campbells. I look for what I need, but there's nothing here. "Um . . . how do you want me to do this?" I ask. You'd think washing dishes would be the same no matter where you are, but I always kept the dish soap on the back right corner of the sink and the sponge on the left. I can't find either here.

Gigi opens a cabinet under the sink, revealing a bunch of things, including a green-and-yellow sponge. She points to a lever next to the faucet and says, "Soap." Stepping behind me, she points next to my legs and adds, "Dishwasher."

"Okay, great," I reply. I open the door of the dishwasher and stare inside. I've never used one of these. Am I going to look like a complete idiot if I admit that? I close the door and search for a button to turn it on, but can't find one. I pull the door back down and scan inside again, but it's not there, either.

"Um . . . can you show me how to work this?" I ask. They're going to think I'm from the backwoods.

"Oh, sure. Just load it up however you want. We each have our own way, and everyone thinks their way is best," she says with a grin. "You do what works for you." She then goes on to show me how to add the soap and turn it on.

"Do I need to wash stuff before I put it in?"

"Just give them a rinse. The dishwasher can take care of the rest."

I follow her instructions and start lining plates in the bottom right, bowls on the bottom left, and glasses on the top. I have no idea what I'm doing, but hopefully it doesn't show.

"Hailey, are you coming to the game with us?" Gil asks, looking up from his phone.

"Um . . . ," I say, buying myself a little time. I've never seen a football game. I don't even know how the game works. The bigger issue, though, is being around all those students and parents at the game. I glance down at my droopy outfit and stained shirt.

"Come on, it'll be fun," Gigi says, spooning leftovers into a plastic container. "You saw the clothes in your closet, right?"

I nod.

"I think there's a Pinecrest Patriots T-shirt in there you can wear. And some jeans. You'll fit right in."

How did she know what I was thinking?

"You load it like Brad," Gil says, nodding toward the dishwasher. "I've got to have the bowls up top so I can turn them completely over. I hate when they still have water in them afterward."

"Oh, I can move them," I tell him, starting to rearrange.

"Leave her alone," Gigi says, swatting him with a towel. "The way you're doing it is fine. You can fit more dishes in this way."

"So," Gil says, "are you coming to the game?"

"Um . . . I guess so," I answer, when all I want to do is go to bed early and sleep for twelve hours. I don't feel like that's an option, though. They're all going, and I can't really stay here alone on my first night. Besides, I'd be a little freaked out in this huge house by myself.

"Great! We'll leave in about twenty minutes," Gil responds.

I nod.

At least if I'm not here, Chase can't get me kicked out. Maybe I'll finally spend an entire night in a foster home.

CHAPTER 5

I'M SITTING IN THE STANDS, WATCHING THE TEAM RUN UP AND down the field. I can't really follow the game or the rules, but I do know we want a touchdown. Or, another touchdown, that is. It's twenty-one to seven with the Patriots in the lead. Luckily, it's easy to know when to cheer or groan with hundreds of eager fans around you.

I shove my hands into my pockets and try to ignore the smell of popcorn coming from the guy in front of me, but it's nearly impossible. My mouth waters every time the wind blows and sends another buttery whiff my way.

"Do you want something to eat or drink?" Gigi asks, nudging my shoulder. She must have noticed me staring.

"No, thanks," I say, focusing back on the game. I'd love some popcorn, but I don't have any money and it doesn't feel right to use theirs, especially when I barely know them.

"Are you sure?"

"Here's twenty bucks," Gil says, reaching into his pocket. "Go raid the snack bar."

"I can't take your money," I reply, pushing his hand back as my stomach growls and makes me question my decision.

"It's for food. We told you we'd cover all your food expenses." He hands the bill back to me.

"That's for meals. Not snacks at a football game."

"Food is food in my book, but if it makes you feel better, you can grab me a Coke while you're down there. Then anything you get for yourself is payment for doing me a favor."

Just then, something happens on the field and everyone starts cheering. Gil shoves the bill into my hand and then jumps up, pumping his fists overhead and cheering. Gigi joins him as I stare at the money. I guess I could at least get him a Coke.

"Do you want anything?" I yell at Gigi to be heard over the roar of the crowd.

"I'll take a water. And do you want to share a popcorn? I'd like one, but I can't eat an entire box."

"Oh, um, sure. I guess so," I reply, drawing my eyebrows together. They totally just tricked me into spending their money on snacks at a football game.

"Get yourself a drink, too!" she yells as I start to make my way down the stands.

With everyone excited about the current play, it's difficult to move as fans jump around and constantly bump into me. Finally, I'm at ground level and have an open path with everyone crowded around the fence.

The bright lights and smells coming from the snack bar summon me, and I'm glad I agreed to share with Gigi.

"Hales?"

I turn toward the voice and find the last person on earth I want to see tonight.

"It *is* you. I've been waiting all day for your call. Where the hell you been? What are you wearing?"

"Chase." All the good things that have happened today suddenly seem like a dream. That's not my life. Chase, with all his drama, is my life. Somehow, he'll make the Campbells kick me out before the night is over, and I'll be right back where I belong.

"What are you doing here?" I ask, moving forward to keep my place in the line.

"My brother's dating a girl from Northern Moore. Told me we could score some Molly here."

Drugs. Of course.

"You a Pinecrest girl now?"

I tug on my T-shirt, wishing I could hide the logo plastered to the front of it. "It was the only placement Sherry could find for me."

"We gotta change that. Come with me tonight," he says, grabbing my hand and trying to tug me out of line. "No one will find you."

"Sherry knows where you live," I reply, holding my spot.

"We'll stay with Axel."

Axel is his best friend and supplier. There's no way I'd ever stay at his house.

"I can't, Chase. I'm sorry."

"What you mean, you can't?"

"I can't. I need to go to school and graduate. I can't hide away in Axel's apartment."

He narrows his eyes at me. "What kind of lies these people been feeding you?"

I ignore him, so he continues, "You think you gonna go to college? Get some ritzy job? Ain't never gonna happen. You'll end up just like your momma."

I feel the sting of tears and have to look away from him.

He tries to pull me out of line again, but I yank my arm away. "Please, leave alone."

"Never gonna happen," he repeats, but I don't know if he's talking about my future or leaving me alone.

The person in front of me steps aside, and it's time to place my order. When I pull out the twenty, Chase's eyes grow wide. "Add a pretzel and a Three Musketeers to that."

"No," I say, shaking my head. "This isn't my money, Chase."

"Who cares?"

The price of a pretzel is about the same as the Coke I ordered for myself, so I ask the cashier to swap that out. When she hands me the drinks and food, I pass Chase his pretzel. The cashier tries to give me my change, but Chase grabs the money for himself.

"Chase, I really need that."

"Doesn't look like it. You've got nice clothes and plenty of food."

"Please," I beg. Gigi and Gil are going to think I stole from them and kick me out. The tears finally begin rolling down my cheeks. "Don't ruin this for me. I need that money back. It's not mine. I have to return it."

"Is there a problem here?"

The deep voice sounds familiar. I turn to find Brad's friend Adam coming toward us.

"No, no problem," I reply, wiping away the tears.

"Are you sure?"

"She said there ain't a problem," Chase says, puffing out his chest.

Adam nods and then licks his lips, as if he's thinking about his next move. Without warning, he says, "Hailey, I want you to meet my sister. Come on." He puts his hand around my back and turns me away from Chase. I start to move, but then worry about the money again. I can't show up empty-handed.

I stop and look into Adam's eyes. "He took Gil and Gigi's money," I say. "I have to get it back."

"How much?"

"Ten bucks."

He reaches into his pocket and then hands me a ten.

"I can't take your money."

"Think of it as a loan. Pay me back whenever you can."

I glance over my shoulder at Chase, whose eyes are shooting daggers at us. There's no way I'm getting the money from him, so this is my only option. "Thank you," I whisper.

He shrugs off my comment. "If you're Brad's sister, then you're practically my sister. I'll look out for you when he can't."

That one little sentence is like a lightning bolt, striking the ground and forming a big old chasm that separates my past from my present. People I met only hours ago are looking out for me, while my boyfriend of a couple years and someone I've known practically my whole life is trying to get me into trouble. Again. My shoulders slump with that realization. I'm glad Adam did what he did, but it sucks that Chase was . . . being Chase.

I sigh and steal one last look at him. The face I used to find welcoming is downright hostile, and I'm torn. I'd be furious if he walked away with another girl, but this is different. This is about my placement. Shouldn't he know that? Shouldn't he want to help me? Isn't that what a boyfriend is supposed to do?

Yes, yes, and yes.

I clench my jaw as the disappointment turns to anger. I want to kick something—Chase, myself—but I know it won't do any good.

"My sister is over this way," Adam says, pointing to the right.

"Actually," I say, shaking my head to clear thoughts of Chase, "I should probably get Gil and Gigi their snacks."

"Sure thing. How about we find you after the game?"

"Oh, okay. Thanks again for helping me out."

"No problem."

I make my way back to Gil and Gigi and then hand them their snacks and Gil his money. He pockets it without even looking.

"Didn't you get anything for yourself?" he asks.

"Gigi and I are sharing the popcorn," I say.

"Good," he replies, and then focuses back on the game.

I try to pay attention, but I can't stop thinking about Chase and how angry I am with him. He almost ruined my third placement in three days. If Adam hadn't shown up, he would've.

It's almost like he's doing it on purpose.

Crap.

I sigh when I realize the problem. He saved me from my mom a million times, and now he's trying to save me from DSS and my foster homes. It's sweet in a Chase sort of way.

The only problem is I kind of want to see what a normal family is like. Once I explain that to Chase, he'll back off, especially if I promise him we can meet up somewhere after I get settled.

Feeling like I have a plan, I'm able to enjoy the rest of the game. The Patriots end up winning thirty to seven. True to his word, Adam joins us with a girl who looks a lot like him with dark skin and hair, although hers is pulled into twists with a tie low on her neck. He's also got a pretty blond girl with him.

"This is my sister, Abbie, and her best friend, Michelle," Adam says.

"Nice to meet you," I reply. "I'm Hailey."

"You're in my geometry class," Abbie says. "God, I hate that subject."

"Me, too," I agree, smiling.

"You're a senior?" Michelle asks.

I nod.

"And in geometry?"

I nod again, but more slowly this time. I don't like where she's going with her comment.

Confirming my thoughts, she says, "That class is usually for freshmen, like Abbie."

"That's not true," Adam replies. "There are plenty of upperclassmen in there."

"But it doesn't look good on your college applications," Michelle says, tipping her head as though she's letting me in on a big secret.

I remain silent as her words tear open the earlier wound from

Chase. As much as I'd love to go to college, I'm sure Chase was right. There's very little chance of that ever happening, so it really doesn't matter what my nonexistent application looks like.

"Anyway," Abbie says, breaking the tension, "Adam mentioned you're living with the Campbells now."

I nod again.

"Looks like I'm your new next-door neighbor, then," Michelle says with a fake smile. I'm sure the smile I give her in return looks just as fake.

"We all live in the same neighborhood," Abbie says, "but the Campbells' house is the nicest, so we spend a lot of time there. It will be fun having someone new around. It's kind of boring with just the four of us."

"Great," I say to be polite. Adam and Abbie seem nice, but I'd prefer to spend as little time as possible with Michelle.

"We've got to get going if you want ice cream before your curfew," Adam says to Abbie.

"Want to come with us?" Abbie asks me. "My brother can drop you off afterward."

"Sorry, I can't," I reply. In addition to having no money, I don't want to deal with Michelle's evil glare, which has been on me nonstop since we met.

"Okay, next time, then. Tomorrow is movie night at Brad's house. We'll see you then!"

"Ready?" Gil asks after they leave.

"What about Brad?"

"Coach is very long-winded. By the time Brad showers and the team has their postgame review, we'll all be home and in bed."

I'm glad we don't have to wait. I'm exhausted and ready to fall into a coma so I can forget about everything for a little while.

I follow Gigi and Gil out but stop suddenly at the gate when my eyes land on a familiar figure lurking in the shadows under the bleachers.

Chase.

CHAPTER 6

I PAUSE, THINKING ABOUT WHAT TO DO. I WANT TO ASK HIM TO back off for a while, but not with Gigi and Gil here. I have no idea what he'd say to them. Can I just ignore him, though?

I'm still undecided when Gigi and Gil go through the gate. Gigi turns around and asks, "Are you coming, Hailey?"

"Yes," I finally say, taking long strides toward her. I'll just pretend I didn't see him. I do sneak one last peek, but he hasn't moved. It looks like he has no intention of talking to me or the Campbells, either. I let out a relieved sigh. I'll call him tomorrow and explain everything so he won't mess up this placement for me. There's no way I could handle moving to another home and another school and having to go through all this again.

We return to the house, and I fall into a deep sleep within moments of climbing into bed. I'm used to sleeping on a sofa, not a queen-size bed that makes me feel like I'm floating on clouds. It's weird how you never know what you're missing until you get it. I had plenty of complaints at home, but my sleeping situation never made the list. Now I realize it should have.

I wake up feeling rested and . . . optimistic. It's the first placement where I've made it through the night without getting kicked out. Yesterday was tough, especially seeing Chase, but I feel like I might actually be able to make this work. When I roll over and look at the clock, I have to blink my eyes a couple of times to make sure I'm reading the time correctly. How can it already be eleven? I don't want everyone to think I'm super lazy. They've probably been up since the crack of dawn. I need to seem like I fit in.

I jump up, find a Patriots sweatshirt to throw over my tank top, and step into the hallway. Glancing past the gallery, I see that Brad's door is closed. Maybe I was wrong. Maybe he's a late sleeper, too.

Tiptoeing downstairs, I find every room I pass empty. When I get to the kitchen, there's a note from Gigi and Gil on the counter saying they had to run some errands and Brad is working out. So I was right about all of them waking up at the crack of dawn.

They also tell me I should help myself to breakfast. I'm sure they weren't expecting me to wake up closer to lunchtime.

I open the fridge door, but it feels strange, like I'm snooping, so I close it. I try another door, which turns out to be a pantry, but it's the same feeling. My fingers tap against the doorknob. I'm starving. I have to eat something. I open the pantry a slit and spot a box of granola bars in the front. My hand darts in, and I grab one in record time, as though my skin will go up in flames if I'm not fast enough.

Satisfied I have enough food for a few hours, I slip back into the living room. I suppose I could watch TV. The only problem is I don't see a television. I wander around the downstairs, trying not to feel too nosy, but don't find one anywhere.

I'm about to give up and go back to my bedroom when a thumping beat begins pounding through the walls and floor. I follow the sound to a mostly closed door and wonder if I should go through. I knock in case it's Gil and Gigi's bedroom, even though they're not here. When no one answers, I scoot my foot so the door opens a little wider. That reveals even louder music, now with lyrics, and stairs. They must lead to a basement.

As I go down the carpeted steps, the music grows louder. At the bottom, I find a wide room with a sofa in the shape of a horseshoe, a bunch of beanbag chairs, the most gigantic television I've ever seen, a pool table, and a Ping-Pong table. There's also a small kitchen in the back of the room. To my left is a hallway with two other rooms, one of which seems to be the source of the music.

I walk in that direction and peer in the open doorway. Standing in the middle of the room is a shirtless Brad with sweat beading up on his muscles.

Muscles that are much more noticeable today than yesterday.

He bobs his head in time with the music as he lifts weights, switching between his left arm and his right.

My eyes move up his back to his dark hair, which is soaking wet and curling around his ears. Opposite him is a mirror, which gives me a nice view of his striking eyes. I've never known anyone to have eyes that shade of blue before.

And they're intense. He's focused on what he's doing, his eyes following each movement. Sometimes his brow furrows and then moments later, it levels out as a hint of a smile appears. It's as if he's critiquing every little move he makes, even though they all seem the same to me.

Without warning, he drops the individual weights on the floor, grabs a long bar with weights attached to each end, holds it squarely on his shoulders, and then squats. Repeatedly. I feel my face redden as my eyes wander to his backside. I'm used to Chase's nonexistent butt, not Brad's well-defined, muscular one.

"Oh my God," I whisper, turning around and leaning against the wall. I cover my eyes with my hand. I have to get it together. Brad is my foster brother. Brother. I cannot be thinking about his butt. Or his eyes. Or his muscular arms.

This time, it might not be Chase getting me kicked out; I might do it all on my own.

"Hailey?"

No, no, no. Did he see me? I want to crawl into a hole and die. This is so embarrassing. I'm a guest in his home, and I was gawking at him during a workout.

"Hailey?" he says again.

I'm tempted to make a run for it, but as soon as I take a step, he appears in the doorway.

"Hey," he says. "You're up."

I feel the heat rising in my cheeks, and I can't imagine what he's thinking.

"I was looking for a TV," I reply lamely.

"Over there," he says, pointing to the television that's bigger than some cars.

"Right."

"Nice sweatshirt. It was mine from middle school."

My face gets even redder with that comment.

"Have you had breakfast?" he asks.

"Yes." I hold up my half-eaten granola bar as proof.

He frowns. "That's not breakfast. I'll be done in a few minutes, and then we can make lunch together. How's that sound?"

"Um . . . fine," I reply, hoping to end this conversation. I need to go dunk my face in a bowl of ice to get it back to its normal color.

"Want to keep me company while I finish up?"

Oh God. Then he'd really see me gawking at his body. I definitely can't do that. "I should probably shower. I'll meet you in the kitchen in a few minutes."

"Okay."

He strolls back to the weights, and I make a quick exit up the stairs.

Fifteen minutes later, I'm shampooed and buffed with the nicest soap and shampoo I've ever used, my skin no longer looks like a tomato, and I'm ready to face him again. I wander to the kitchen and find him at the counter with a variety of meats, cheeses, breads, and condiments laid out in front of him. He's got one sandwich on his plate and is working on a second.

He barely looks in my direction before saying, "Help yourself."

I take a piece of wheat bread, add a slice of American cheese and a couple pieces of turkey. He finishes making his second sandwich and then pushes the condiments my way. I shake my head as I flip the halves together.

"No mayo?"

"No."

"Mustard?"

"No."

"What do you want? We probably have it."

"Nothing, thanks."

"You eat sandwiches plain?"

"Yes."

"Why?"

"Why not?"

"It'll taste like shit."

He clearly has never had to struggle to find food if he thinks a plain sandwich is so bad. There have been more times than I care to remember when my only food for the day was a handful of mustard, ketchup, or mayo packets I had managed to snag from a fast-food restaurant. I'm not about to ruin this lunch with tastes that bring back the worst of the worst memories.

"So, what's your deal?" Brad asks, leaning against the counter. He bites off some of one sandwich and eyes me, waiting.

"I've got no deal," I reply. There's no way I'm getting into what landed me here. He wouldn't understand. He's got wonderful parents, loads of money, and great friends. A perfect life. Mine is the exact opposite.

"Everyone has a deal."

"What's your deal, then?"

"I'm a textbook only child. I'm spoiled rotten, a classic over-achiever, selfish, and have an insatiable need for instant gratifi-cation."

My jaw drops open. Literally drops open. Who thinks stuff like that? And who would share it with a stranger?

"Dad's a psychiatrist," he says with a shrug. "And I'll be one, too, someday."

He's acting all casual, but I don't buy it. "Your choice or his?"

Brad points his finger at me. "Ahh . . . you're pretty insightful yourself. So, are you an only child, too?"

I notice he fails to answer my question, which probably gives me the answer. I nibble on my lunch for a moment while deciding how I want to reply. After swallowing, I say, "Kind of. I've got a half sister, but I never see her."

"Same mom or dad?"

"Mom."

"Is she in foster care, too?"

"Not that I know of."

"How's that work?"

"It's hard to explain."

He wipes crumbs from his mouth and says, "I'm pretty smart. I bet I can keep up."

"She's been living with someone else since she was born."

"Who?"

I shrug.

"You don't know?"

"She was kind of adopted as a baby."

"That doesn't seem hard to explain. Adoptions happen all the time."

"I don't think it was totally legal."

"Oooh," he says, drawing out the word. He takes a drink of Gatorade. "Actually, I don't understand. Your mom gave her baby away to someone?"

I nod. I don't want to get into the specifics. Knowing my mom sold her baby will just make me seem like even more of a loser compared with him and his perfect life. I always hold out hope someone threatened her and that's why she did it.

"How long ago?"

"Ten years." That was when things really started to go down-hill. Until then, my mom was able to keep things mostly okay. Sure, we never had three-course meals, but we usually got at least two decent meals a day. That's also when she started using more regularly.

Brad stuffs the rest of his lunch into his mouth. After a couple minutes of silence, he swallows and asks, "What about your dad? What's his story?"

"No idea."

"Not part of your life?"

I push crumbs around my plate. "He was more of a temporary sperm donor."

"You're a test-tube baby?"

"What?" My head jerks up to see him studying me. "No," I say, "more like a casualty of my mom's revolving door of boyfriends."

"Oh shit," he replies.

I look away. "I don't need your pity."

"It's not pity. Anyone with half a heart . . . a quarter of a heart . . . hell, an eighth of a heart would feel bad."

"That's pity."

"Yeah, maybe it is," he agrees. Pushing against the counter, he hauls himself up and sits facing me. "Sorry, but come on. No kid should have to deal with that kind of shit."

"Okay, you can stop right there," I say, holding up my hand. "I'm fine. It's life. Some of us are dealt a good hand"—I motion around the room—"while others are dealt a crappy hand. Nothing I can do about it other than try to make the best of a bad situation."

"You're right. I'm sorry." He gathers both our plates and sets them in the sink. "Want to go to the mall today?"

"The mall?" I ask, surprised by his change of topic.

"Yeah. It's Mom's birthday next week, and I need to get her something."

"Um . . . okay. I guess so." It's not like I have anything else to do.

The squeak of a door interrupts us, followed by a thud and jingling of keys. Seconds later, Gigi and Gil enter the kitchen.

"All fixed," Gil says, tossing Brad the keys.

Brad snatches them out of the air. "Thanks."

"You're sure it didn't happen at the game?" Gil asks.

"Positive. I would have noticed, plus the rims would've been damaged if I had driven home like that."

Gil sighs. "You're right. I just don't like the idea of someone breaking into our garage and slashing your tires."

No. No, no, no, no.

My fists clench at my sides, and my nails dig into my palms. It couldn't be Chase. He wouldn't do that, would he?

Normally, I'd say no, but after the last few days . . . I wouldn't put it past him. How would he even get here, though? Did he follow us home last night?

"What happened?" I ask, hoping my voice doesn't reveal how nervous I am.

"It looks like someone got into our garage and specifically targeted Brad's car. The others were fine."

"Did they steal anything?" I ask.

"I don't think so," Gil says, then pauses. "Well, I don't know. We haven't checked."

"Shit," Brad says. "I left my iPad in there last night."

He runs out of the room, and Gil shakes his head. "Don't worry, Hailey. This is a safe neighborhood. Nothing like this has ever happened before."

Until I came along, I think. I always bring trouble with me. Should I tell them? Probably. Will they kick me out if I do? Yeah.

Maybe this was a onetime thing. Maybe he did this as a warning because I walked off with Adam. I should've talked to him last night. Told him I'd find a way to see him, just not here at their house.

"I need to make a call," I say urgently. "Do you have a phone I can use?"

CHAPTER 7

"HEY, CHASE. IT'S ME," I SAY WHEN HE ANSWERS. MY VOICE IS calm, but my eyes narrow at the person on the other end of the line. Messing with Brad's car is a new low for him; one that even I didn't expect.

"Yeah?"

"Did you follow me last night?"

"Maybe."

He did. I was hoping there was some other explanation for what happened, but I guess deep down I knew there wouldn't be. I curl and uncurl my fist, trying to keep my voice even. "You can't do that," I say.

"I can do whatever the hell I wanna do."

"Please," I beg, taking a different approach. "I appreciate what you're trying, but I don't want to get kicked out of here. I need this. I need a normal family for a while. If you can just leave me alone until I'm settled, I promise we can meet up again. I'll get to Carthage, or we can meet halfway. Please."

It's quiet for a moment and then he says, "You know who you belong to, right?"

My mouth drops at his words and then tears well up in my eyes. He's never asked me that before, but I've heard Mattie, my mom's boyfriend, say it to her plenty. I respond like she does every time, "You. I'm yours. Forever. You know that."

"Did you fuck him?"

"No," I say as the tears start rolling down my cheeks. *Does he mean Adam? Or did he see Brad last night?* I guess it doesn't really matter who he's jealous of. I just can't believe he'd honestly think I'd go around sleeping with random people. "I would never do that. I don't even like him that way."

"Good. If you lay a finger on him, I'll know. I'm watching you."

More tears fall onto my cheeks. "I know. I won't. I promise."

"You gonna call me?"

Wiping my face, I reply, "Yes, once I'm settled and things calm down, I'll call you a couple times a week."

"Make it every night, starting tonight."

Then, without so much as a good-bye, the line goes dead.

I put the phone back in my pocket and take a shaky breath.

It's Chase, the Chase I've known almost my entire life, but I'm 100 percent freaked out by him right now. This is a whole new level for him. What comes after a tire slashing? I have no clue, but I also don't want to find out.

I feel like I'm in one of the fun houses where you never know what's around the corner. One night it could be nothing, but the next night it could be a crazed Chase who jumps Brad in a dark alley. And I'll never know until it happens. Which means one thing . . .

Without warning, the flood gates open.

I have to call him every night. I have to truly convince him I'm his forever.

That's what it comes down to. I'm ready to be done with him and that part of my life, but I can't. I'm stuck. There's no way out.

I'm never going to escape my past. The Campbells and their house are a nice distraction, but that's all it is. Sooner or later, I'll be back where I belong, lying next to Chase in the trailer park where I'll need him again.

I should've known that from the beginning. I should have never been lured in by what the Campbells have. It's not mine, never has been, and never will be. I wipe my eyes one last time and shake my head at my ridiculous dreaming. Normal and family will never go together in my world.

When I open the door to Gil's office, hoping to escape to my room without seeing anyone, I run straight into Brad.

"Everything okay?" he asks.

"Yeah, sorry," I say, dropping my gaze.

"What are you sorry for?"

"Um . . . crying in front of you, I guess."

"You don't have to apologize for that."

"I don't usually cry like this."

Brad shrugs and then says, "So, the mall?"

I nod and reply, "Just let me change first."

A few minutes later, after any evidence of my tears has been washed down the drain, we meet in the garage. I'm wearing jeans and a button-down shirt I found in my closet. The only external reminder of my past is the holey sneakers on my feet. Internally, it's a completely different story after my call with Chase.

Brad opens the car door for me, which causes me to look at him out of the corner of my eye. Why would he do that? I've never had a guy do that for me before, and I'm not sure how I feel about him doing it.

"I was raised to be a Southern gentleman," he says, walking around to the other side. After joining me inside, he adds, "Mom would kill me if I didn't open doors for you."

"That's kind of . . ."

"Old-fashioned?" he asks, turning the key in the ignition.

"No."

"Chauvinistic?"

"No."

He opens the garage door and backs out. "Caveman-esque?"

"No, I was going to say sweet."

"Oh," he says, staring straight ahead with a small grin.

* * * *

"An art book?" I suggest.

"She has every art book ever published," Brad complains. We've been walking around the mall for an hour, and he doesn't seem to have a clue what to get his mom.

"Some canvases and paints?"

"She doesn't make art. She just buys it."

"What else does she like to do?"

"I don't know. . . ."

"She likes to watch you play football."

"Well, yeah, but that doesn't really help with a gift."

"You could get her a life-size poster of you in your uniform," I say with a half smile.

"Yeah, that wouldn't be weird at all," he says, rolling his eyes.

"Does she ever complain about going to games?"

"Not really." He pauses. "Actually, when it was really cold last year, she complained there weren't good enough gloves or enough coffee in the world to keep her hands from freezing."

"How about gloves, then?"

"She has gloves."

"Better gloves. Those obviously don't work."

"I guess we could see what they have. Let's go to Dick's."

After a couple of turns, we enter a mega sports store that carries everything from fishing poles to tents to soccer balls. As we walk through the aisles, I run my fingers along all the fabrics, stopping at a blue fleece on the clearance rack. It's the softest material I've ever felt. I bite my lip and reach down for the tag, glancing at it for only a second before letting it fall back in place. Five bucks. I don't know why I even looked. It's not like I have any money. My shoulders sag, and I continue down the aisle.

"You want this?" Brad asks to my back.

I turn around to see what he's talking about, but immediately blush when I realize he's holding the fleece.

"Have you gotten your clothing stipend yet?" he asks.

"No."

"This is a really good deal."

I shrug.

"You'll probably get the money soon."

Maybe, maybe not. One thing I've learned is not to count on anything. I shrug and continue down the aisle, running my hands over each item. I can appreciate them even if I'll never own any of them.

"This is the clearance rack," he says. "There's a good chance it won't be here when you come back."

"Then it wasn't meant to be," I say without facing him.

"Or I can pay for it now, and you can pay me back later."

"No," I reply, turning around to face him while shaking my head. I already owe Adam ten bucks. I'm not going even more into debt over a silly fleece when Gigi has a closet with plenty of clothes for me.

"I don't mind, really," he says.

"I do." I abruptly turn away from him.

He must take the hint because it's quiet behind me. I walk past a few more clothing racks and then something catches my eye. "Hey, look at this," I say. "It's a hand warmer. Maybe this is what your mom needs."

Brad joins me and picks up one of the small packages to study it. Then he also grabs a pair of gloves lying next to the display.

"Thanks. I think we're done here," he says.

A few minutes later, we're back in the mall. "Do you want to go to the ice cream place?" he asks, looking at the food court across the way from us.

"Sure," I reply. I'm not getting any, but I'll sit with him while he eats it.

"What do you want?" he asks when we're standing in front of the counter with countless flavors and toppings.

"Actually," I say, looking down at my shoes, "I'm not hungry."

He orders an extra-large hot fudge sundae and says, "Are you sure you don't want anything?"

I shake my head.

When we sit down, he asks, "You don't have some sort of eating disorder, do you?"

My eyes grow wide with his question. No one's ever asked me that before. I always figured people thought I was skinny because I didn't have a lot of food, not because I didn't want to eat it.

"No," I whisper, then study a family sitting at a table a few feet away.

"It's the money, right?" Brad asks.

I nod but still won't look at him.

"It's only a couple bucks, Hailey. It's really not a big deal."

"To you," I whisper, still focusing on the family. The little kid is now demanding to feed himself, which is leading to a huge mess. His face is covered in vanilla ice cream, and it drips from his chin onto the table below, forming a pool. I expect the parents to yell or take over, but they just sit there patiently while he proudly spoons ice cream into his mouth.

"Are you and your boyfriend serious?" Brad asks out of the blue.

His question breaks my focus on the little boy. Why is Brad interested in Chase? Does he know that's who slashed his tires?

I cautiously turn to face him. "Why do you want to know?"

"Just wondering."

"Do you have a girlfriend?" I ask.

"Nope. I haven't found the right person yet."

"Ever?"

"Nope."

"You've never had a girlfriend?"

"Nope."

"You've got to be kidding me," I say, staring at him in disbelief. "You're the star of the football team. You're . . ." My face heats up, stopping me before I say something stupid about how hot he is. "Your family is loaded; you're, like, the nicest person I've ever met; and you've never had a girlfriend?"

He swallows a bite of ice cream and gives me a huge smile, revealing his dimple. "Sorry to disappoint you."

"So, like, you've never . . ." I blush again and shake my head when I realize what an inappropriate question I was about to ask. "Never mind."

"What?"

"It's not important."

"Your red cheeks make me really want to hear the end of that sentence."

"It's kind of personal."

"I don't mind personal."

I think for a moment and then decide to go for something a little less inappropriate. "You're seventeen and have never . . . kissed a girl?"

"Eighteen," he replies with a smile. "And I didn't say *that*. It's a big jump from kissing on a date to having a girlfriend."

"Do you want a girlfriend?"

"Someday. Eventually. Is your boyfriend all you dreamed he'd be?"

"He's . . . okay." At least he used to be okay. He was never Mr. Romantic, but he made me feel important in his own way.

"That doesn't sound like a match made in heaven."

"Every couple has issues." And ours seem to be getting worse and worse.

"What are yours?"

"It's personal." There's no way I'm getting into me and Chase with Brad.

"Hey, I answered your personal question! I just told you all about my experience with girls."

"Kissing is all your experience?"

He shrugs and gives me another grin, which brings me right back to the original question I had for him. "You mean . . . ?"

"Spit it out, Hailey," he says with a smile, leaning back in his chair with his arms behind his head. "What do you want to know?"

I lean forward on my elbows, getting the best view of his face I've had since we met. He's got a faint scar under his left eye. It runs all the way to his nose and makes him look kind of rugged, like someone who could just as easily survive in the wilderness as in his fancy house.

"You're a . . . a . . . ?" I whisper, still not able to say the word.

"A football player? Yes."

"No, a . . ."

"Math nerd? Yes."

"No—wait, really? You're a math nerd?"

"Yes, why? Need help?"

"Maybe. With geometry."

"Okay. It's settled. Your foster brother is a math nerd who will tutor you."

I roll my eyes and cross my arms. "Don't make me say it."

"Why?"

"I don't have conversations like this, especially with guys I just met and whose houses I live in."

"Then you'll never know."

"We both know what I'm talking about. Yes or no?"

"I have no idea what you're talking about. Am I a cat person or a dog person?" He grins. "A little of both, actually."

I throw up my arms. Why is he being so difficult about this? "Fine," I huff. "I don't care."

"But you do," he says, pointing his spoon at me.

"I only care because you're a walking contradiction."

"What do you mean?" he asks, lowering his spoon and focusing on me.

"Rich, but generous. Smart, but popular. Friendly, but picky. Hot, but not a player."

"Did you just call me hot?" he asks, lowering his elbows on the table and leaning closer. His eyes twinkle, and his dimple has never been bigger as he smiles at me, clearly enjoying my momentarily lapse in judgment.

I roll my eyes. "That's what girls at school were saying, not me," I lie as my cheeks heat up yet again.

"You don't think I'm hot?"

"I've kind of had a lot on my mind lately. No time to really think about the hotness level of my foster brother," I say, trying to play it cool.

He grins again and says, "I'm not rich. My parents are."

"Same thing," I reply with a wave of my hand.

"So, you're not a virgin?" he asks, laying the word out there since I obviously can't.

My reaction is immediate. My already pink cheeks darken to crimson, and I lower my eyes to the tabletop, too embarrassed to even look at him.

"Your decision?" he asks.

"What?" I say, momentarily meeting his eyes before glancing down again. "Of course it was my decision. He's my boyfriend. I . . . love him."

"Really?"

"Yes, really," I say quietly, focusing back on the family, which is now mopping up the pool of ice cream on the table.

"Okay. Just remember, if I ever need to kick his ass, I'm happy to." I glance back to him. He's smiling, but his eyes are as intense as they were in the weight room this morning. It's almost like he wants me to ask him to do it.

Did Adam tell him what happened at the game? Does he know Chase is the one who slashed his tires? I have a feeling a meeting between the two of them would not end well, which is all the more reason to keep Chase happy.

CHAPTER 8

AFTER OUR TRIP TO THE MALL, I'M HAPPY TO HAVE A LITTLE time to myself. Brad is friendly and nice, but way too easy to talk to. My face turns to a tomato just sitting here thinking about the things I've told him. My mom. Chase. Sex. Groaning, I rest my head in my hands. What is wrong with me all of a sudden? Why can't I seem to keep my mouth shut around *him*?

Other than dinner, I've spent the last three hours in my room trying to outline a story for my creative-writing class and attempting geometry proofs, but my brain isn't cooperating. I'd rather obsess over Brad—both what he now knows of me and the surprising things I've learned about him. He's the star of the football team and probably one of the most popular guys at school, but has never had a girlfriend? Really? How is that possible?

"Hailey, everyone's here!" Brad's voice echoes through the hallway outside my door.

Right. Movie night with his friends.

I appreciate them including me, but spending a whole night

with Michelle judging me sounds about as fun as my visit to the health department yesterday morning. Luckily, Brad offered to invite Brittany, probably because he thinks we're close friends. Better that than the truth. At least now there's someone else new here to take the attention off me.

I leave the safety of my new room and catch a view of Brad's butt as he rushes down the stairs. I've been catching way too much of his backside today. First in the weight room and then at the mall, when he leaned over a rack trying to find a sweater for his mom. Not to mention when we got back and he decided to mow the lawn directly outside my window. Without his shirt. Again. The boy has a serious problem keeping his clothes on. And I have a serious problem ignoring him when he's not fully clothed.

I need to get a grip. Brad is off-limits for many reasons.

Maybe I can just secretly ogle him and hope, someday in the distant future when I'm finally free of Chase, I might find someone half as nice and cute. A girl can dream, at least.

When I get downstairs, Brittany engulfs me in a hug like we're best friends. It's unexpected, but it does make the glare I receive from Michelle sting a little less.

"Hey, Hailey," Abbie says from behind the edge of the refrigerator door. "Soda?"

"No, thanks. I'm good."

Brad is busy in the kitchen, microwaving popcorn. Michelle walks over to him and stands uncomfortably close while he tries to move between the cupboard and the microwave.

"Action or blood and guts?" Adam asks, holding up two movies.

"Action," Brittany, Abbie, and Brad say.

Michelle pouts. "I was going to vote blood and guts."

Adam says, "I vote action, so you're outnumbered. Better luck next time." He's smiling the whole time and says it in a friendly way, but Michelle still gives him a dirty look. At least I'm not the only one receiving those.

While Adam starts up the movie, we settle ourselves onto the ridiculously large sofa. Brittany and I take one end, with Abbie close by. Adam takes the middle and Brad sits next to him, stretching his legs out to the end. Michelle eyes all our positions and then squeezes herself between Brad and Adam, even though there is much more room other places.

"I like your shirt," Abbie says, passing the popcorn bowl to me.

"Oh, thanks," I reply, my face heating up. No one has ever complimented my clothes before. Not that these are my clothes, but still. I take a handful of popcorn and pass the bowl back to her.

"So, how's foster life treating you?" Brittany whispers to me, as the others talk about someone from school.

"Okay, I guess."

"Are the Campbells as great as they seem?"

"Yes."

"Please tell me you uncovered something crazy about Brad," Brittany whispers with a devious smile. "He's too perfect. He *has* to be hiding something epic."

I laugh, wondering if she's right. He and his parents do seem perfect.

"Any girly underwear in his dresser drawers?" she asks.

"I wouldn't know," I reply with a smile.

"Any crack hidden under his bed?"

"I doubt it." Crackheads I can identify from a mile away. I hate that I have that skill, but it comes with the territory when you grow up where I did. It's essential for survival, really.

"Any STD meds in his bathroom?"

"Brittany!" I whisper. I can't believe she'd even suggest that. What if he heard her?

"So that's a no?"

"Yes, that's a no." At least it seems like it'd be a no based on what he told me at the mall.

"A third nipple?"

I give her a look to let her know how crazy she sounds right now. "No, he doesn't have a third nipple."

"You know for sure?"

"Yes."

"You've seen him without his shirt?"

I nod as I bite my lip and try to hide the smile I seem to have no control over.

"Yum."

"Oh my God. Be quiet!" I whisper.

After a moment, she whispers, "You like him."

"Sure. He's nice."

"That's not what I mean." She nudges me with her elbow and then catches my eye.

He *is* nice. The nicest guy I've ever met. But I can't like him in the way she's thinking.

When I don't respond, she whispers, "You could do a lot worse."

I have done worse, much worse.

Chase and Brad are complete opposites. It's like my mom's Frito-and-hot-dog casserole compared with Gigi's chicken cordon bleu we had for dinner tonight. My mom didn't cook much, but her casserole was always one of my favorites. I just never knew any better until now.

That's the same thing with Chase. I always thought he was pretty good, but that's just because I didn't know any better. He saved me from my mom, which, at the time, was all that mattered. Now I'm seeing the complete jerk he can be when he doesn't get his way.

And I'm getting a glimpse into who else is out there.

Brad actually seemed to take an interest in me today, asking me questions to get to know me. Chase has never done that. Then again, we grew up together, so what did he have to ask? He knows everything about me.

At least he did until I was placed here, where he can't keep an eye on me.

Oh my God. I completely forgot to call him tonight. He's going to freak on me.

I glance at the clock on the wall. It's still early. I could excuse myself for a few minutes, but Gil was sitting in the library reading when I passed by a little while ago. I don't know of another phone, and I don't want to talk to Chase in front of him. I decide to wait until after the movie to call. It's a Saturday night, so he's probably out getting blitzed anyway. He's got better things to think about than what I'm doing.

An explosion in the movie draws me out of my thoughts to focus on the people around me. The guys are mesmerized by the fight scene. Abbie and Brittany are on their phones, their fingers moving at lightning speed. Michelle's been inching closer and closer to Brad every minute that passes. He doesn't seem to notice, though. Instead, he hollers whenever something blows up and then dissects the scene with Adam.

The two of them couldn't look any more different. Besides their skin color, Brad's big with bulky muscles while Adam's only a little taller than me. He's plenty built, too, but his muscles don't stretch his shirt like Brad's do.

One thing that's similar is their clothes. Like Brad, Adam and Abbie clearly have money. It's not like they're dressed up in fancy outfits, but I can tell their jeans and tops are not from Goodwill or Walmart, where I'm lucky to shop. The materials look softer and the clothes fit better, almost like they were custom made for them.

From my angle, I see Michelle from the side. She's got a pointy nose and chin. Her blond hair falls in curls over her shoulders, and her eyes are made up with smoky lids and black-as-night eyeliner, like she's attending a red-carpet event. The makeup, her short skirt, and tight sweater all seem a bit much just to watch a movie.

Brad must sense my gaze because he turns his head and lifts his chin at me. I focus back on the movie, but not before I catch his smile. It seems real and genuine, like he's happy I'm here.

"I'm cold," Michelle says. I glance back in their direction and see her inching even closer to him.

"Grab a blanket," he says, not taking his eyes off me.

Michelle stands, frowning, and then walks around the back of the sofa.

"You okay?" he mouths to me.

I nod, just as Michelle returns. She lowers herself practically on his lap and then spreads the blanket over the two of them. I can't tell for sure, but it seems like her hands may be roaming up and down his leg under the blanket. From the expression on his face, he doesn't seem to even notice. He's still got his eyes on me, despite Michelle's best efforts.

I can't look at them anymore. It's painful. I tell myself that's because she's trying to get the attention of someone who's clearly not interested, but I worry that might not be the only reason. For the rest of the movie, I keep my eyes plastered to the screen, so I don't have to see them again.

During the final chase scene, in between the explosions and roaring engines, a soft *tap-tap* comes from someplace other than the speakers. We all look around the room.

"You expecting anyone else, man?" Adam asks.

"No." Brad stands up and turns on the light.

Adam pushes himself off the sofa, picks up two pool cues, and then tosses one to Brad. They hold them like baseball bats as they march toward the sliding glass door, which puts me on edge. The other girls must agree, because they scoot closer together.

Tap-tap.

"What is that?" Michelle asks, craning her neck to try to see around the boys, but it's useless. It's a curtain of black outside.

"The wind?" Abbie suggests.

"That's not the sound the wind makes," Brittany says.

"Maybe it's causing a tree branch to hit the glass," Abbie says.

Brittany turns and faces her. "Are there any trees right next to the glass?"

"No, not really . . ."

Tap-tap.

As the girls continue to argue over the source of the sound, the boys peer out the door.

"Oh hell," Brad groans.

CHAPTER 9

BRAD FLIPS ON THE OUTSIDE LIGHT SO EVERYONE CAN SEE who's there.

Chase.

My stomach drops and my palms grow clammy at just the sight of him. I should've called.

"You gonna let him in?" Adam asks.

"I'm not sure," Brad replies.

"Who is that?" Michelle asks.

"It's for me," I say quietly, and slide off the sofa. I need to get him out of here quickly before he can majorly screw something up.

When I get to the glass, Brad holds my arm. "You're not going out there alone," he says.

I glance down to his hand on my arm. It's warm and strong and gives me a sense of safety I've never felt in my life. Despite that or maybe because of that, I unwrap myself from his grip and say, "I'll be fine. That's Chase . . . my boyfriend."

Brad doesn't seem at all surprised, which is odd. It's almost like he already knew. "He can come in," Brad says, opening the sliding door. To Chase, he adds, "Don't be a dick."

"Calm down, bro," Chase says, sauntering through the door like he owns the place. I've seen this attitude from him before, and the situation usually ends up with fists being thrown. I cannot let that happen here.

"I'm not your bro," Brad replies through clenched teeth, which makes me cringe. I get the feeling he'd be just as happy to fight.

"Why are you here?" I ask, dragging Chase across the room to put a little space between him and Brad.

"You didn't call tonight."

Ugh. I should've called before the movie. What was I thinking? Oh right, I was thinking about Brad while trying to do my geometry homework. That's exactly what Chase is worried about.

"I figured you'd be busy this early," I lie. "I was going to call in a couple hours."

"Or maybe you were too busy with your new friends," Chase says. The scowl he gives me hurts as much as a slap to the face. He doesn't buy my story one bit. It's like he knows exactly what I was thinking about Brad earlier today.

Chase's scowl transforms to a smirk as he glances at Brad across the room.

I follow his gaze to find everyone watching us with wide eyes and gaping mouths. I feel the heat rising in my cheeks. I so don't want all these strangers getting a front-row seat at the drama that is my messed-up life.

Grabbing Chase's hand, I lead him around the corner and into the hallway.

"You can't stay here," I say.

"Your mom wants to see you."

Those words cause my heart rate to spike. "No." I can't see her. She'll blame me for getting taken away and I'll have to deal with all her crap.

"It's done. She already talked to Sherry."

I slump against the wall. Why would Sherry do that? She knows what will happen if we see each other again.

"Let's join the party," Chase says, tilting his head toward the other room.

"You can't stay here," I whisper again.

"Why not?"

"Come on, Chase. Don't get me kicked out of here tonight. I told you I'll come see you once I'm settled."

"I'll be a good little boy," he says with a wicked smile that makes it clear he absolutely will not be good.

"Chase . . ."

"What? If you're not fucking him, then you shouldn't care if I stay."

"Oh my God. There's nothing going on."

"Prove it."

I close my eyes and knock the back of my head against the wall.

"Stop acting like a spoiled princess," he says.

Taking a deep breath, I slowly open my eyes. "You're not going to start anything?"

"No."

"You promise?"

"Yeah."

I can't believe I'm letting him do this, but if I don't, it could be worse. He'll cause a huge scene and confront Brad about sleeping with me, which would be mortifying.

When we return to the group, I say, "Can Chase stay for the next movie?"

"Is that what you want?" Brad asks.

I nod but can't meet his eyes.

"The more the merrier," Adam says. "Help yourself to a Coke in the fridge."

Chase strolls over to the kitchen area and raids the refrigerator and pantry like he's stockpiling for the end of the world. He's got two ice cream bars, Twizzlers, Doritos, and a Slim Jim piled into his arms. Then he lowers himself onto the couch next to me, setting his bounty on his lap. I look straight ahead so I won't have to see the stares I'm sure he's getting from everyone else.

It's eerily silent for a few moments, and then Brittany says, "'Sup?" I glance in her direction and find her raising her chin in greeting to Chase. Abbie and Michelle have moved as far away from him as possible, making it clear how uneasy they are with him.

Chase reaches into his pocket and pulls out a plastic bag with weed. "Anyone want some?" he asks. I close my eyes and lean my head against the back of the couch. This night will not be over soon enough.

"You can't smoke that here," Brad says.

Chase shrugs and pockets the weed before extending his arm over my shoulders, pulling me much closer than I want.

"So," Brittany says, trying to break the tension. "You up for a gory movie?"

"Always," Chase says.

We start the movie, but I can't get into it. I'm worried about Chase and what the others must think. He stuffs his face for the first half of the movie, and then, when the food is gone, he starts touching me. It started off innocently enough with his hand on my knee, but now his hand keeps moving farther and farther up my thigh.

I lean over and whisper in his ear, "Not here. Later."

That satisfies him for about fifteen minutes, until he abruptly stands and pulls me up by my arms. "You got a place we can be alone?" he asks Brad.

My face goes up in flames, and I can only imagine what Brad's thinking.

Confirming my thoughts, he stands and replies, "No. I think it's time for you to leave." He flexes his fingers a few times, and I get a terrible sinking feeling in my gut.

"It's okay," I say, stepping between them to prevent an all-out brawl. "He just wants to talk to me for a couple minutes and then he'll leave, right?"

"Sure thing, babe." He smiles at Brad. "We're just *talking*, bro."

"Stop calling me that."

"The weight room?" I ask.

He nods and then says, "If you hurt her, I will fuck you up. Understand?"

My eyes grow wide. I've never heard Brad talk like that. In fact, I've never heard anyone talk like that about me. It sends a warm rush through my body, and I have to fight back a smile.

I glance at Chase to make sure he didn't see my reaction, but he's smirking at Brad with pure hatred in his eyes. That quickly crushes my hidden smile. I need to convince him I'm his and get him out of here ASAP before he can cause any serious trouble.

I pull him into the weight room and away from Brad.

"Really quick," I say, unbuttoning his pants. "And then you have to go." My plan is to make him happy without actually having sex. I can easily have him out of here in two minutes.

"What's the rush, babe?" He reaches for my jeans and starts to unbutton them.

I cover his hands with my own. "I'm having my period," I lie. That usually does the trick with him.

"I don't mind."

"I want to focus on you," I try again. I unzip his pants and reach through the fly. That gets his attention and he seems to forget about me. He moans and then says, "I've missed you, babe."

"Me, too," I lie again. It seems I have to lie a lot around him, and it's happening more and more lately. That probably should have been my first sign we were doomed to fail. Actually, him stealing food stamps from my mom should have been the first sign. Or threatening my chemistry partner after seeing us talking during lunch. *Okay, there have been a lot of signs.*

I start giving him what he likes, and he responds as he always does. In my mind, I'm counting down the seconds until he's done and can finally leave. Ten. Nine. Eight. Seven. Six. Fi—without warning, he whips my shirt over my head.

"Chase!" I whisper as he reaches for my bra.

"Come on, baby," he says, sliding the material down and gliding his hands over my chest. "Don't stop now."

I glance down to my fingers, where they've stilled. I need to finish this quickly and get him out of here. I do as he asks, but he suddenly moans really loudly. Too loudly. All the blood drains from my face as I realize what just happened. He's never acted like that before. He did it on purpose. To make a scene.

"Get out of my house!" Brad yells, barreling into the room with Adam right behind him, giving Chase the exact reaction he wanted.

I reach down and grab my shirt, trying to get it on before Brad and Adam can see anything, but it's like I've got extra fingers and they don't know how to work together. My arms get stuck in the material and it ends up hanging around my neck while my bra's still around my waist.

Brad tackles Chase. He hits the floor with a thud followed by a loud crack as his head lands on a stack of weights.

"You bastard," Chase spits out, reaching for his temple, where a small gash is oozing blood.

I finally get my shirt on and then shove my bra into my waistband as I move to the corner of the room, away from the boys.

Chase jumps to his feet. Brad pulls back his fist, and I cringe, ready for the hit, but Adam gets to Chase first. He grabs his hand and twists his fingers back. Chase falls to his knees, gasping for breath.

"I gave you the benefit of the doubt," Adam says, "and you let all of us down. This is the warning. Next time, we won't be so easy on you."

With that, Adam releases his fingers, but then grips his forearm behind his back and walks him back through the door with Brad following. Chase's zipper is still down, and I can only imagine what the girls in the other room think.

I slip into the hallway and see that everyone is watching Adam and Brad throw Chase outside. I make a beeline for the stairs, sprint up them, and then head straight for the front door to escape the wreckage of this night.

CHAPTER 10

I RUSH OUT THE FRONT DOOR AND AROUND TO THE BACKYARD
with the safety of the forest beyond. I'm not wearing shoes, but the
pinecones and fallen limbs under my feet don't slow me down one
bit. The embarrassment, shame, and disgust I have for myself keep
me running until I can no longer see the lights from the Campbells' house. Then I finally let myself slow down to a walk, pulling in ragged breaths from my first exercise since gym class two
years ago.

When I'm no longer focused on running, the last hour replays
in my head over and over again. As if that's not bad enough, the
part when Brad saw me halfway naked is played in slow motion,
just to make sure I realize how bad it really was.

Finally, the tears start falling. I've been embarrassed tons of
times about how skinny I am or my awful clothes or something my
mom did, but none of those compare with this. Brad saw me naked
from the waist up. That alone would be bad enough, but he also
knows what we were doing. Brad, Mr. Goody Two-Shoes who's

never had sex, saw what I was doing to Chase. I cradle my head in my hands. Brad would never hang out with someone like him. He's got to be completely disgusted by me right now.

I reach a dark and quiet street and lower myself to the curb. There's a house down the road a bit, but I'm alone right here.

Drawing my knees to my chest, I wrap my arms around them and watch the tears drop onto the pavement, forming shiny small dots that reflect the full moon above. My hair falls in a curtain on either side of my face, complete with bits of brittle leaves that got stuck during my trek through the woods. They scratch my cheeks every time I sob.

I sit like that for a long time. I don't have a watch, but the moon has moved behind a group of trees, which makes me think it's been at least half an hour, if not longer. I stare at my dirty socks and finally wonder what I'm going to do. I was so eager to run away from the Campbells, but what's my plan now? Stay here until morning and wait for someone to call the cops on me? Go to the house down the road and ask to use their phone so I can call DSS? Go back to the Campbells? None of those seem like a good option, so I hug my knees tighter and pray an answer will magically appear before I'm forced to make a decision.

Just then, two headlights come into view at the end of the street. I lower my hands to the curb, getting ready to push myself up and scamper back to the cover of the woods, when the car stops on the side of the road. Worried any movement would make me even more obvious, I sit still as a statue, hoping they made a wrong turn and will soon leave.

Instead, two doors open and close, as loud as gunshots in the otherwise silent night. Figures emerge, a tall one and a short one, but I can't make out any details until they walk into the yellow beam of the headlights.

Brad and Brittany.

I lower my head and start crying again. There's no way I can avoid them now.

"Where's Chase?" Brad asks, when he's standing directly in front of me, his blue Nikes practically touching my feet.

"How would I know?" I reply, wiping my face with the heel of my hand. Why is that his first question? He was the one who kicked Chase out.

"You didn't meet up with him?" Brittany asks.

"No." I saw his motorcycle in the driveway but ran the opposite way so I wouldn't have to deal with him.

"You weren't planning on leaving with him?"

"No, but I'll be out of your lives as soon as I talk to Sherry." I turn toward Brad. "Can I use your phone?"

"What do you mean out of our lives?" he asks. "You've only been here two days."

"I'll get a different placement when your parents kick me out."

"Why would they kick you out?"

I sniff and wipe my nose with my sleeve. "Because I broke one of their rules."

"They don't know the whole story. And, even if they did, they wouldn't kick you out. You'd lose some privileges, but that's all."

"They have no reason to keep me."

"Yeah, they do. They want to help. We all want to help."

I take a deep breath, trying to pull myself together before I speak again. "I can't stay here."

"Why?" Brittany asks.

I shake my head, not wanting to talk about it. Just thinking about it makes my neck and cheeks turn a blotchy, red mess.

"I didn't really see anything," Brad says, obviously getting it.

"Right," I reply, scoffing.

"I was so angry at Chase; he was all I could focus on."

"I don't believe you."

Brad takes a deep breath and then says, "Let's just pretend tonight never happened."

"Like that's even possible."

Brad shrugs. "I've already done it."

I shake my head. "How can I stay here if I can't even look at you anymore?"

"You can look at me."

"No."

"Yes."

He squats down in front of me, places his thumb under my chin, and tilts my head up. I continue to force my eyes to the side, avoiding his face, as fresh tears fall.

"Please don't cry. It's okay. This doesn't change anything. You fooled around with your boyfriend. That's all. I shouldn't have barged in there. It's all my fault. Let's go home and get a good night's sleep." He holds out his hand, but I refuse it.

"This isn't my life. I need to go back where I belong."

"You belong here," he says.

"No, I don't. You don't get it."

"Get what?" he asks, resting his hand on my shoulder.

I glance at his hand, surprised he'd touch me after what he saw and what he must think of me. "Chase slashed your tires."

"I know."

"He wanted to cause a scene tonight."

"I know."

If he knows, why does he want me to stay? It makes no sense for him to bring this into his perfect life.

"He'll keep causing problems."

"No, he won't," he says with a shake of his head. His blue eyes are serious, and his jaw is clenched tight. It seems there's no doubt in his mind we could be done with Chase.

"Yes, he will," I push. "You don't know him."

"I have a pretty good idea of what he's like."

"I wouldn't be able to live with myself if he damaged anything else of yours or hurt you."

"First of all, Dad is getting a better security system, so you don't have to worry about our stuff. As far as me, I think I can hold my own against him."

"I don't know. . . ."

"Really, Hailey?" he asks, his lip twitching as though he's fighting back a smile. "I've got at least sixty pounds of muscle on him. You honestly think I'd let him get away with anything?"

"He's just . . ."

"What?"

"Not really into fighting fair." That's an understatement. I'm surprised he didn't pull out a knife tonight.

"I'm not worried. Between my size and Adam's killer karate

moves, we're safe. You're safe. Just say the word and I won't let him near you again. I promise." He squeezes my shoulder, and I get that same sense of safety I felt back in his basement before Chase came in.

"Why?" I ask, still not understanding why he'd want to deal with all my crap.

"I'm your foster brother," he says with a shrug. "That's what we do. Protect our foster sisters from assholes."

"This is my life and my drama, not yours." I sigh and add, "I'll never be able to escape it, but that doesn't mean you should have to deal with it."

"Dammit, Hailey!" Brittany yells. "Don't act so helpless! You can change things. Go home with the Campbells. Cut ties with Chase for good. Graduate high school. I've been there. I know it's hard and it seems impossible, but it's not. You're in control of your life."

She meets my eyes, and we stare at each other for a few moments before I have to look away. She reaches for my hands. "Do you want more from your life? That's all you need to ask yourself."

She's right.

It's that simple. If I want to live like my mom, then I keep on doing what I've been doing. If I want something better—college, a good job, a decent home and car—it's time to make a change. A real change for once. I can't count on people like Chase.

My spine straightens. I pull my shoulders back. I take a deep breath. This is it.

"I don't want Chase to bother me again," I say to Brad.

"Done," he replies, stone-faced, as if it will be as easy as taking out the trash. The funny thing is, I completely trust him. I met him yesterday but have absolute faith he will do whatever he says.

"Group hug," Brittany says, motioning with her hands as Brad and I rise to our feet. The three of us stand there, on the side of the street, in a three-way hug, as I shed yet more tears. This time, though, they're happy tears. These are the type of people I need around me—people who believe in me. My life might actually be on the right track for once.

CHAPTER 11

"YOU UP, HAILEY?"

I hear Brad's voice through my bedroom door and moan. Even though last night ended well, I'm still embarrassed by what happened. Plus, to make matters worse, Gil and Gigi were in the car. They didn't ask for any explanation when I got in, but I'm sure it's coming. The fear of telling them feels like a freight train sitting on my chest.

"Mom made pancakes, if you're hungry."

My stomach growls at his words. Of course, if I go down there, I'll have to face everyone. Running away would have been so much easier.

"Can you say something, so I know you're in there?"

"I'm here," I reply.

"Okay, good. We're all downstairs, if you want to join us."

Reluctantly, I rise. If I'm staying here, I have to face them. As much as I'm dreading it, it's probably better to get it over with sooner rather than later. I run a brush through my hair, throw a

sweatshirt over my tank top, and rinse my face, hopeful it will help
wash away my crappy yesterday.

When I arrive in the kitchen, everyone is sitting around the
table with not only pancakes but also bacon, eggs, and orange
juice. It's a feast, really. I'm not sure I'll ever get used to having
more than enough food waiting for me whenever I want it. And
the Campbells don't even realize what a luxury it is. To them, luxury is probably a yacht or an expensive sports car. To me, it's a full
plate of food at least once a day.

"Morning," Gil says, pouring syrup onto his pancakes.

"Good morning," I practically whisper, as I keep my eyes
down and find my spot at the table.

"Would you like some juice?" Gigi asks.

I nod, and she pours a glass for me.

"Have you heard back from that scout?" Gil asks Brad.

"Yeah, he called yesterday. They're interested, but he said I'd
probably be offered an academic scholarship, not a football scholarship."

"Why's that?"

"He said I have unusually high grades for an athlete. They try
to save the athletic scholarships for those who really need them."

"But you'd still be on the team, right?" Gigi asks.

"Yeah."

Gigi passes a plate of scrambled eggs to me. "Help yourself,
Hailey." To Brad, she asks, "So, what do you think? Could you
see yourself at Wake?"

"I'm not sure."

"It's a fantastic school," Gil says.

"Of course you're going to say that. It's your school," Brad replies, rolling his eyes. "Both my parents went to Wake Forest," he says, turning to me.

I nod and spoon eggs onto my plate. I'm happy to see they're more interested in Brad and his future than me this morning. Maybe they will act like last night never happened, and I won't have to explain it to Gil and Gigi.

"They have a top-notch premed program and their football program is getting better every year," Gil says.

"I know."

"What's the problem then?"

Brad chews his food thoughtfully. When he finally swallows, he says, "I always thought I'd go someplace new for college. You know, someplace different."

"Wake would be new to you."

"I've been there hundreds of times!"

"As a visitor, not a student," Gigi says.

Brad rolls his eyes. "You know what I mean. I need to think about it and see what the other schools have to say."

"Absolutely," Gigi responds. "So, do you two have plans for the day?"

"Homework," Brad says.

Then they all look at me. The only homework I have left is geometry, and I'm not sure any more time will help me. I don't have anything else to do, though, so I reply, "The same."

"Do you need help with geometry?" Brad asks, as if reading my mind.

"No, you're busy. I'll be fine."

"I'll be done in a few hours if you want to work on it together."

"Oh, okay. Sure," I reply quietly, moving eggs around my plate.

The conversation then turns to football—high school, college, and professional. I eat my breakfast and smile and nod whenever they try to include me in the discussion, but I have no idea what they're talking about.

As Gil clears the table, Gigi asks, "Can I talk to you for a minute, Hailey?"

And just like that, the freight train sitting on my chest starts up its engine and tries to suffocate me with its weight.

I don't answer, but Brad and Gil make a quick exit, leaving me alone with her.

"Do you want to tell me what happened last night?" she asks.

"Not really," I mumble, smashing a crumb on the tabletop with my finger.

"Why not?"

"I messed up."

"We all mess up."

"Not you guys. You, Gil, and Brad are all perfect."

"We're far from perfect."

She has no idea how her family looks to an outsider. "Compared to me, you're perfect."

"That's not true. I'm not going to get angry, if that's what you're worried about."

"Yes, you will. I broke a rule."

"Which rule?"

"Number one."

She thinks for a moment and then says, "You had someone in your room with the door closed?"

"Not my room. The weight room."

"Is there more to the story?"

I nod. There's no way I'm going to be able to tell her. They only asked a few things of me. They were all easy rules, yet I didn't follow them for even two days.

"Did you have sex?" she asks.

I bite my lip. I'm not sure if she'd technically consider what we did sex. "Um . . . maybe?" I say.

Her mouth turns down, either in disgust or confusion. I can't tell which. "It's usually a yes-or-no thing," she finally says, making me realize it's more confusion.

"I . . . we . . . it wasn't like . . ." I bite my lip again and tap my fingers on the tabletop.

"You did something intimate?" Gigi asks, saving me from having to say the words.

I nod.

"Any chance you could be pregnant from what you did?"

I shake my head.

"Get an STD?"

"Um . . . probably not." I look down at my hands. At least I don't think so.

I feel the heat creeping up my neck as the blush rises to my cheeks. "Sorry. I didn't mean to break your rule. I just . . . I . . . I was trying to get him to leave."

"Who?"

"My boyfriend . . . I mean ex-boyfriend. I decided to break up with him."

"You had . . . something close to sex with him to get him to leave?"

I nod again even though I know how stupid it must sound to her.

"Why did you decide to break up with him?" she asks, studying me.

I bite my lip again. "I think he is kind of . . . not great for me."

She gives me a small smile. "Okay," she says, rubbing her hands together. "First, thanks for telling me. I know that wasn't easy, so I appreciate your honesty."

I bite my lip again, waiting for what comes next. Is she going to kick me out like everyone else has?

"I'd like to take you to the doctor to make sure everything's okay," she says, surprising me.

"I—I just went this week," I say.

"Another appointment won't hurt. Plus, I'd like to get you established with a doctor anyway."

"Okaaay," I say, drawing out the word and finally meeting her eyes. She wouldn't make me go to the doctor if she were kicking me out.

"Good. Now that that's settled, we need to decide what to do. When you break rules around here, you lose a privilege for a little while. Do you have any suggestions on what to lose?"

That's it? Brad was right last night? They really aren't going to kick me out over this? The freight train on my chest vanishes into thin air as I realize how lucky I am. She could take away all my privileges, and I wouldn't care. The only privilege I need is to be a part of this family.

"So, what do you think?" Gigi asks.

I'm not exactly sure what she's considering. At home, on a good day, my mom would take away food or lock me out of the house if I made her mad. When she was drunk, she'd get violent.

"I guess I could skip lunch and dinner today," I offer.

"What? No! I'd never withhold food from you." The serious face she's worn this entire conversation turns to a frown and her eyes soften. I know that look well. It's pity, and I wish I had kept my mouth shut. "How about if I take away two days of your allowance?" she asks.

I can't believe what she's suggesting. Since I'm not used to having money ever handed to me, that seems like a very minor price to pay. "That's it?"

"That seems fair since it appears you learned from your mistake and are truly sorry for what you did."

"I am. I promise I'll never do it again."

"I believe you."

She stands and walks around the table to give me a hug. I'm completely floored by how she handled it. She didn't kick me out. She didn't scream at me. She didn't even give me much of a punishment. Is this how normal families work? If so, mine is a hundred times more dysfunctional than I thought.

CHAPTER 12

BRAKES SCREECH AS ANOTHER BUS PULLS INTO THE LINE, BUT it's not mine. Mine usually takes at least ten minutes to get here, so I settle onto the concrete wall to wait.

"Bye, Hailey!" a girl says as she walks past to catch her bus. She's friends with Brittany and we've talked a few times, but I can't remember her name. I hate that she remembers mine when I'm so forgetful. Of course, she only had to learn one new name when I've had to learn a ton.

"See ya later!" I reply with a wave.

As I watch her board the bus, a familiar figure strolls into view. It's Brad, which is weird. He has a car. In the week I've been here, I've never seen him around the bus line.

I watch him as he wanders along the buses, alternating his attention between the students' faces behind the windows and those milling around on the curb. The whole time he's chatting or at least smiling and raising his chin in greeting to those he passes. It's like no one is a stranger to him, which I find hard to believe since there are more than two thousand students in this school.

When he gets right in front of me, he looks in my direction and our eyes lock. The smile he's been wearing grows even bigger, and he strolls over to me.

"Want a ride today?"

"Thanks, but I'm good."

"You'd rather ride the bus?"

I shrug. He's offered to drive me to school every morning this week, but I hop on the bus instead. I figured he was just trying to be nice. It's not like the popular football star really wants to be seen with the foster kid. That's a great way to ruin your reputation in like five seconds flat.

"I don't have a problem with it," I say. Besides, I've been a bus rider since kindergarten, so it's not like I know any different.

"It'll take you three times as long to get home."

"I'm not in a hurry."

"Okay, then," he says, rocking back on his heels and looking around us. "The bus it is." He pauses. "Maybe I should join you if it's so great?"

"What about your car?"

"I can get it tomorrow."

"You can't leave your car here. It makes no sense."

"Good point. Let's go," he says, nodding in the direction of the student parking lot, as if the decision has already been made. I guess it kind of has. If he's not concerned about his reputation, why should I be?

"Has anyone ever told you you're kind of pushy?" I ask.

"Me? Pushy? Never."

I roll my eyes. "Do you always get your way?"

He smiles, revealing his dimple. "Yep. I'm selfish like that. It's an only-child thing."

"I guess there are worse ways to be selfish than demanding I ride home with you," I reply with a grin.

"Exactly. I'm selfish, but in a generous way."

Shaking my head, I say, "I'm not sure selfish and generous are supposed to go together."

"You're the one who said I'm a walking contradiction."

"That you are," I say, pushing myself off the wall and collecting my backpack.

As we're walking, he says, "If your concern is my driving, I'd be happy to provide you with a full background check showing my spotless record."

"Yes, that's what I need to feel better about getting into your car."

He reaches down to his pocket and pulls out his phone. He starts moving around the screens until a document pops up.

"Wait. You're serious?" I ask. I thought he was trying to be funny.

"I'd hate for you to fear for your life while I'm driving."

"I've already been in your car, remember?"

"Did you fear for your life?"

No. Not at all. He's one of the most cautious drivers I've ever seen. "A little," I tease. "I thought that golf cart was going to rear-end us as you crawled through the subdivision."

"Have you not seen the deer in our neighborhood? You have to go slow so you don't hit one."

I've been here a week and haven't seen any deer. I even ran through the woods that one night and didn't see any.

"We have hundreds of them," he continues with a smug look. "And they have no respect for the road."

"You're blaming your grandpa driving skills on innocent deer?"

"They're not innocent!"

"But you admit you have grandpa driving skills?"

"Only because the deer have a death wish," he says, gesturing with his hands like this is common knowledge. Maybe it is for people who grew up here.

"Is that also why you parked as far from the mall as possible last weekend?" I ask, loving the defensive reaction I'm getting out of him. He's usually the calm, cool, and collected one who pokes fun at me. It's fun to see how he reacts when the tables are turned.

"Oh, come ooon," he says, drawing out the words. "It wasn't as far as possible."

"There were like a gazillion closer spots."

"You should be happy," he says, pointing at me. "I got you some exercise."

"Are you calling me fat?"

He rolls his eyes. "Everyone needs exercise."

"Well, thank you, Brad, for looking out for my well-being."

"See? Generous. It's my middle name. Here's the report," he says, trying to hand me his phone.

I shake my head. "I don't want to see it, but why exactly do you have this?"

"Foster licensing. They did a full background check on us. I guess we all passed."

"No skeletons hidden in your dad's closet?"

"Apparently not. Shocking, right?"

We reach the student parking lot, and I glance around, looking for his car, but can't spot it. He walks between two cars to reach the next aisle and then turns left. There, at the end of the row, is his black BMW, many, many spots away from any other cars.

"What is it with you and parking?" I ask, following him.

"The more you make fun of me, the farther away I'll park," he says, smiling at me from over his shoulder.

It takes us less than ten minutes to reach his house. If I had taken the bus, I'd still have about an hour. I don't want to admit it, but this was much better.

"Thanks for the ride," I say.

"Sure. So, I'll drive you home any day I don't have practice?" he asks, hanging his backpack on a hook by the door.

I guess he really doesn't care about being seen with me at school. If that's the case, I'm not about to pass up a ride. "I guess so. Since I know you won't take no for an answer."

"You're learning," he says with a smile. "I can drive you in the mornings, too."

We move into the kitchen, and I start to head for the stairs while he goes to the refrigerator.

"Where are you going?" he asks, opening the door.

"My room."

"Why?"

I don't have a reason. For the past week, whenever I get back from school, I go straight to my room until dinner. In fact, I spend most of my time in my room. It's not like the Campbells have forbidden me from going anywhere in their house, but it's still their home. I feel weird being in other rooms unless I'm invited by one of them. My room just seems like the safest place.

When I don't say anything, he adds, "Want a snack?"

"No, thanks."

"Want to keep me company while I eat?"

Not wanting to be rude, I say, "I guess so," and turn around.

Brad piles three gigantic slices of pizza onto a plate and carries it and a bottle of Gatorade to the table. I sit opposite him.

"You're not hungry?" he asks.

I'm a little hungry, but dinner shouldn't be too far off. Why Brad would eat this much right now is strange. "Won't your mom make dinner in a couple hours?"

"Yeah."

"Won't she be upset if you don't eat?"

"Why wouldn't I eat?"

"You're having an entire meal right now."

He laughs and shakes his head. "You've never seen me demolish an entire pizza. This is nothing." He pauses. "What's your favorite food?"

"Lasagna. Why?"

"What about snack food?"

"Potato chips."

He jumps up from the table and goes to the pantry. I hear him rummaging around in there, and then he sticks his head out. "Plain or a flavor?"

"Sour cream and chive. Why?"

He emerges with a bag and holds it triumphantly overhead. "You're in luck."

After tossing the chips on the table, he sits down and goes back to his cold pizza. I look at the bag and wonder what I should do. It's a brand-new bag. Does he really want me to open it?

As if reading my thoughts, he reaches over and tears it open, then shoves it in my direction.

"Eat up," he says. "Winter's coming. We need to get a little meat on your bones so you don't freeze to death."

"You're trying to fatten me up?"

"Yep."

That should probably make me mad, but it has the opposite effect. For years, I've wanted to look healthy, not like a skeleton. It's reassuring to see him want the same thing without me ever saying a word about my weight. It's another small bit of proof I'm in the right place.

I take a chip from the bag and nibble on it. It's as delicious as expected, and I quickly gobble it up and reach for another. "This may do it," I say as I eat a third.

"What's your favorite color?" he asks.

"Green. Why?"

"How come you're so suspicious of everything I do or say?"

I shrug. Being in foster care puts you in weird situations. Maybe I react to the weirdness by being suspicious of everyone and everything.

"Just trying to get to know you," he says before stuffing a big piece of crust into his mouth.

"What's *your* favorite color?" I ask once he's swallowed it.

"Blue. Favorite holiday?"

I have to think about that. Holidays weren't a big thing at

home, but I loved the parties we had in elementary school. Especially when they involved candy. "Valentine's Day. Yours?"

"Christmas. Most embarrassing thing that's ever happened to you?"

Ugh. The Chase incident. I was hoping to never think about that again. Actually, I'd love to never think about Chase again, but that's probably never going to happen. Every night after I turn off my bedroom light, I peek out the window to make sure he's not lurking around outside. So far, so good. Maybe Brad really can keep him away like he said. I don't know how he's doing it, but I am grateful. Answering Brad's question, I say "That's easy. You saw it last weekend."

"You're lucky then."

I lick the grease off my fingers and ask, "Why do you say that?" I certainly didn't feel lucky at the time. After it was all over, I guess I was lucky because Gil and Gigi didn't kick me out and Brad and I are able to pretend it never happened. And Chase does seem to be out of my life as a result of that night, at least for the time being. Regardless, it's still the most embarrassing thing ever.

"Only two people witnessed your most embarrassing moment. That's nothing."

"Yours is worse?"

"Oh yeah." He takes another bite of pizza, so I wait to hear more. After swallowing, he takes a gulp of Gatorade, and then goes back to the pizza like he has no intention of saying anything else.

"Well?" I finally ask, unable to handle the suspense any longer.

"Well what?"

"What happened?"

"You really want to know?"

"Yes!" It'd be nice to have some dirt on Brad, because right now he seems like a saint. I'd love to have some evidence he's a normal person.

He leans back in his chair and says, "Two years ago, before a game, I was doing squats to warm up and my pants ripped. My ass was hanging out there for the whole world to see, including Mom and my old Sunday-school teacher."

I cover my mouth to hide my smile.

"And you know what Adam did? You'd think he'd come down from the stands and get me a towel or something, right? Nope. He took a picture that somehow ended up in the hands of my team-mates, who teased me forever. They still call me Moonshine."

I don't want to laugh at his most embarrassing moment, but it's a good one.

"Go ahead," he says, holding his hands out. "Make fun of me all you want."

"Sorry," I say. I lose my internal battle and laugh. "That is bad."

"No kidding. At least only two people witnessed yours."

"Still, I was horrified. It happened in front of the cute boy I just met and will see every single day."

He raises his eyebrows. "Cute? I thought I was hot."

I hold up my finger. "I never said you were hot." I remember specifically telling him that was other girls, not me.

"That's right," he says, nodding. "You had too much other stuff on your mind to think about me that day. It's good to know your mind's emptying out so you can focus on more important things like whether I'm hot or cute."

I roll my eyes. "I have so not been doing that." Okay, I have, but he doesn't need to know. He's hot. Definitely hot.

He shrugs and gives me an innocent look. "Somehow you landed on cute. Seems like you must've put some serious thought into it."

"Nope. It just sounded nicer than 'pushy, walking-contradiction boy I'll see every day.'"

He laughs and stands. "Well, if it makes you feel better, I think you're cute, too," he says with a quick smile before loading his plate into the dishwasher.

My mouth drops open.

He did not just say that.

Why would he say that?

Before I can collect myself, he returns to the table and points to the chips. "You done?" he asks, as if nothing out of the ordinary just happened. Maybe it didn't. Maybe I imagined it. There's no way Brad would find me cute. I must've heard him wrong. Or maybe he was just saying it to be nice. Yeah, that has to be it.

It meant absolutely nothing.

I nod and try to hand him the bag, but he shakes his head. "This is your home, too. You need to start acting like you live here."

"I don't know where it goes," I say quietly. I need to just pretend the last few minutes of our conversation never happened. He's Brad. My foster brother. Not cute Brad or hot Brad. Just Brad my foster brother.

"In the pantry," he says, clearly already forgetting about our conversation. Seeing him acting totally normal makes it easier for me to forget it, too. He was just being nice. Like he always is.

I open the door of the pantry and peer inside, getting my first good look. It's organized like shelves at a grocery store, with everything perfectly aligned and labels facing forward. On the top left are four bags of different kinds of chips. Two are opened and have a clip on the top to keep the bags closed.

"Hey, Brad?" I ask.

"Yeah?" he says, coming up behind me. I turn around, but he's standing way too close and I practically crash into him. My free hand flies up to stop me from falling. It lands right in the middle of his chest. His very muscular chest that feels just as nice as it looks whenever he parades around with his shirt off.

My hand whips back. I so didn't need that right now. "Sorry. D-do you have any more of those clips?"

"Yep. In the drawer under the oven." He just stands there, so I take a deep breath before heading to the drawer. When I get there, I see only cookie sheets.

"It's not here."

"Try the cabinet next to the microwave." I give him a confused look over my shoulder. This is one of the few cabinets I've actually been in because it holds the plates I always put away after dinner. Still, I open the door. No bag clip.

He says, "The drawer next to the fridge?"

It's full of pens and pads of paper.

"The corner cabinet?"

It's filled with small appliances, including a blender and a waffle maker.

"Maybe the cabinet above?"

Coffee mugs.

I put my hands on my hips and stare at him. "What are you doing?"

He grins. "I don't know what you're talking about."

"You're either totally clueless about where things are stored or you're purposely making me snoop through all your cabinets."

"Or helping you learn where things are other than our dinner dishes."

"You really want me just digging through all your cabinets and pantry?"

"Yes. And hanging out downstairs." He pauses. "Why do you spend so much time up in your room anyway? Are you into some weird satanic shit I should know about?"

"Very funny."

"I'm serious. You hide out up there until dinner, then scamper back as soon as we're done. My parents had the basement redone as a hangout place. You've been down there twice in a week."

"It's not like you've invited me down there," I point out. Granted, the first time I went down there I wasn't invited, but look what my curiosity got me—drooling over a shirtless Brad.

"It's *your* home. No invitation needed."

I get what he's saying. It's looking more and more like I'll be here for the long haul, but it's hard not to feel like a guest. When you're a guest in someone's home, you don't just go into their fridge or head to the basement to watch television. "So, you just want me to wander around your house, anywhere I want to go?"

"Yes. Well," he says, frowning, "you might want to be careful with Mom and Dad's room. I stay away from there. No one needs to know what happens in their parents' room."

"Ewww," I say, grimacing. "Don't put images in my head."

"Gross, right?" He disappears through the doorway with an overhead wave while I still need to find the clip for the chips. I search through a few more drawers before finally finding it next to the plastic wrap. After adding it to the bag, I store the chips in the pantry.

Looking around the kitchen, I realize it doesn't feel as foreign as it did a week ago. What used to be scary and intimidating is starting to feel familiar and comfortable. And it's not just the surroundings. Brad and I are figuring things out. We're slowly getting to some sort of friend or foster-sibling place, although I never pictured myself with a brother or a friend who looked and acted quite like Brad. Even so, it's actually starting to feel like maybe this is the place I belong.

CHAPTER 13

"HAILEY!" SOMEONE CALLS FROM BEHIND ME.

I turn around to find Brad leaning against the wall of the auditorium. We're having a guest speaker today, and all the other students are filing in. "What are you doing?" I ask, stepping to his side and letting people behind me pass.

"Waiting on Adam. Want to sit with us?"

"Sure," I reply, searching the sea of faces for Adam. I was originally thinking I'd sit with Brittany, but she's scheduled to watch the second presentation instead.

"Yo, Moonshine!" a guy says, walking up to Brad and knocking him with his elbow. His nickname brings a smile to my face.

"Hey, Carlos," Brad says. "This is Hailey. Hailey, Carlos. He's cocaptain of the football team with me."

I recognize him. He sits at Brad's table during lunch every day and even though I don't sit there—by my choice, not because Brad hasn't invited me—I see all his friends when I walk by. Brad, Abbie, and Adam always smile at me; Michelle either ig-

nores me or makes a face like she's just taken a bite of the worst
lunch ever.

"Nice to meet you, Hailey," Carlos says. "You're new here,
right?"

I nod. "Nice to meet you, too."

"So," he says, looking at Brad with a smile, "you've taken it
upon yourself to make the cute new girl feel welcome at Pinecrest,
huh?"

My face heats up at the word "cute." I'm not used to people
talking like that about me, especially when I'm standing right
here, and now it's happened twice in two weeks.

"I have," Brad says, grinning back at him before focusing on
me. "Is it working?" he asks me.

"Um . . . yeah . . . I guess so," I stammer, feeling totally caught
off guard. He and Brittany have been awesome. I rarely see Brad
since we aren't in the same classes, but anytime we pass in the hall,
he goes out of his way to talk to me, even if it's just for a couple of
seconds. It's been a huge relief having both of them help me not
look like a total loser in a new school.

"You going in?" Carlos asks.

"Yeah, let's go," Brad says. "I'll text Adam and tell him to meet
us inside."

The three of us find a mostly empty row in the back of the auditorium and take our seats. After texting Adam, Brad opens a
video on his phone. "Have you seen this?" he asks me, shoving it
in my direction.

It's a collection of guys doing stupid things and failing. Like
trying to jump from a roof onto a trampoline and into a pool,

but bouncing over a fence and landing in an overgrown weedy field instead. Brad laughs, while I cringe. "That had to hurt," I say, as another guy does a somersault over the handlebars of his bike.

"But it's hilarious, right?" Brad asks, laughing as someone falls through a frozen lake on his motorcycle.

I close my eyes and turn my head when it's clear nothing good is going to come of a guy trying to pick up a massive snake.

"Seriously? You don't like this?" he asks, snatching his phone away and showing it to Carlos. "Funny, right?"

"Yeah, I saw that last night. Laughed my ass off."

Brad types on his phone, then pushes it back to me as a new video pops up. Baby pandas rolling around on the floor. "How's this?" he asks.

I smile at a tiny baby trying to climb over another to reach its mom. "Much better."

"Okay, quiet down," the principal says from the stage. "We have a great speaker today, so stop texting and playing games on your phones. Ms. Reynolds is going to talk about the struggles she faced growing up and what we can do to promote diversity not only at school but also within our communities. Please help me welcome her."

I lower the phone to the armrest between us and clap with the rest of the students as the speaker steps to the podium and begins her speech. Adam slips into the now dark auditorium and sits down next to me. Brad fist-bumps him and then picks up his phone and types something onto the screen.

A moment later, he hands it back to me as an adorable little otter drinks from a baby bottle. "Awww," I whisper. "I might need to get one of these as a pet."

.“Dad’s probably allergic,” he whispers. “He ruins all my pet dreams.”

“Ahem,” someone says from behind us. We both turn around to find the vice principal there, holding two slips of paper. She hands one to me, then the other to Brad.

I take a look at it, and my stomach drops. It’s a detention slip for this afternoon. The reason scrawled into the open space is: *Using phone during assembly.*

I shoot Brad a freaked-out look, but he rolls his eyes and shakes his head, completely unfazed by what just happened. I’ve never gotten a detention. Ever. How in the world did Brad, king of the Goody Two-Shoes, land us both in detention?

I turn to stare at the speaker, afraid I’ll get in even more trouble if I look anywhere else. Brad nudges my leg with his own. I shake my head, still staring straight ahead. He does it again and whispers, “This is nothing.”

I ignore him.

He then bumps my arm with his elbow.

I ignore him again.

He then pokes me in the ribs.

I ignore him again. At least I try to. He hits a ticklish area, and I scrunch over to the side and bite my lip to prevent a laugh.

“Stop it!” I whisper-yell to him, scooting as far to the other side of my seat as possible. We already have one detention; we don’t need another.

“Just trying to get you to smile,” he whispers back. “Don’t be mad about the detention. I’ll take care of it.”

I roll my eyes. There’s no way he can take care of it. We earned it fair and square.

After a couple of minutes, he whispers, "You're not mad, are you?"

I shake my head, still staring straight ahead. I'm not angry with him, more like myself.

That must be all he wanted, because he leaves me alone for the rest of the assembly.

When the speaker finally thanks us for our attention and leaves the stage, I turn and look at him. "Your parents are going to kill us."

"No, they won't," he says, standing. "Let's go talk to Mrs. Little."

Adam smiles and shakes his head. "Twenty bucks says you won't even have detention after Brad works his magic."

"What?" I ask, glancing between the two of them.

"He's a pro at negotiating his way out of these situations."

"There's nothing to negotiate," I say. "They told us not to use phones, and we were playing on one."

"That's where you're wrong," Brad says, leading us out of our row and then through the doorway. "The principal told us to stop texting and playing games. We were doing neither."

"That seems like a minor technicality."

"Minor, but important," Brad says with another smile. "Come on."

I follow him to the office, where we wait for only five minutes before being let into the vice principal's office.

"What can I do for you two?" Mrs. Little asks.

"Thanks for seeing us, ma'am. We'd like to discuss the detention slips you gave us," Brad says, sitting in a chair opposite her desk. I take the other one and swallow against the lump in my throat.

"What's there to discuss?"

"We were watching an important video on the phone, not texting or playing games."

She raises her eyebrows. "And?"

"No one said we were not allowed to watch videos, especially important ones."

She takes a deep breath and says, "That was inferred."

"With all due respect, inferred rules can be confusing for students. If we were not allowed to use our phones at all, perhaps it would have been better to tell us to turn them off rather than 'stop texting and playing games'?"

She shakes her head and asks, "Why was the video you were watching so important?"

"We were considering options for pets. You know that Hailey is in foster care, right?"

"Yes."

"It's been scientifically proven that pets can help heal trauma, especially in adolescents and teens. This could be an important piece of the puzzle for Hailey's growth and development."

"So, let me get this straight—you're claiming that you weren't aware that phone use was prohibited during the assembly because of poorly worded instructions? And, furthermore, that what the two of you were doing was more important than the speaker because it could have lifelong ramifications for Hailey?"

"Yes, ma'am," Brad says with a smile, his dimple dancing with pride.

I sit motionless, staring at the two of them. I can't believe Brad is even trying to argue this. It's ridiculous. Of course they didn't want us on phones. And baby pandas and otters are not going to change my life.

She taps her fingers on the desk for a few moments. "Considering your outstanding academic and athletic record, Bradley, I'll let you two off with a warning this time. Let's show more respect for our guests from now on, though."

"Yes, ma'am," Brad says, standing. "Thank you."

I stand, my mouth gaping, and follow him outside, too stunned to say anything.

Adam's waiting in the hall for us. "Well?" he asks.

"I—I guess I owe you twenty bucks," I say, finally finding my voice.

"Nah, you don't," Adam says, rocking his shoulder into mine. "But I told you. He has everyone at this school wrapped around his little finger."

He really does. I can't believe how smooth he looked in there, getting us out of a punishment we absolutely deserved.

"Well?" Brad says, holding his hands out. "What'd you think?"

"That was impressive."

"Glad I could help you out."

"You do realize you're also the one who got me *into* trouble, right?"

"Only because you have no sense of humor," he says with a twinkle in his eye, teasing me. "If you had just laughed at the first video, I wouldn't have had to find the others."

"So, I'm completely responsible for getting us into trouble, and you're completely responsible for getting us out of it?" I ask with raised eyebrows.

"Something like that," he says with a smile, laying his arm across my shoulders. "We make a good team."

I shake my head and smile. I wouldn't call what we did today good teamwork, but at least I can still claim I've never had detention. I look up at his beaming face and say, "Well, thank you, Brad, for saving the day."

"Anytime. That's what I'm here for."

He's trying to be funny, but there's some truth to what he's saying. I used to lie awake at night, picturing a knight riding in on a white horse to whisk me away from everything. The face of the knight changed from my dad to Chase to people I didn't know, but no matter who I pictured, I was always met by disappointment in the morning when my mom stumbled out of her bedroom and my stomach grumbled for food I wouldn't get.

As I got older, I realized what a ridiculous dream that was. That's what happens in movies, not real life. In real life, you wake up every morning and trudge through your day, hoping nothing too horrible happens. That was my life. I had accepted it. I figured it was the best I could ever hope for.

But maybe that doesn't have to be my life. A few weeks with the Campbells and my life has taken an abrupt U-turn. Who would've thought a couple good decisions could change so much? The bleak, miserable future I had accepted is transforming before my eyes. All it took was surrounding myself with people I could count on. Like Brad, who now has his arm casually draped over my shoulders.

I smile up at him and say, "Thanks."

"You're welcome," he replies, not realizing I'm thanking him for a lot more than just saving me from detention. He squeezes my shoulder and leads me down the hallway toward the cafeteria while more than a few people do a double take.

I have to bite my lip to stop myself from smiling. This is what life is like when you're not simply trudging through your day.

CHAPTER 14

"WRITE DOWN YOUR GIVEN," BRAD SAYS, BANGING PRETEND drumsticks along with the music coming out of his speakers. We're sitting on the floor with our backs against his bed.

I write down my given, then stare at the geometry proof, unsure of what to do next.

"What's the definition of a parallelogram?" he asks.

"Um . . . give me a second." I scan the glossary at the back of the book and find it. "A four-sided flat shape with straight sides where opposite sides are equal in length and opposite angles are equal."

"So, what do you need to prove here?"

"Well, I'm given that the opposite sides are equal in length, so I guess I need to prove the opposite angles are equal?"

"Exactly."

I raise my pencil, ready to do just that, but then realize I don't know how.

"Search for congruent figures," he says without even looking

at me. He tells me that at least twenty times during each tutoring session. Apparently, geometry is all about finding identical
figures.

"It's just one shape," I complain. "How can it be congruent?"

"It can't. Think about it."

My brain hurts. These sessions over the last few weeks have
been good for me, and my grade has gone from a D to a C, but it's
been painful. I don't know what it is, but my mind does not process
geometry. At all.

He grabs my book from me and flips to an earlier problem. He
points to it and then lowers the book back on my lap. Along the
way, his arm ends up between us, resting against my hip. It's not
like he's trying to cop a feel. It's just the innocent placement of
his arm between us, and the back of his hand happens to touch
my hip.

I try to focus back on the problem, but it's impossible. My eyes
are drawn to his hand.

My brain knows it means nothing. So why does my stomach suddenly feel like it's full of butterflies trying to bust their way out?

I glance back to my book, figuring he'll move his arm once he
realizes, but he doesn't. It just sits there, burning a hole through
my jeans.

I swallow, take a deep breath, and try to focus on the problem
before me. "So, I need to draw in a line to make two triangles?"
I ask, finally remembering what we did for the earlier problem.

"Yep."

I do it, but then stare at the problem again. His closeness is
making it even harder than normal to concentrate.

After a moment, he says, "This is exactly like the other problem."

"Right," I say, glancing down at his arm again, which still hasn't moved.

What is wrong with me? I cannot react to him like this. Besides, as nice as he is to me, he would never be interested in me. We're totally different people. Incongruent figures, really.

Oh my God.

I'm using geometry humor. What has happened to me? I giggle without even thinking.

"What's so funny?" he asks.

Crap. Was that out loud?

"Geometry's funny," I say, tapping my pencil on the book, not really wanting to get into the details with him.

"No, it's not."

I smile. "I made a weird geometry observation. That's all."

"Care to share?"

"Not really."

"Come on. I love a good math joke."

"It's not really a joke," I say with a shrug. "I was just thinking about congruency and how . . . incongruent the two of us are."

He frowns. "I wouldn't say that."

"You're a straight-A student, an athlete, have the best parents ever, will be invited to college with open arms, and I'm . . . none of those."

"Okay, so maybe we're incongruent, but I wouldn't say we're incompatible. Sometimes congruency is overrated. Congruency is boring. Incongruency makes things interesting."

"Like the whole opposites attract thing?" I say with a smile, then catch myself. "That's not what I meant," I continue as my face heats up. "I'm—"

"Brad! Hailey!" Adam yells, leaping into the room. "Come downstairs—we're all here."

Thank God. I jump up and away from Brad.

"Hey, Adam, you're early," Brad says, standing.

"Yeah, my mom was pissing me off. I had to get out of there."

"Uh-oh. What's going on?"

"College crap."

"Sorry, man," he says, patting Adam's shoulder.

"Are the girls downstairs?" I ask.

"Yeah, Abbie's starting the popcorn," Adam replies.

"I'll help her," I say before racing through the door and away from my embarrassing words to Brad.

When I join the girls, Abbie and Brittany are talking while waiting for the microwave to ding. Michelle is sitting on the sofa, playing on her phone.

"Hey," I say to everyone as I walk to the fridge. "Anyone want something to drink?"

"Coke," Brittany says.

"Sprite," says Abbie.

Michelle ignores me.

I pull out their drinks and grab a Sprite for myself.

"You have to come to our gig next Saturday," Brittany says, looking at me.

"Where is it?"

"The Arboretum. They're having some sort of festival. We're on from one to two."

"Want to go together?" Abbie asks.

"Sure, that sounds like fun."

"Hey, Brad," Michelle says, drawing my attention back to her. She's forgotten about her phone and is headed toward the stairs as the guys come down.

"Hey, Michelle. Abbie. Brittany," he says, stepping into the room.

Abbie and Brittany wave while Michelle sidles up next to him. "We got a romantic comedy today. We figured it was time for a girly movie, since we always watch explosions and aliens and all that boy stuff."

"Fine by me," he says, stepping around her to grab a Gatorade from the fridge.

Beeping from the microwave pulls me back to the kitchen area. Abbie pulls out the steaming bag and pours it into a huge bowl already halfway filled with popcorn, then we all take our seats.

I sit on the end like usual with Brittany right next to me. Abbie is between her and Adam. Brad and Michelle continue standing, rather than taking their normal spot at the end.

"Hey, Brittany," Adam says, "want to share some Junior Mints?"

"I'll get them for you," Brad offers, heading back to the kitchenette. He returns with not only those but also Sno-Caps, my favorite.

After Brad tosses the Junior Mints to Adam, Brittany gets up and sits next to him. "Are you trying to get lucky tonight?" she asks with a sideways glance.

"Do Junior Mints hold that much power over you?" Adam asks, handing her the box.

She smiles and accepts it. "In your dreams, buddy."

While I'm watching the two of them, Brad plops himself down right next to me, his leg touching mine. His freaking leg pushed up against me from hip to ankle. If I thought his arm was bad during tutoring, this is a thousand time worse. The pressure of his hard muscles, muscles I shouldn't even be thinking about, is like a gigantic fluorescent billboard. It commands all my attention, and the more I try to ignore it, the more noticeable it becomes.

"Sno-Cap?" he asks, holding the opened box between us.

I take it and pour a couple pieces of candy into my hand. He's not fazed at all. Of course not. He's not the least bit attracted to me, so he probably doesn't even notice the contact.

After handing the box back to him, I curl my legs under my body and scoot to the very edge of the sofa, practically on top of the armrest. It's uncomfortable, but at least it puts a few inches between us.

A loud huff draws my attention back to Michelle, who is still standing in the middle of the room. She shoots me an evil glare, then lowers herself next to Abbie, who holds out the bowl of popcorn. Stuffing kernel after kernel into her mouth, she stares at the television.

Great. She'll probably take her evilness to a whole new level now.

While chewing on a Sno-Cap, I try to focus on the drama of the movie and not the drama going on right around me. I have no idea what's up with Michelle and Brad, but I'd prefer to stay out of it. Maybe I should have Abbie remind Michelle how Brad and I are foster siblings and nothing more. Maybe it's all a simple misunderstanding that's leading to her nasty attitude.

Although a misunderstanding would be nice, I kind of doubt that's the problem. Michelle hasn't liked me from the minute we met, and at this point, I don't think there's anything I can do to change that.

As I pop another piece of candy in my mouth, I think about my options for dealing with her. I could dish it right back at her, but there's no way I could ever be as mean as her. I think you're either born with the mean gene or not. She was; I wasn't.

Really, my only other choice is to ignore her. From now on, I need to completely ignore everything she says and does.

And that's exactly what I do for the rest of the movie. I ignore both Michelle's attitude and Brad's closeness, Unfortunately, that's easier said than done, especially ignoring Brad.

CHAPTER 15

WALKING INTO THE GYM, I'M BLOWN AWAY BY ALL THE
decorations. I've never gone to a school dance before, let alone
homecoming. Brittany and I stroll under an arch of yellow and
white balloons to find the party in full swing.

A deep bass pounds through my chest, and flashing lights reflect off the shiny green and gold streamers. From a distance, my
dancing classmates seem to move as one, like some weird creature
with hundreds of arms spilling across the floor.

"Let's dance," Brittany squeals, dragging me to the center of
the creature.

I follow her lead, bouncing to an upbeat hip-hop song as we
wave our arms overhead. Everyone around me is shouting the
words. When it gets to the chorus, I join them, singing the part I know.

The energy in the room is overwhelming. There's no way I can
avoid getting drawn into it. Even Michelle must agree because
when she and Abbie join us during the next song, she smiles at me.
It's a first, and I wonder what's going on.

Brad and Adam are right behind them. I watch Brad out of the corner of my eye as he dances. He's a pretty serious guy, so I'm surprised by how relaxed he looks moving to the beat. I wouldn't say he's a great dancer, but he's cute. He's not embarrassed to try out some interesting moves, and I find myself grinning at the way he rocks his hips.

He catches my eye and smiles back before weaving through the crowd to appear right in front of me.

"Having fun?" he yells, still bouncing to the music, but in a more restrained way.

I nod. I'm glad I let them all persuade me to come. I didn't want to at first. I was worried I wouldn't fit in, and there was the issue of the dress and dinner beforehand. I've been with the Campbells for five weeks, so I have a little money saved up, but I didn't want to waste it on something frivolous like a dance. Luckily, Abbie had an old dress I could borrow, and Gil gave me some money for dinner. I still hate when they pay for stuff for me, but he reminded me it was food and I would never be expected to pay for my own food.

Now I realize how ridiculous I was being. This is fun. And no one cares how anyone dances. That's clear by Brad's newest move. His arms are out to the side, practically hitting the poor girl standing there, as his body jerks one way and then the next.

Despite that, he's still hot as can be. He's wearing khaki pants, a pin-striped button-down, a blue blazer, a green plaid tie, and loafers. It's very preppy. I never thought I liked that style because I'm usually attracted to the bad-boy look, but it definitely works on him. Although, I think any look would work on him. It's not the clothes. It's what's beneath the clothes.

Just then, the song ends and a slow one starts. I glance around me as people start pairing up, and try to find a quick exit off the dance floor. I find an opening and begin to head that way, when a hand lands on the small of my back.

Turning around, I find Brad, all smiles. "Want to dance?" he asks.

Because that wouldn't be weird at all.

We've become close friends, but is it normal for close friends to slow dance together? To me, it seems like that might be crossing some invisible line.

He raises his eyebrows, waiting for an answer.

"Seriously?" I say.

His face shifts from expectation to amusement in a fraction of a second. "What?" he asks. "Am I so disgusting you can't bear the thought of dancing with me?"

It would be nice if he were gross. It definitely would make things easier. "Yes, that's it," I reply with a grin. "I don't want to get your disgusting cooties on me."

He laughs and moves his hands to my waist. "Going old-school, huh? I haven't heard the word 'cooties' in at least ten years."

"I haven't said the word in at least ten years," I reply with a smile, lightly laying my arms on his shoulders and clasping my fingers behind his neck. This is the closest we've ever been and it feels way too intimate, just like I thought it would. "Is this really a good idea?" I ask.

He reaches for my right hand and lays it on top of his. With a finger from his other hand, he traces shapes on my palm while saying, "Circle, circle, dot, dot—now you've got a cootie shot." Then he replaces my arm where it was but moves our bodies even closer. "Feel better?" he asks. "You're now fully vaccinated against my disgusting cooties."

I laugh at his seriousness and then bite my lip. Does he not notice how awkward this is?

Apparently not, because he starts swaying our bodies to the music. "You look nice tonight," he says.

"Thanks." I glance down to my black-and-silver dress and stay focused on the skirt swaying from side to side because it's easier than watching his face so close to mine.

He's quiet for a few minutes, and I wonder what he's thinking. All that's running through my mind is how my chest brushes against his every time we lean to the left. Under normal circumstances, I'd enjoy the fluttering in my stomach, but right now, I want to kick myself for having it with him.

"So, how's it feel to be a Pinecrest girl?" he asks, obviously not sharing my messed-up thoughts.

"Fine," I reply, taking a half step back.

"That's it?"

"What did you expect?"

He peers down at me with a grin. "I don't know. Maybe more than a one-word answer?"

"It's fine."

He laughs and shakes his head. "I love when I can draw out smart-ass Hailey. It's rare, but always a special treat."

Just then, a pop song starts. My fingers snap apart like they're made of springs, and I step away from him, grateful our dance is over.

As soon as I turn to the side, I realize I'm not the only one. Michelle is standing there, hands on hips and evil in her eyes. I guess our momentary truce is already over.

"I was supposed to get the first dance," she says, transforming the glare to a pout as she focuses on Brad.

"My bad."

"Next one?" she asks.

"Sure, if I'm around."

His answer brightens her mood. She twirls, flipping her hair in my direction, and goes back to Abbie.

"She hates me," I say to him, watching her bubble over with excitement as she whispers something in Abbie's ear.

"Possibly."

I whip my head toward him and stare in disbelief. "Really?" I ask with a laugh. "You're supposed to say something like, 'No, she doesn't. She's just moody. She treats everyone like dirt.'"

"Right," he says, nodding his head. "Let me try again. She's moody. She treats everyone she hates like dirt."

I laugh again and gently smack his arm. "You're not making me feel any better."

"Is that what you wanted?"

"Yes!"

"Okay, okay," he says, holding up his hands in surrender. "You should've said so. Michelle is immature and moody. As soon as she finds a new villain in her life, you'll be spared."

"When will that happen?"

"As soon as somebody wrongs her."

"Like who?"

"Could be anyone. Want me to do it?" he asks, his eyes lighting up with excitement.

"What would you do?"

"Ditch my dance with her tonight."

"That's mean. You told her you would."

"I told her I would if I was around. If you want, I'm more than willing to take the bullet for you."

"For me or for yourself?"

"There are lots of benefits to this plan," he says with a lopsided grin before leading me back to Brittany and Adam, who are dancing together. Actually—I do a double take—more like grinding together. This is a surprising new development.

Brad and I form a circle with a couple of other people near us, and luckily, we all leave plenty of space between our bodies. There's no way I could dance like Brittany. I'm pretty sure I would die of embarrassment.

After a couple more songs, my legs grow sore, and I've got sweat beading up on my forehead. I need a break. "Come with me to get a drink?" I ask Brittany.

"Sure!"

We wave to the guys and head over to the refreshment table, where I pour two cups of punch and hand one to her.

"What's up with you and Adam?" I ask.

"I could ask you the same about Brad."

"Uh, no," I say, shaking my head. "We had one slow dance together as friends. You and Adam are all over each other."

She laughs at me. "He's cute, isn't he?"

"Yeah."

"We'll see what happens," she says with a shrug before crushing her cup in her hand and tossing it into the trash can. "Ready for another—"

I don't hear the rest of her sentence because Brad barrels into me, grabbing my hand and pulling me away from her. "Come on, come on, come on—I've got to disappear."

"Wait! What?" I yell, trying to dig in my heels, but it's no use.

"Slow song. Michelle," he says, still dragging me. It's then I notice the change in music. It is much slower. I can't believe he's really going to hide from her. He can't do this all night.

I wave to Brittany, who's watching us and shaking her finger at me like she's warning me to be good.

I finally stop fighting him and let him lead me through the crowd to a back door. We slip outside, leaving the chaotic sounds and lights behind us, although my ears still ring from the music.

"We're going to hide in a back alley?"

"Yep."

"From some silly girl?"

"Yep."

"Just so you don't have to dance with her?"

"Yep."

"I've never been more impressed by your bravery," I say with a roll of my eyes.

"I can't slay dragons every day. Sometimes, it's easier to run from them. Come on, let's go this way," he says, starting to walk into the dark night.

We're silent as he leads me around some dumpsters, between two tennis courts, and to the football field. He flips a lever on the gate, and it swings open.

We climb to the top of the stands and sit on the edge of a bench. It's a different view than I'm used to with his games, because Gil and Gigi like to sit in the front. Although I wonder why we're here, it is nice. It's peaceful with a bird's-eye view of the forest beyond the field and a small lake to the left, shimmering in the moonlight.

"So, why exactly are we here?" I ask, turning to face him.

"Michelle? Ring a bell?"

"We didn't have to come all the way out here."

"It's my favorite place," he says with a shrug. "It has lots of good memories."

"It is nice. Much more peaceful than on game days."

"Yeah. I love all the energy of games, but sometimes I need to come up here by myself to clear my mind."

"You needed to clear your mind tonight?"

"It helps me deal with Michelle," he says with a grin.

"She likes you."

"Not really. She likes the idea of me."

"Huh?"

He sighs and says, "She'd donate a kidney to land a popular senior as a boyfriend. It doesn't have to be me. In fact, we have very little in common. She needs to focus on someone else."

"Is she always like this?" I stare at his profile. The moonlight casts deep shadows along his nose and cheekbones, making his features look even more chiseled than usual.

"Not this bad. She's just jealous."

"Of what?"

"You," he says, turning to face me.

"Me?" I ask with wide eyes. That's impossible. No one has ever been jealous of me. "There's no way."

"She's generally not a fan of girls who are prettier than her."

I laugh. "That's clearly not a problem."

"What do you mean?"

"She's gorgeous. I'm ordinary."

"That's not the word on the street."

My heart drops to Abbie's silver sandals on my feet. "What street?" With my mom's reputation for a new boyfriend every week, I don't want my name attached to any street. Ever.

"The guys' locker room."

Oh my God. That's just as bad. Why are they talking about me? I have done nothing since coming here that should make me the subject of trashy locker-room gossip.

"Don't worry!" he says, rocking his body into mine as he takes in my petrified face. "It's nothing bad. A few of the guys were asking me why the cute new girl was hanging out with my parents at games. I told them you're a family friend and your mom got really sick so you have to stay with us for a while. I kept it vague. One of them wanted to know if he could ask you out," he says, arching an eyebrow at me. "Aiden. He's in your creative-writing class. Says you guys talk sometimes."

I know who he is. Our teacher makes us partner up almost every day to critique each other's work. Aiden sits in front of me and always offers to be my partner. He's nice and has a wild imagination. My stories are about as ordinary as me.

"I told him you've just gotten out of a relationship, so he should wait."

"Oh." That's true. But even so, I'm not remotely interested in Aiden. He's good-looking and nice, but I've never felt . . . "it" around him. I'm not exactly sure what "it" is, but if I'm going to date someone, I'd like for thoughts other than "Is this class ever going to end?" going through my mind when we talk.

"Was that okay?" Brad asks.

"Yeah, I guess so."

"If you want to go out with him, I can tell him you're ready."

"No," I mumble. This whole conversation is starting to make me feel uncomfortable.

"Are you sure?"

"Yeah."

"Is the problem Aiden or dating in general?"

I'm not against dating again, although I would first need to find someone suitable. The only guy who's gotten even close to making me feel "it" is definitely not suitable. "Why are we talking about this?" I ask, fidgeting on the bench.

"Just trying to see where your head is."

"Why?"

"I could always take you out on a 'practice' date if you think it'd help."

He's got to be kidding. I study his face, but he's staring straight ahead and gives nothing away. Is he trying to be funny? Supportive? My mind swirls in different directions, but I can't come up with a good reason for him to say something like that.

When I don't answer, he says, "Tell me something good about your childhood."

I'm about to object, when he turns toward me and holds up his hand. "Don't tell me there's nothing good. You have to have at least one good memory from being a kid."

It doesn't take me long to come up with my best memory growing up. When things got really bad, I used to hold on to that memory like a raft in a raging river. It gave me hope that if I survived the current rapids, we could turn things around again.

"On Fridays, after school, when I was young, like five or six, my mom used to get me one of those little bottles of Sunny D and a new coloring book and crayons. Then we'd spend an hour together, just me and her, coloring and talking. It was the only time I ever remember her focusing on me."

"That's nice," he says.

"It was. Years later, I learned she had to walk to the Dollar Store, three miles round-trip, every Friday to get those things."

"She really went out of her way to do something nice for you."

"Yeah. It was sweet. Of course . . ."

"Stop right there," he says, holding a finger to my lips. "This is a fun night. Let's save the negative talk for another time."

I know his movement is to shut me up and the casual touch means nothing, but my mind and heart can't seem to get on the same page. It's like my heart is sending texts to every cell in my body, telling them to turn to mush. It's so inappropriate, and I begin to wonder if there's something seriously wrong with me.

"Ready to get back to the dance?" he asks. "You looked like you were having fun in there."

I think that's an excellent idea. Any more time out here and I might do or say something really stupid.

When we reach the main entrance to the gym, he holds the door open for me. I walk through and then wait for him, but he stands outside, waving. "I'll meet you at the car when it's over."

"What? Why?"

"You must be repressing Michelle from your memory for some reason."

I roll my eyes. He's not usually this immature. "You're seriously not coming back in because of *her*?"

"Yep."

"What are you going to do?"

"Watch the game," he says, tilting his head toward a group of guys crowded around a tablet. Their faces are bathed in blue light from whatever is playing. "Have fun!" he says, before strolling over to them.

I shake my head. Apparently he's not as mature I thought.

Wandering through the crowd, I find Brittany and Adam. When they see I'm alone, their dancing becomes PG-rated and they welcome me into their little circle. I can't stop thinking about Brad. I've never had a close guy friend before. It's different. And confusing. Lines are blurred. Actions are overthought. Reactions, at least on my part, are messed up. It would make me feel better if I thought he was dealing with it, too, but I don't get that impression. He's the perfect foster brother and has taken his role seriously.

So, why can't I have only sisterly feelings around him?

What is wrong with me?

CHAPTER 16

THE CAFETERIA LINE CRAWLS TODAY. I TAP MY FOOT AS I WAIT for the girl in front of me to decide between pizza and wings. It's not that hard of a decision. They're both delicious. She sticks her hand in, almost grabs a slice, but shakes her head and walks away empty-handed. I grab a basket and, after keying in my code, rush toward my usual table.

I have to talk to Brittany. This whole Brad thing is messing with my head. For the past four nights, I hardly got any sleep as homecoming kept replaying in my mind. I finally decided I needed help. Maybe someone on the outside can provide me with a better perspective and get my stupid hormones in line.

"Can we talk?" I ask, sliding in next to her and her friends.

"What's up?" she replies.

I motion for her to follow me to the other end of the table so we can have some privacy.

"This must be big," she says, pulling a fruit cup out of her lunch bag.

"I like Brad."

There. I said it. You can't fix a problem until you admit you have one, right?

"No kidding," she replies, rolling her eyes.

"This is a huge problem!"

"How so?"

"He's my foster brother! What is wrong with me? How can I even think of him like that?"

She opens her fruit, then says, "Because he's hot as hell and the nicest guy in school?"

"And also my brother."

"Come on," she says, waving the plastic lid in her hand. "He's not really your brother."

I stare at her like she's got a unicorn horn coming out of her forehead. "He is as long as I'm living in his home with his parents. Do you ever think about your foster brother's gorgeous eyes?"

She cringes. "No, gross."

"Exactly my point."

"Jonas is ten, Hailey."

"Oh." I thought he was older. "I need to figure out a way to only think sister thoughts around him."

She empties the fruit cup in three bites. "I'm pretty sure he's not thinking brotherly thoughts around you."

"What? Of course he is. He's been the perfect big brother."

She searches in her lunch bag for something while saying, "I saw the way he looked at you at homecoming." She pulls out her hand, holding a plastic bag of Oreos. "Michelle wishes she could get that look. Want one?"

I grab an Oreo. "You're being ridiculous. He was acting nice. Trying to make me comfortable."

"Uh-huh," she says, laying the cookies on the table and reaching down to her backpack on the floor.

"What are you doing?"

"Texting a friend. I want to know if there's a DSS rule about dating your foster sibling."

I practically spit out my Oreo. "Of course there is!"

She shakes her head. "I'm not so sure. They want us to be normal. They aren't going to tell us we can't date."

"Dating in general is way different from dating the boy whose house you live in."

She types a message and then lays her phone on the table. "Maybe."

When I'm done with the cookie, I turn to my chicken wings. After swallowing a bite, I ask, "How do you convince yourself a guy is physically repulsive?"

"Never gonna happen with Brad."

"It has to happen." If not, I'll end up driving myself crazy.

Her phone vibrates on the table and she picks it up. After scanning the screen, she says, "Bummer."

"What?" I ask, licking sauce off my fingers and craning my neck to see her phone.

"There were two foster kids in the same house who started dating a while back. DSS moved one of them somewhere else. So, you've got to decide—Brad or your placement."

"There's nothing to decide. Brad's not into me. I just need to get my hormones under control."

She smiles. "Maybe if you convince yourself he's a serial killer?"

I frown. "That's the best you've got?"

"Yeah, sorry."

❋ ❋ ❋ ❋

Later that afternoon, I get to try Brittany's idea when Brad comes home from school. I'm sitting at the kitchen table doing my homework like usual when he walks through the door, hair still wet from a shower after practice. He's wearing a T-shirt and athletic shorts, which reminds me of that first morning when I watched him working out. He still looks just as good, if not better, and I force my eyes to the side.

"Hey, Hailey," he says, hanging up his backpack.

"Hey."

"Where's Mom?"

"In her office. She's negotiating on a new piece of art."

After strolling over to the oven where Gigi has a roast baking, he opens the door and looks inside. I stare at his back and try to convince myself he might have murderous tendencies, but it's impossible.

"What are you looking at?" he asks, joining me at the table. I blush, realizing I must have been staring at him the entire time.

"Oh, sorry. I was daydreaming."

"About what?"

"Chemistry," I say, lowering my gaze to the book in front of me.

"Chemistry does that to me, too. Calculating the number of moles in a gram of hydrochloric acid is just so exciting."

"Zero-point-zero-three." I only know because that was the last problem I did.

He smirks as he sits down. "You're such a nerd."

"That means a lot coming from the straight-A student."

He grins at me again. "Soooo," he says, drawing out the word. "I was thinking about our talk at homecoming and . . ."

I sit back in my chair, fold my arms across my chest, and wait for him. I assume he's going to talk about Michelle. As far as I know, they still haven't discussed his lack of interest. Maybe he needs help coming up with a way to let her down easy.

"You know that practice date I mentioned?"

My eyes grow wide and my arms drop to my sides. *No, no, no,* I silently pray. *Let's not talk about this.*

"Uh-huh," I say with a gulp.

"How about tomorrow? We have a half day, and I don't have football. The timing is perfect."

"I don't think I need a practice date."

"Sure you do. Aiden could ask you out any day."

That would be just my luck. "I don't want to go out with Aiden."

"Why not? He's nice."

"Yeah."

"According to the girls, he's good-looking."

"Yeah."

"So, what's the problem?"

"He's not my type," I say with a shrug, and turn the page in my chemistry book. My eyes scan the page, but I don't bother to make sense of the words. I wish he would just drop the subject. Why is this so important to him?

"What's your type?"

I shrug again.

"Chase?"

"No." I wouldn't say he was necessarily my type as much as someone who filled a void I desperately needed. It probably could've been filled by anyone who gave me a little bit of attention.

"What is it then?"

"Brad," I say with a deep breath, and then close my book. "I'm not comfortable talking to you about this. I'm sorry."

Leaving him in the kitchen, I climb the stairs and spend the next thirty minutes in my room while I wait for dinner. It was a wimpy thing to do, but I never claimed to be strong. If I'm going to survive around him, I need to know when to walk away.

* * * *

Luckily, everything returns to normal, and it's as if he never mentioned the practice date when he drives me to school and we pass in the hallways during our half day. After the early-dismissal bell rings, I go to the front of the building and wait for him like usual.

I take a seat on a bench and watch as other students are picked up by parents. After ten minutes, when only a handful of us remain, I start to get worried. Brad's generally out here by now. I glance back to the door but don't see him. I do, however, see a scowling Michelle.

She immediately starts doing something on her phone, although I'm pretty sure she saw me. Regardless, she walks to the other side of the waiting area from me and leans against the wall, still playing on her phone.

Since she's ignoring me, I have no problem doing the same. I focus back on the line of cars, as students, one by one, head out to enjoy their free afternoon. It's a gorgeous, sunny day, and I think about what I could do. I could do my homework outside. Or read a book on the Campbells' hammock. Or take a nap.

The last car pulls up, then drives away, leaving only me and Michelle. I glance in her direction again, but she's angled away from me as if purposely trying to pretend she doesn't see me. It's ridiculous. We're only ten feet from each other. Obviously, she knows I'm here.

"Hey, Michelle," I finally say, trying to be nice.

Her head snaps up, as if she's truly surprised to hear my voice. I have to fight the eye roll.

"Oh, hey, Hailey," she says.

When she doesn't say anything else, I add, "What's up?"

"Just waiting on my mom."

I nod. "I'm waiting on Brad. He's usually out here by now."

"Have you texted him?"

"I don't have a phone."

Her eyes light up. "Do you want me to do it?"

"No, that's okay. I'm sure he'll be here soon."

"I don't mind," she says, suddenly chatty. She frantically moves her fingers over the screen of her phone and then lowers it. "I'll let you know what he says."

"Thanks," I reply. Kind of. It would be nice to know where he is, but we both know the reason she offered and it has nothing to do with helping me.

She nods and then gets quiet again. After a moment, she bites her lip and shifts from one foot to the other.

"Want to sit down?" I offer, scooting to the edge of the bench. She shakes her head.

We're silent for another moment before she picks up her phone and looks at the screen. "He says his calculus teacher was nagging him to enter a math competition. He's on his way out now."

"Oh, okay. Thanks."

We're silent again, and it feels so incredibly awkward that I have to say something. "So, any plans for the afternoon?"

She twists her lips, as if thinking about what to say, then shakes her head. "Nope."

More silence. More awkwardness.

"How long have you and Abbie been friends?" I ask. It's the only thing I could come up with.

"Since preschool."

"That's nice."

More silence. We seem totally unable to have a real conversation.

"I like your shoes," I offer. They're black ankle boots that look brand-new.

"Thanks." She picks up her phone and starts typing again, making it clear she doesn't mind the silence between us.

I make a face at her since she's clearly not paying attention to me, then glance back to the door, just as Brad strolls through. Finally.

"Sorry," he says, as he approaches me. "Ms. Kay would not take no for an answer."

"So, you're joining some math competition?"

"Apparently. At least it's not until January, after football season. Hey, Michelle," he says as she steps next to us, suddenly no longer treating me like I've got a deadly disease. "Why didn't you catch a ride with Adam?"

"Mom's taking me to visit Nana."

"Visit?" Brad asks, his eyebrows drawn. "Is she not living with you anymore?"

"No, Mom moved her to a nursing home a couple weeks ago."

"Oh, sorry. I didn't realize."

"That's because we don't hang out like we used to." She gives me a much dirtier look than I gave her a couple minutes ago. Plus, it's actually to my face, unlike what I did to her back. How can one person be so freaking mean?

"Is she getting worse?" Brad asks, stuffing his hands into his pocket.

"Yeah," she replies.

"I'm sorry. Please tell her I say hi."

"She won't remember you. She only recognizes me half the time."

He bites his lip and nods, clearly not knowing what to say. Luckily, a silver minivan pulls up at that moment, saving him.

"See ya later," she says with a wave that's clearly only for him.

"See ya," we both say, as I stand.

Once she's gone, Brad looks at me with a smile. "I bet the two of you were having fun before I got out here," he says, rocking his body into mine. "She seemed her overly friendly self today."

"Oh my God," I reply, rolling my eyes. "She's impossible."

He smiles again. "I didn't realize her grandmother was doing worse. She's got Alzheimer's. That might be part of the reason she's acting like this. She doesn't handle stress well."

As bad as I feel for Michelle, it doesn't really excuse her behavior. I've had plenty of stress, but I don't take it out on people I barely know.

"They were really close when she was growing up," he continues, as we walk toward the student parking lot. "Her grandmother basically raised her because her mom had such a crazy work schedule at the hospital."

"This must be hard, then," I say. Still, no excuse to treat me like she does.

"Yeah," he replies. "So, are you going to come cheer me on during the math competition?" he asks with a silly grin.

"You do realize how nerdy a math competition sounds, right?"

"I do, but I learned long ago to embrace my inner nerd."

"Reeeally?" I reply, drawing out the word and giving him a sideways glance. He's about the least nerdy nerd I've ever met.

"Yep. I have a pocket protector, glasses, even a protractor at home. I've been saving them for a special occasion, just like this."

Smiling, I ask, "Are there specific nerdy math cheers I should practice for this big day?"

He grins. "I'll trust you to come up with some."

I think for a moment, then say, "Like 'Brad, Brad, he's our man, if he can't multiply, no one can!'" I clap my hands, then raise them overhead like the cheerleaders do at the football games.

He laughs. "I think it will be less multiplication and more finding derivatives and integrating functions."

I have no clue what that means, but I still come up with another cheer. "When I say derivatives, you say Brad. Derivatives!" I turn around and walk backward so I can watch him.

He laughs and shakes his head.

"Brad!" I answer for him, throwing my arms up again. "Oh! I've got a good one," I say pointing at him. "Two, four, six, eight,

Brad's gonna integrate!" I wiggle my fingers in his direction like the cheerleaders do when a player's getting ready to kick the ball.

"On second thought," he says, playfully swatting my hands down, "maybe you should stay home during the competition."

"You don't think I'd make a great cheerleader?" I ask with a laugh. There's no way I could ever be a cheerleader.

"Well," he says with a smirk, "as good as you'd look in the outfit, I'm not sure all the nerds could handle it."

My stomach does a little flip at his words, and then I shake it off. He's just being his usual nice self. Like always.

"So, want to grab lunch?" he asks, unlocking my door and opening it for me when we get to his car only moments later. "Just lunch. No pretend date, because I'd hate to make you mad like yesterday."

"I wasn't mad."

"You sure seemed mad."

"I was uncomfortable."

"Uncomfortable," he says, rolling the word around on his tongue like it's a foreign concept. I'm sure Brad has never felt uncomfortable in his life, other than his one embarrassing moment. "So, lunch?" he asks again. "Mom's treat, since she didn't plan ahead and leave us anything at home."

"Okay, fine," I relent, taking a seat and buckling up. I'm starving, and it'd be nice to get something quick and easy.

He circles around the car and joins me. "Where to?"

"I don't care."

"What kind of food do you want?"

"It doesn't matter."

"Mexican? Pizza? Fast food?"

"Whatever."

He starts up the car. "You narrow it down to two, and I'll pick."

"Mexican or McDonald's," I offer, giving him two fairly cheap and quick options.

"Mexican it is," he says, backing out of his parking spot.

Five minutes later, he pulls into a strip mall close to his house, and we enter the small restaurant. It's got sombreros, guitars, and striped blankets hanging on the walls. There are only two other customers this time of day, so we're seated immediately and given chips and salsa.

I dip a chip and watch Brad study the menu as I chew. His brows are drawn, causing a crease to form between his eyes. It's like this one decision about what to eat for lunch is a matter of life and death.

Glancing quickly at the menu, I see a lunch special for under five dollars. Easy decision.

Brad continues to scrutinize every word. He must be reading the entire thing line by line, although his eyes aren't moving. It seems like he's just staring at one spot on the menu. I nibble on another chip and wait.

And wait.

And wait.

Finally, he closes the menu and meets my eyes. "I've decided," he says.

"It's about time."

"It wasn't an easy decision."

"Lunch is a serious matter," I reply with a grin.

Just then, the waiter appears and asks, "What can I get for you?"

"Combo number three," I say.

"Um . . . give me a sec," Brad says, opening up the menu again. What in the heck is his problem?

"Um . . . I guess I'll go with the fajitas."

"Chicken or steak?"

"Steak."

We hand over the menus and I stare at Brad, trying to figure out his bizarre behavior. "You forgot what you spent like five minutes deciding on?"

"Nope." He reaches across the table and rests his hand on mine. My head snaps down to the contact as my stomach starts filling with butterflies. "I wasn't deciding on lunch. I decided I just need to do this. I'm sorry I made you uncomfortable yesterday, and if I'm reading you wrong, I'm even more sorry for what I'm about to do."

The butterflies stop in midair at his unexpected words, and my eyes drift back up to his face. What in the world is happening?

"But I like you, and I think you like me," he says in rush. "I've decided I just need to lay it out there and see what happens."

I stare at him with a blank face.

"So . . ."

I can't respond. I can't even form any thoughts.

"Just laying it out there," he repeats, squeezing my hand.

I glance down but still can't make sense of what's going on. It's like I'm in some alternate universe where everything is turned upside down.

"To see what happens."

I remain silent, focused on where our hands meet. His fingers are strong and rough against my skinny ones—another reminder of how different we are.

"Which apparently is nothing good," he says, dragging his hand away. The loss of warmth draws my eyes up to his face again. There's a faint red tint to his cheeks. I've never seen him blush before, and it makes him even cuter.

"Sorry," he says. "I honestly thought you felt something." He stuffs a chip in his mouth. "I should've waited until after lunch. Now I've got to sit here for like twenty minutes trying to pretend I didn't just humiliate myself in front of you. This is officially my most embarrassing moment now. God, where is our food?" he asks, looking toward the kitchen.

Meeting my eyes again, he asks, "Should we just go? We don't need to sit here and pretend like everything's normal."

He starts to stand, and I finally find my voice. "No, let's stay."

He raises his eyebrows and slides back into his chair. "You sure?"

"Yes."

"Okay," he says slowly. He drums his fingers on the table and continues watching me, his cheeks still red while mine are probably white as snow, since all the blood drained from my face about a minute ago.

"I'm really sorry," he says again.

"Don't be," I murmur, my eyes dropping to the table. I can't believe he's been feeling the same thing as me this whole time. It's . . . shocking. Shocking, but reassuring.

"No. It's completely wrong of me. I thought . . . never mind. It doesn't matter. This won't change things. I promise. We'll be . . . foster siblings," he says with a slight cringe.

"You like me?" I whisper, afraid if I say it any louder he'll come to his senses and realize his mistake.

"No," he says, shaking his head.

I frown.

"I mean, yes?"

"Which is it?" I ask, starting to get even more confused.

"Yes, unless that's not what you want. I'll leave it up to you," he says, resting his hand on mine again. "You tell me—which is it?"

This is it. It feels like another defining moment in my life. I'm given the choice of two paths—a safe but difficult one or a dangerous but exhilarating one. My brain tells me to go with the safe option, but my body has been hijacked by my heart.

"Yes," I whisper. "It's a yes."

CHAPTER 17

"OKAY, THEN. THIS IS GOOD," BRAD SAYS, HIS WHOLE DEMEANOR transformed from a couple of minutes ago.

"Yeah, I guess so," I reply, a shy smile spreading across my face.

He squeezes my hand, causing my stomach to flip and the smile to grow even larger. I can't believe it. Brad, Bradley Campbell, one of the most popular boys at school, actually likes me. Me, of all people. I feel like I'm in some cheesy romantic comedy.

"So, maybe we could go out tonight? Dinner and a movie? I'm paying. Don't even think about protesting."

That's when reality comes crashing down on me like a monstrous tidal wave. I can't go out with him. We can't be seen in public on a date. I snatch my fingers from his and hold them in my lap. "Wait," I say as my brain takes charge. My frown causes his smile to fade.

"What? I'm a Southern gentleman, remember? I'm not letting you pay."

"This isn't a good idea."

"Seriously? You're going to fight me about who pays for our dates?"

"No, not that," I say, shaking my head. "Us. Together. It's a terrible idea."

"No, it's not. You like me. I like you. Let's give it a try to see how it works out."

The sound of our arriving food causes him to pause. The waiter lowers Brad's sizzling skillet of fajitas in front of him and my burrito combo in front of me. Brad starts loading a tortilla with steak and peppers, clearly not getting it.

"Um, Brad?"

"Yeah?" he asks, looking up.

"You're forgetting one very important thing."

He glances at his fajita. "What?"

"You're my foster brother. I can't date you!"

He stares at me like I'm the most complex geometry problem he's ever seen. "But I'm not your brother."

"Yes, you are."

"Not biologically."

"So?"

"Brothers dating sisters is wrong because they're actually related—the whole incest thing. You and me," he says, motioning between the two of us with his finger, "no similar DNA. Not related. Nothing gross or against the law."

"Except I live in your house."

"Which will make dating that much easier," he replies, smiling.

"Come on. You have to admit it would be weird."

He tilts his head back and forth a few times as though considering the idea. "Not really. What if you were staying somewhere else and we had met at school? Would it be okay then?"

"Yes."

"What if I was in college and came home on weekends? Would it be okay then?"

"Where am I living in this scenario?"

"With my parents."

"Then no."

He takes a bite of fajita, then follows that with a gulp of water. "So the issue is my parents?"

"And sharing a house with you."

"Why?"

For such a smart guy, he's being awfully dense. "I can come up with about a million reasons. You can't come up with one?"

He takes another bite while deep in thought. After about a minute, he says, "Got one. The kiss good night would be confusing. Should I do it at the front door or the door to your bedroom?"

I roll my eyes. "Why are you not taking this seriously?"

"Sorry, sorry," he says, giving me a smile that doesn't look apologetic at all. "We don't have time to go through your million reasons. Can you give me the top two?"

"There's no way DSS or your parents would allow it. I'd get kicked out. And what happens when we get into a fight or break up? We'd be forced to talk at dinner even if we hated each other."

"Wow. Okay. Nothing like planning for a very bleak future," he says, leaning back in his chair.

"Be serious."

"Mom and Dad would never kick you out. I won't let them."

"What about when we break up?"

He grins at me. "Can't we enjoy the benefits of dating for a while before we start talking about our imminent breakup? Like for at least five minutes?"

I try not to smile but fail. I blame it on his dimple, which looks way too cute right now. All his earlier shyness is gone, replaced by his normal confidence. A confidence that I find way too appealing. "And what benefits exactly would you like to enjoy for five minutes?" I ask, crossing my arms.

He twists his lip for a moment, as if deep in thought. "I'm kind of partial to the kissing benefit, but," he says, glancing around the restaurant, "this might not be the right place for that."

"You think?"

"A close second would be the hand-holding benefit." He lays his hands on the table. I give him a look that I hope lets him know what a bad idea this is as I lightly place my palms in his. His smile grows even larger as he squeezes my fingers.

This is a terrible, terrible idea, my brain reminds me.

Yet I can't stop the fluttering in my chest that's telling me it might not be *that* terrible. We're just holding hands, my heart rationalizes to my brain. It's innocent. Nothing horrible can come of something so sweet and innocent. Right?

Right. I gulp and squeeze his fingers back. By the look on his face, I get the impression he could sit like this the rest of the day. And I'd probably love every minute of it. My heart takes a big victory lap around my brain at the idea.

Then my stomach grumbles loudly, and I realize I need my hands to eat.

"I'm kind of hungry," I say, glancing between his pleased face and my plate of food.

He laughs and lets go of me. The loss of contact causes my brain to take control again. It trips my heart at the finish line and then stands victoriously over the beating pile of mush.

"I'd hate to be responsible for you missing a meal," he says.

We both take a bite of our food and chew slowly, watching each other. I have no idea what's going through his mind, but mine is obviously a mess if I'm visualizing my heart and brain battling it out in a track-and-field event.

After a moment, he says, "We're two minutes in and so far, so good. No fighting. Maybe we could try it for a little longer before we completely scrap the idea?"

"You honestly don't have any concerns about this?"

He shakes his head. "Nope."

I take another two bites while my heart scrambles up from the ground. My brain tries to tackle it, but it sneaks away and sticks out its tongue from somewhere in the corner of the room. "I guess I could think about it," I finally say, accepting the long-distance high five from my heart while my brain does a facepalm. So much for all the good decisions I had started making.

* * * *

"Start up the fire!" Abbie yells later that night as we step onto the patio in her backyard. Rather than dinner and a movie with just Brad, we're having dinner with his friends at Adam and Abbie's house. Brad and Adam are lounging around the fire pit. When we approach the table behind them, they both stand.

"I'm starving," Brad says, grabbing hot dogs and buns, which are balanced precariously on a bag of marshmallows in my arms.

We lower the food to the table as Adam makes a mile-high fire appear out of nowhere with just the turn of a knob.

"Who's thirsty?" Brittany asks, setting bottles of soda and cups on the table.

"Me," I answer, reaching for the Coke and then pouring myself a cup. "Sprite?" I ask Brad. He nods, so I fill a cup for him and then take orders from Abbie, Brittany, and Adam. Luckily, Michelle isn't here. I don't know why, and I don't care. I'll just enjoy the peacefulness while it lasts.

As if reading my thoughts, Brad asks, "Where's Michelle?"

Abbie replies, "She's at UNC Wilmington, visiting her cousin for the weekend. She won't be back until Sunday."

I try to hide a smile at the news but must fail because Brad pokes me in the side with his elbow. "Don't look so happy," he whispers.

"Sorry," I reply, now smiling even bigger, "I'm just tired of her evil glares."

He rolls his eyes. "She's not evil. She's just . . ."

"Yes?" I ask as I stop my pouring. It's childish and ridiculous, but I can't stop myself from feeling a little irritated he'd defend her. I realize we're not together, but I still don't want him standing up for her of all people.

"You're right," Brad says, taking one look at my face. "She's evil." He tears open the package of hot dogs and then begins spearing them with metal skewers.

"Good answer," Brittany says, slapping him on the back. Then she winks at me.

I roll my eyes. Since our talk yesterday, she's been looking for every opportunity to point out anything he does that could remotely be taken as a sign he likes me. I haven't told her signs are no longer needed since he flat-out told me earlier today. I thought about telling her but realized it would open a whole can of worms I don't want to get into with her or anyone else.

"You better be careful," Abbie says, reaching for a skewer from Brad. "First high maintenance and now evil? If she finds out what you've been saying, there will be hell to pay."

Brad holds tight to the skewer as she tries to pull it away. "How do you know I called her high maintenance?"

"Adam told me," she says, yanking the hot dog from him.

Brad glares at Adam.

"Dude, you know I don't gossip," he replies, turning around to focus on the fire and clearly distancing himself from the drama right here.

We all stare at Abbie. "Well, technically I overheard you telling Adam."

"Overheard or spied on us?" Brad asks.

"Don't even give me that. You read my entire diary when I was eleven. This doesn't even compare!"

He smiles. "Stephen is sooooo cute! I hope he'll sit next to me in choir. Maybe he'll be my first kiss," Brad says in a girly voice, and then makes kissing noises in her direction.

"You're such a pain in the ass," she says, reaching around me to smack his arm.

He smiles at her and then turns serious again. "Don't tell Michelle, okay?" he says.

"I won't," Abbie says, giving him an annoyed look before taking her hot dog over to the fire.

He hands me and Brittany each a skewer and then the three of us join Abbie and Adam. I sit on the edge of a sofa. Brad stands next to me and we start cooking our dinner over the flames.

"Did you really read Abbie's diary?" I ask.

"Yeah. Adam and I both did while she was at gymnastics practice."

"That's not very nice."

With a shrug, he replies, "That's the kind of shit brothers do to their little sisters."

He lowers himself to the sofa, much too close, and makes it really hard for me not to think about what tonight could have been if I had only listened to my heart earlier today. We'd be having a nice dinner, just the two of us. I wonder if he would've dressed up like he did at homecoming? Would I be staring at a preppy Brad rather than the casual Brad in jeans and a T-shirt next to me? Not that it matters—his jeans and T-shirt emphasize all the right places.

I feel my cheeks heating up and have to scoot away from him.

"What are you thinking about?" he asks.

"Nothing."

He gives me a sexy smirk. "I don't believe that. Are you still making your decision?" I know exactly what he means—the decision about us. "Because I'd be happy to try to influence you."

"How exactly would you do that?" I ask.

He finishes his hot dog in two bites, then lays his skewer down and leans back on the sofa, draping his arm over the cushions. He's not touching me but would be if I leaned back.

"First, I'd make a list of all the positives," he whispers while the others are caught up in a conversation about weekend plans.

I raise my eyebrows.

"Number one: You need a boyfriend who doesn't treat you like shit so you know what a real relationship is." He holds out his hands, like he's waiting for me to argue. When I say nothing, he smiles, probably assuming I've given him the point.

"Number two: We're adorable together."

I laugh at his smug attitude while he grabs his phone out of his pocket. He sweeps his finger across the screen a couple of times and then turns it toward me so I can see a photo of us at homecoming. We are adorable, especially him. "You do look pretty good," I whisper.

He smiles again, taking this point, too.

"Number three: We'd have good . . . chemistry."

I gulp. "You're not talking acids and bases, are you?"

"Nope." He scoots over until his side is touching mine again.

I abruptly stand. "I need a bun." And some space.

I head back to the table and take my time loading ketchup onto my hot dog so my racing heart can find its normal rhythm again.

Joining me, Brittany says, "You two looked pretty cozy over there."

I shake my head and take a bite.

She gives me a smile like she doesn't believe me for a second. Luckily, though, she lets it go. "How are you adjusting to the whole foster-care thing? Feeling better about it?"

I nod. "It's pretty good. The worst part is I have to meet my mom in a couple weeks."

She wrinkles her nose in disgust. "Sorry."

It's nice to talk to someone who gets it. "What should I expect?" I ask. "Will it be good or a waste of time?"

"It was different for me because I was pulled when I was only six. I didn't know any better, so I looked forward to seeing her. Of course, she missed most of our meetings."

"But it was good when she was there?"

"I guess. As I got older, it changed, though. I stopped making excuses for her. And then it hurt more when she didn't show."

"That sucks."

"Yeah, I used to self-medicate on those days."

"Really?" I had no idea she was into drugs. She certainly doesn't look like she uses now.

She shrugs. "It was a bad time."

"And now?"

"A much better time."

"No more self-medicating?"

"Not in two and a half years."

"Good."

She nods. "Your situation will be different since you already hate your mom."

"I wonder if she'll put on an act or treat me like she normally does?"

She shrugs. "No matter how bad it is, remember, when you're done, you get to go home to the Campbells and forget about her again for a while."

I nod and take another bite. That's true. It's only an hour of torture. I used to put up with it twenty-four-seven, so an hour is nothing.

After swallowing, I say, "Hey, are you going to that LINKS training this week?" It's foster-kid training on money management, which would probably be good for me. Plus, they're taking all of us to a bank to get checking accounts. Since I've been getting an allowance from the Campbells, it would be nice to put the money someplace safer than my underwear drawer.

"Yep," she says after finishing her hot dog. "Joelle's making me. She said I need to learn how to budget."

"Why?"

"She got mad at me for buying these," she says, sticking out her leg and modeling her new shoes. They're yellow Vans that have a retro look to them. "They were expensive, but totally worth it, right?"

I shrug. As cute as they are, I wouldn't have paid more than about ten bucks for them. I bet she spent a lot more.

"Definitely worth it," Abbie says, walking by us with a bag of chips she got from inside. "It's getting cold out here. Come back to the fire."

I finish my hot dog, and then we follow her. I have to decide where to sit. Brittany chose next to Adam on the love seat, and Abbie took the opposite end of the sofa from Brad. I can take the middle of the sofa between Abbie and Brad, the rock wall, or a lounge chair on the opposite side of the fire.

I know where I want to sit, but I also know it's a bad idea. Instead, I head for the lounge chair.

Over the next hour, as the sun sets, we talk and joke and eat s'mores. It's fun and relaxing, especially without Michelle. I feel guilty thinking this, but I wish she wasn't part of their group. Everyone seems much less tense when she's not around.

"Can I take a look?" Brittany asks. Adam and Abbie were telling her about the Thunderbird their dad's restoring.

"Sure. It's in the garage," Adam says, standing.

He asks, "Want to come, Hailey?"

"No, thanks." It would take something much more interesting than a car to pull me away from the warmth of the fire.

The three of them leave, and then it's just me and Brad sitting about a mile away from each other. He smiles and waves.

I wave and then lean back on the lounge chair, closing my eyes and enjoying the sounds of crackling fire and chirping crickets.

Suddenly, high-pitched yipping fills the night, followed by a lower and longer howl. It kind of sounds like a dog, but not really.

"What is that?" I ask, sitting up.

"Coyotes."

"No, it's not." Why is he messing with me? We don't have coyotes around here.

Do we?

The sounds continue. "Is it really coyotes?"

"Yeah."

I pull my legs up to my chest and scan the backyard, but it's black as coal out there. "Where are they?"

"They live in the woods behind our neighborhood."

"Seriously?"

"Yeah."

I try to lie back again, but the continued noises are nerve-racking. How many are there? How far away are they? I shiver, realizing the fire is no longer warm enough to keep the goose bumps from my arms.

Sitting up, I scan the backyard again.

"There's plenty of room over here," Brad says, motioning to the sofa.

Just then, a loud howl cracks through the night, sounding like it's practically in the backyard. I jump to my feet without a second thought and leap onto the sofa next to him.

He laughs and puts his arm around my shoulders. "They're mostly harmless," he says.

"Then I should go back over there," I reply, motioning to the chair.

"I mean, they're vicious animals," he says with a squeeze. "Stick with me and I'll keep you safe."

He's joking, but I do feel safer. I always feel safe next to him. Whether it's coyotes or Chase, he seems to know exactly what to do. I'm not sure how he convinced Chase to stay away, but I haven't seen or heard from him since that awful night.

"Thanks," I murmur.

"Anytime. I'd hate for your beautiful face to be mauled by a coyote."

I wasn't talking about right now, but I don't want to discuss Chase and how Brad kept him away, so I nod and snuggle into his side, enjoying how he called me beautiful. It's stupid, I know, but I'm not used to someone talking to me like that. It makes me feel different. Better. Like I finally really matter to someone.

He rests his chin on the top of my head and rubs my shoulder. In the back of my mind, I think this should be awkward, but it feels completely comfortable. Like this is just a natural extension of our friendship. I sigh and enjoy his warmth and his clean scent mixed with the smell of campfire as I let my heart take control again for a few minutes until the others return.

"This is nice," he says. "Did my list of pros win you over?"

"No. I'm still taking everything into consideration. There's the list of cons, too, you know."

"Right. The con that at some point in the future we might have a fight that might somehow make things a little awkward. That definitely outweighs *all* the pros," he says, rolling his eyes.

"You forgot the con of me possibly getting kicked out."

"My parents aren't going to kick you out."

"DSS might."

"They don't need to know."

I angle my body toward him to see his face. "For real?"

He grins at me. "Yeah, we'll have a covert relationship. We'll be like spies living two different lives: friends whenever anyone else is around and . . . more when it's just us."

"How very James Bond of you," I reply with a laugh. He can't be serious.

"I am a big fan of James Bond."

"Well, you do have the dashing good looks and a way with the opposite sex."

"Don't forget how good I am at handling myself in a brawl, too."

"Right."

"So, a secret relationship, then?" he asks, his eyes filling with hope.

"People would find out."

"How?"

"Abbie could hear you talking to Adam, and then she could tell Michelle, and then the whole world would know."

He shakes his head. "I won't tell Adam."

"Don't you tell him everything?"

"Yeah," he replies with a shrug, "but I can make an exception for this."

I'm not sure, but I think there's a rule against dating someone if you can't tell your best friend about that person. If not, there should be. It probably means it's the exact opposite of what you should be doing. "It still seems like a really bad idea."

"Then you haven't thought about it long enough. Keep thinking."

I smile at his answer. He's going to be persistent. I should probably find that annoying, but knowing someone cares enough to keep trying has the opposite effect. It sends a warm rush through my chest.

"This is nice," I reluctantly say, scooting closer. It's just snuggling. That's not so bad, right? We're just sitting next to each other, talking, and his arm happens to be around my shoulders and my head happens to be on his chest.

"Would you be totally opposed to me kissing you right now?" he asks.

And there's the problem with snuggling.

I tip my head up, and we lock gazes. He's wearing a shy half smile, and his intense blue eyes bore a hole straight to my soul, looking for an answer.

"It *would* be nice," I reply.

"But it's not going to happen?"

I shake my head, thankful I'm able to find at least a shred of self-control tonight. I can't risk my placement and everything good that's happened in the last month. Not even for him.

He nods. I expect him to move away from me, but he just holds me tighter. "This is good enough for now."

The warm rush from earlier turns into a flood, spreading throughout my body and settling in my stomach, where it sits there feeding my heart and tormenting my brain. As much as I love his words—because they're so unlike anything I ever heard from Chase—the problem is this: Snuggling on the sofa when no one is around really can't be good enough for now.

It has to be good enough forever.

CHAPTER 18

TWO WEEKS LATER, I'M AT DSS IN A ROOM WITH KIDS' TOYS
and my mom. This is the first time I've seen her or even talked to
her in almost two months. She's sitting on the sofa when I enter.

Looking at her is no longer like looking in a mirror. We have
the same coloring and are the same height, but my once dull and
brittle hair is thick and shiny, my cheeks have filled out, and my
tiny legs and chest are fuller. She seems to look even worse than I
remember, with more wrinkles and dark bags under her eyes. She
looks fifty but is only thirty-three. It's a side effect of the drugs
and alcohol. They really should show before and after pictures
during health education. That would definitely persuade most of
the girls to stay away.

"Hailey, honey, I've missed you so much," she says all sing-
songy. She never talks like that, so I immediately know she's putting on a show for Sherry. She jumps to her feet and wraps me in a
hug, but I let my arms hang by my side. I haven't missed her one
bit. I don't even want to see her now.

"I'll be back in thirty minutes," Sherry says, leaving the room.

As soon as the door closes, my mom crosses her arms and narrows her eyes at me. "Where'd you get the fancy clothes?" she asks in her usual nasty way.

I look down at what I'm wearing. Jeans and a pink T-shirt. Far from fancy, but much nicer than anything in her closet. "I got a clothing stipend from DSS."

"Must be nice having someone handing money to you."

"It's not for long. I'll be on my own in March."

She sits back down and pats the cushion next to her. "I wanted to see you weeks ago."

I stay standing. "I know, but I wasn't ready."

"Weren't ready to see your dear old mom?"

"No."

"You've gained weight."

"Why did you want to see me?" I ask.

"I talked to Chase."

My stomach drops at her words. Nothing they talk about could lead to anything good for me. When I don't say anything, she continues, "He said you're living in some billionaire's place now."

"They're not billionaires."

I actually don't know how much money the Campbells have, but they aren't billionaires.

"He saw all the paintings they have hanging up."

Crap. How did Chase see the artwork? He was in the basement but never made it up to the gallery. I guess the floor-to-ceiling windows in the living room might give a view to that area if he was in the backyard.

"I don't know what you're talking about," I lie, studying the bookshelf filled with brightly colored toys.

"Don't play dumb with me. Chase talked to his cousin, and he said we might could get a hundred grand for a few of those! We'd be set for the rest of our lives, Hay-Hay," she says, switching her tone from angry to sickly sweet. She only calls me Hay-Hay when she wants something from me, and I know exactly what she wants from me right now.

"They're not worth nearly that much," I say. I have no idea what they're worth, but she needs to think they're worthless. "Mrs. Campbell paints as a hobby. She's not very good. It's just for fun."

"That's not what Chase's cousin says."

"He's wrong."

"I don't think he is."

She stands up and wraps her arm around my shoulders. "Hay-Hay, it's our big break. Why can't you see that? We'll sell the paintings and be free. We can start over."

"You forget I'm in DSS custody. There's no starting over for me."

"Sure, there is. We'll move to Atlanta. I've already got something lined up. As soon as we leave the state, they can't touch you or me."

I'm not sure that's how it works, but I know she won't listen to reason right now.

"I can't," I say.

"You won't."

"Fine, I won't."

She removes her arm, and her body crumples onto the sofa.

Her shoulders shake with fake tears. This is predictable. If I don't do what she wants, she tries to guilt me into it.

"I—I just need some good luck," she sobs. "This is our chance, Hay-Hay. We can turn everything around. We don't even need you to do much. Just let us in sometime when no one is home. That's it. Chase and his cousin will do the rest."

"No."

"Baby girl, you need to think about it for a while. They have tons of money; they can part with a little. We have nothing."

"That's stealing."

"It's called charity."

"It's called a felony."

"Your hands will be clean."

"I said no, and I mean no. That's it. End of discussion."

I start to turn around, but she jumps up from the sofa and rushes at me, her fake little crying act over. "I never should have had you, you ungrateful little bitch!" she yells, spit landing on my arm. It's the same thing I've heard at least once a week for as long as I can remember.

She reaches up and yanks on my hair hard enough to jerk my neck. I try to smack her hand away but hit her face instead.

"Fuck you!" she says, smacking my cheek with her open palm. It stings, and I have to fight back the tears. I haven't let her see me cry in five years, and I don't want to start now.

"Okay, okay!" Sherry yells, barging through the door with a large man. "Break it up, you two." The man steps behind my mom and holds her arms tight to her side. Sherry stands next to me with her arm over my shoulders.

The security guard ushers my mom out, and then Sherry sits

me down on the sofa. "Sorry," she says. "I didn't know it was going to be this bad."

I shrug. I could have told her that, but since I never offered the information, I can't really hold it against her.

"How did you know what she was doing?" I ask.

She points to a mirror on the other side of the room. "Two-way mirror."

Of course. It's good to know they take some precautions. "Could you hear her, too?"

"No, we don't have a microphone in here. Is there something you want me to know?"

I think about her question. Should I tell her what my mom wants me to do? Probably.

But what if they move me to a different foster home to try to protect me? I'd never see the Campbells again. It's not like Chase can get into the Campbells' house anyway. After Brad's tires were slashed, they updated their security system. There's no way Chase is smart enough to get through it.

"No," I finally say. I'm not willing to give up everything for that small risk. I know I'm being selfish, but I can't bring myself to tell Sherry what my mom said. Doing so would mean no more Gigi, no more Gil, no more Brad. I can't give them up.

"Okay," Sherry says with a sigh. "You've got my number if you change your mind."

I nod, and then she continues. "I no longer think it's in your best interest to be reunified with your mother."

"You think?" I reply with a smirk.

She smiles in return. "Our options are for you to seek emancipation or stall on future visits until you age out."

"How does emancipation work?"

"You'd be considered an adult and would have to support yourself. I don't want you quitting school, which means things could be challenging. We could find some financial support for you, but I'd rather you stay in foster care until you're eighteen."

I nod. That's what I want, too.

"I'll suspend your mother's visits. Do you think she could regularly pass weekly drug screens?"

"No."

"Then six consecutive clean screens will be a requirement for further visits. That should be enough to stall until your birthday."

"Thank you," I reply, hugging her. Hopefully, I'll always remember today as being the last time I ever saw my mom.

* * * *

Ten minutes later, I stare out the door of DSS, looking for my ride. Gigi usually drives me to foster-care things, but Brad volunteered today. He's been going out of his way to spend time with me, which is nice, but also stressful. Every time, I worry Gil or Gigi will see right through it and accuse me of liking their son.

There he is—way at the back of the parking lot, of course. He's standing next to his car, talking to someone. I start to head outside, but when the other figure turns around, I stop dead in my tracks.

It's Chase.

Crap, crap, crap. How did this happen? I haven't seen him in weeks. How did he end up at DSS the same day as me?

I step to the side and lean against the wall, watching the two of them. They're both tense, but at least no one's throwing punches.

I start chewing on my nail as my stomach grows queasy. They seem to just be talking, but I wouldn't put it past Chase to try something.

Just then, Brad puffs up his chest, says something with a murderous look, and pushes Chase. He stumbles backward and my heart stops. This is it. Chase is going to hurt him.

I turn around and sprint to the receptionist. "Excuse me," I say, tapping on the glass. "There are two guys fighting in the parking lot. Can you call the security guard?"

"What?" the middle-aged woman asks, standing up.

"In the parking lot. Hurry," I urge.

She jumps up and rushes from her office. When she's at the front door, she says, "I don't see anything."

"In the back," I reply, joining her. Once I look out the window, I realize she's right. Chase is gone, and Brad's back in his car. What in the world happened?

"Um . . . I guess they left," I murmur, feeling like an idiot.

She gives me an annoyed look before returning to the office.

I take a deep breath and step outside, afraid I might be ambushed by Chase at any moment. I stand there for a few seconds and scan the parking lot, but don't see him. I take a few tentative steps, still wary, but there's no one here.

I speed up, not exactly running, but getting to Brad's car much quicker than I normally would.

"How'd the visit go?" he asks when I climb inside.

I search his face for a black eye, his arms and legs for blood, but there's nothing. He looks just as good now as he did an hour ago. "What happened between you and Chase?" I ask.

He grimaces. "You saw that?"

"Yeah. I saw you shove him, and then I tried to get help. As soon as I got back, he was gone."

He frowns. "I didn't need help."

"I didn't want you ending up hurt."

"I'm not hurt."

"Good," I reply, blowing out a long breath.

"Look," he says, locking his eyes onto mine and grabbing my hands. "I told you Chase won't be a problem. That means he won't be a problem ever again. I made a promise to you, and I always keep my promises. He's not going to hurt you. He's not going to hurt me."

I nod. I believe him.

"Did you . . . hurt him?" I ask.

"No."

"Then why'd he leave?"

"I threatened to call the cops and tell them he was selling weed in the parking lot."

"Was he?"

"Hell if I know," he says with a shrug. "It got him out of here, though."

I nod again, then drop my gaze to my lap as the fear subsides and is replaced by relief. Relief Brad's okay. Relief I didn't have to talk to Chase. And, annoyingly, relief Chase isn't hurt. As much as I dislike him, I don't really want him getting beat up because of me. "Thanks," I say.

"No problem. So, how'd your visit go?"

"Don't ask," I mumble, buckling my seat belt.

"That good?"

I turn and point to my still-stinging cheek.

"What the hell?" he asks, gripping my chin and angling my face to get a better look. "Your mom did this to you?"

"Yeah."

He rubs his thumb over the sore area. "Does it hurt?"

"Not too bad."

Clenching his jaw, he says, "You need ice."

"I'm fine. Really."

He ignores me and puts the car in drive, heading for the exit of the parking lot. He turns into traffic and asks, "Sherry let this happen?"

"She stopped her. It could've been worse."

While we wait at a light, he glances over at me, his neck muscles tight as guitar strings. "Did your mom do this a lot?"

I shake my head.

"Really?"

I nod. "It's more of a recent thing," I say with a shrug. The first time she hit me was just over a year ago, and it didn't happen regularly until a few months ago.

"Is this why DSS got you out of there?"

I nod again.

The light turns green, and he makes a left into the parking lot for Bojangles.

He pulls into a spot close to the door, between two cars. He never parks between cars. I glance behind us and see an entire row of empty spaces.

"I'll be right back," he says, opening the door and rushing inside.

I watch him through the glass. There's no one at the counter, so he goes straight to the cashier. He says something, nods, and then hands the woman a credit card.

While he waits at the counter, tapping his foot, I lean my head against the window. Why did I tell him what happened? He doesn't need to know this kind of stuff about me. And now he's worried for no reason. I really should have told him the meeting was great and left it at that.

A couple of minutes later, he's back outside and digs through his trunk before climbing into the car with a cup, a grease-stained bag, and a crumpled T-shirt. He dumps ice from the cup into the T-shirt, then balls it up and hands it to me.

I say, "I'm okay. Really."

"It will help with bruising. Trust me. I have a little experience with this stuff."

"Really?" I guess I can believe it with the way he handled Chase, but it's not like he goes around picking fights.

He shrugs. "Football can get kind of physical."

Oh, of course.

"Anyway, you probably don't want to have to explain a big bruise on the side of your face to Mom and Dad or anyone at school."

I grab the T-shirt from his hands and press it to my face without any more arguing.

"Chicken?" he asks, passing a box to me.

"We just had lunch a little while ago."

"I couldn't go in there and ask for only ice," he says, laying the box on my leg and then handing me a biscuit, too. Next, he pulls out an even larger box and sets it on his lap.

I watch him as he opens the lid and downs a drumstick in no time. When he moves on to a second one, the smell of fried chicken finally gets to me and I take a bite.

"You didn't need to get all this food," I say, licking the grease off my fingers. "You could've just ordered a biscuit and a cup of ice."

"I couldn't pass up the opportunity for fried chicken. You know," he says, looking at me, "you should feel special."

"Why?"

"I never let anyone eat in my car. Ever. Not Adam. Not Dad. No one."

That I believe. He keeps his car as spotless as Gigi keeps her kitchen and Gil keeps his office. It must be a Campbell trait.

"I do feel special," I say with a smirk. I'm trying to be sarcastic, but it doesn't work. He makes me feel special practically every day and doesn't even realize it. It doesn't take much. A smile from across the cafeteria. Holding a door open for me. Switching the music to something I like whenever I'm in his car. He's sweet and considerate, and it seems like it's just second nature for him. He's not putting on an act, it's just who he is.

"Good. You are," he says, squeezing my knee and making me grin. Sometimes I feel like such a giddy little girl around him.

After finishing our second lunch of the day, we start to head back to his house, but Brad makes a detour after turning into his neighborhood.

"The park?" I ask.

"Yep. Unless you have something you need to do?"

I shake my head and smile at his suggestion. Over the past two weeks, we've made a few trips to the park. It's always empty and is set back from the road quite a bit on three sides. The fourth side borders a pond, so there's plenty of privacy. Not that we've done much that requires privacy—just some hand-holding and sitting way too close to each other as he tries to convince me to give him a chance. Even so, it's been nice to spend time alone with him, talking and getting to know each other better without expectations, like I always had with Chase.

After parking, he reaches into the backseat and grabs a bag of sliced bread. "I came prepared today."

"Lucky turtles." There's a dock that extends into the pond and whenever we sit on it, tons of turtles come up to us, sticking their heads out of the water, begging for food.

As we stroll down to the water, I reach for his hand, surprising myself with my boldness. This is so not me. I always let him initiate any contact. As soon as he winds his fingers through mine, I know it was the right decision. All the anger and disappointment from my visit with my mom and the fear of seeing Chase disappear in a puff of smoke. It's just the two of us, alone, and suddenly everything feels right with the world again.

He grins and says, "Feeling brave, huh?"

"Well, we never see anything but turtles here, and I don't think they'll be telling anyone anytime soon."

"If they do, the world has bigger problems than you and me."

"Right. Mutant talking turtles are definitely a bigger problem."

"Exactly."

He leads me down to the dock, where we sit next to each other, our legs dangling above the water, its surface smooth as glass. Not only is this place private, but it's peaceful.

We wait for the first turtle head to appear. It doesn't take long. Within a few seconds, there's one, then two, then three, all keeping their distance as they study us. Brad opens the bag and tosses a pea-sized piece of bread to the closest one. It hits the surface, but before the turtle can grab it, a fish darts up and gets it.

"Aww, man," I say, reaching for my own bread. I tear off a piece and try to feed the turtle myself, but the same fish steals it. "That little . . ."

"Shithead?" Brad offers.

I smile. "I was going to say jerk."

"Of course you were. You have a much cleaner mouth than me. One of the many things I like about you."

I turn and watch him. Over the past couple of weeks, I've thought a lot about what he sees in me. I'm clearly not in his league, but I genuinely believe he likes me. There's no reason for him to pretend he does if he doesn't.

"What?" he asks, smiling down at me.

"Just wondering what the other things are."

"What other things?"

"That you like in me."

"Oh."

He doesn't say anything else, and I start to worry he's realized his mistake.

"Do you want to know?" he finally asks.

"Well, yeah."

He scoots closer until our legs are touching, and then he puts his arm around my back, his hand at my waist. "You're strong."

"I'm not strong."

"Yes, you are. You're the strongest girl I've ever met."

I push up my sleeve and flex my tiny little bicep. "Not strong," I say.

He laughs and hugs me tighter against his side. "Not physically. Emotionally. I realized it the night you ran away."

"Running away from problems seems pretty weak to me."

"But you changed your mind. Plus, you're hot as hell. Don't forget that."

My cheeks heat up at his compliment. Chase only ever told me I was hot when we were messing around, so it's weird to hear it from someone when we're just sitting here feeding turtles and talking. It's nice, but strange, and makes me feel like he's already committed himself to a relationship if he's saying those kinds of things to me.

I tear off another piece of bread and toss it to a brave turtle who has swum closer. Once again, a fish steals it. "Poor turtles," I complain. "They're not going to get any."

"Maybe I can lure him in," Brad says, extending his arm out as far as he can reach. The turtle paddles in closer and closer until he's right below Brad's fingers. He drops the bread and the turtle opens his mouth, but misses. The food falls into the water, where it's gobbled up by fish.

"Almost," I say, forming a mountain of bread balls. My plan is to throw them all in at once to overwhelm the fish. Once they're busy chowing down, I can throw in more for the turtles.

"Okay, ready for this?" I ask, cupping most of the bread in my hands.

"Let's see what you've got."

I throw in the pile, and once the fish are preoccupied, I toss a couple of pieces to nearby turtles. They dive and grab them, eating them in one gulp each.

"Nice technique," he says, rocking his body into mine.

Over the next ten minutes, it turns into a game—who can feed the most turtles. We each try our own method and eventually we get them both to work. Mine ends up feeding more turtles but wasting a lot of bread. Brad ends up with a small group of loyal turtle friends, who look like a pack of puppies following him around wherever he moves on the dock.

"They're going to miss you when we leave," I say, motioning to his pack when we run out of bread.

He sits down next to me and curls his fingers around mine. "We'll just have to come back often."

"Your mom might start to wonder why all the bread is disappearing."

"I can secretly pick some up at the store."

I laugh at that image. "Most high school guys secretly shop for condoms, not bread."

"Yeah, well, our . . . relationship is a little different," he says, looking out at the water. A flock of ducks swims on the other side, a few of them diving down with their rear ends pointed straight up. "Of course," he says, "I could pick up some condoms if you think they might be necessary at some point."

He's looking straight ahead, but I get a glimpse of a little pink across the bridge of his nose. Knowing his lack of experience with girls, it's cute to see him react like this. "That might be jumping the gun a bit," I reply with a laugh. "Considering I haven't agreed to a secret James Bond relationship yet, and we haven't even kissed."

He turns to face me, a large grin plastered on his face. "We could fix that right now. Both things. Just say the word."

I stare at him. He looks playful, but his eyes give him away. He's serious, even more so than he was in Adam's backyard a few weeks ago. He really wants to kiss me right now. The realization causes my insides to flutter with excitement, despite knowing what a terrible idea it is.

"Your cheek looks much better," he whispers, running his thumb along my face. It stays on my chin, causing the butterflies to start darting around in a panic.

"That's good," I murmur, and wonder if I should stop him. I want to, but the butterflies are distracting.

He nods and continues watching me, giving me plenty of time to tell him no. The problem is I can't form the words. I know I should. And I want to, but my mouth suddenly feels like a desert. I can't get any words out. Or maybe I just don't want to.

He leans in, his gaze momentarily lowering to my lips before landing back on my eyes, making it perfectly clear what he plans to do.

I gulp, trying to ignore the race-car pace of my heartbeat, and prepare myself to tell him it's a bad idea, but my heart hijacks my body at that very moment. It's like I no longer have any control over what happens. I lean in, and my lips find his very gently.

He's still at first, and my stomach drops. This was a mistake. He doesn't really want to do this.

I start to pull away, but he reaches up with his hand and lightly holds the back of my head, keeping me in place. His lips press against mine, and I respond immediately. When I do, his gentle contact becomes more. More deliberate. More intense. More mind-numbingly amazing.

Which is not good. *What am I doing?* I shouldn't be kissing him. Why can't I stop myself? It's like I'm an alcoholic and his lips are top-of-the-line hard-core booze.

I close my eyes as my head grows light. Despite my internal battle, my hands roam down his back, enjoying parts of him I've admired but never felt before.

His muscles are solid and firm and . . . very nice. The more my hands wander, the more aware of it I become. He's not bony, scrawny Chase. He's rock-hard, sexy Brad, who has always made my insides turn upside down, even with a single, innocent touch. Right now, nothing's innocent, and my insides are quickly turning to mush.

Zzzzt . . . Zzzzt . . . Zzzzt . . .

The sound of a vibrating phone startles me and forces me to spring away from him. All thoughts of mush and sexy Brad fly out of my head like a torpedo. I automatically scan the area around us, sure someone has seen us and already told Sherry or Gigi. Brad moves much slower and doesn't seem to have the same concerns as me. Groaning, he reaches into his pocket and fishes out his phone. With one look at the display, he cringes. I'm positive I'm right.

"It's Mom. She wants to know where we are."

"She knows."

"She doesn't know."

"Yes, she does. Someone saw us and told her."

"You're paranoid."

"I can't be kicked out."

"Calm down," he says, brushing hair behind my ear before kissing my temple. "I told you—I'll never let them do that to you."

He begins typing on the screen, so I lean over to see what he writes: Went to Adam's after Hailey's visit. On our way home now.

"Let me give Adam a heads-up, just in case," he says, typing another message.

"Don't tell him what we were doing," I say, trying to fight back the panic. This could be how everyone finds out. One stupid mistake and the entire town is going to know and my life will be turned upside down before I even have time to pack my bags.

"Calm down," he says again, rubbing my leg. "I'll keep it vague. He won't ask questions."

"You're positive?"

"Yes."

I take a deep breath, then lower my palms to the dock and lean back, focusing on the pine forest across the pond. There's no one there. There's no one in the playground behind us, either, and I haven't seen a single car go by. Brad has to be right. There's no way Gigi could know. She's probably just curious why we're taking longer than expected.

That has to be it.

I sigh, running my hand through my hair. Did I just ruin everything for a couple of minutes of fun? Okay, it was more than a couple of minutes and more than fun, but that's beside the point. I'm getting in too deep. I can't let that happen. I need to get control of myself, or I'll lose the one good thing that's happened to me in seventeen years.

I can never lose sight of that.

CHAPTER 19

"THERE YOU ARE," GIGI SAYS, WHEN WE WALK INTO THE KITCHEN. "How was your visit with your mom?" She's working on her computer while something cooks on the stovetop.

"Fine," I say, as my hand sneaks up to rub my cheek.

"Do you think you'll see her again soon?"

"Um . . . probably not."

"Oh. Why not?" she asks, her face falling.

I look at Brad, then back to Gigi. I don't want to tell her what happened, but I have to tell her *something*.

"Wasn't it Sherry's idea?" Brad asks, walking over to the stove to see what's in the pot and giving me a little more time.

"Yeah. She . . . she . . ." I don't want to lie to Gigi about this. I've already got this thing—whatever it is—with Brad weighing me down. I don't need to add more deceit on top of that. "She didn't think the meeting was helpful," I say with a shrug. That's true. It just leaves out some of the unnecessary details.

"I'm sorry," Gigi replies, closing her computer. "Do you want to talk about it?"

I shake my head. In fact, I'd like for it to never be mentioned again.

"What's for dinner?" Brad asks, lifting the lid. He can't possibly be hungry. We just finished our second lunch only an hour ago.

"Brunswick stew. Oh, Hailey," Gigi says, holding out a phone to me. "Brittany called for you a little while ago. She wanted you to call her back as soon as you got home."

"Okay, thanks." I grab the phone and sit at the table.

Gigi starts discussing a list of landscaping chores she wants Brad to do while I dial.

"Where have you been?" Brittany asks as soon as she answers.

"Meeting my mom."

"That was two hours ago. I've been waiting to hear how it went, you know."

"Sorry. It wasn't great," I mumble.

"Were you with her this whole time?"

I pause, not wanting to lie to her, but also unwilling to tell her the truth. "Mostly."

She's silent, waiting for me to say more. When I don't, she asks, "Why are you being so secretive?"

Crap, crap, crap. She's going to know something's up with me and Brad. "I'm not," I reply.

"Yes, you are. Did something happen with your mom?"

I almost smile at her question. She's giving me an easy out. "Kind of."

"I'm coming over," she says, and then hangs up without saying good-bye.

I take a deep breath and hand the phone back to Gigi. I don't really want to talk about what happened with my mom, but if it keeps us off the topic of me and Brad, I'll happily do it. Plus, if I have to talk to someone else about my mom, Brittany is my best option.

"What did she want?" Brad asks.

"She's coming over."

"Great," Gigi says. "See if she wants to stay for dinner."

I nod and plan on making a beeline out of there, but Brad sits down at the table and starts talking to her about football. Is he not worried that the longer we sit here, the more likely she is to realize her two kids were just kissing a few minutes ago? Apparently not, because he's reclined in the chair like he has nothing better to do.

I slide into my seat and start studying my nails. They have pink polish on them, but it's old and chipping away at the edges. I use my thumbnail to scrape off even more as Brad and Gigi chat.

"Did you see Smith rushed for three touchdowns yesterday? Number-one fantasy running back in the league," he says.

Gigi purses her lips and gives Brad a sideway glance. "You better hope he avoids the injury bug."

He laughs. "You're just jealous."

Pointing at Brad, she says, "You knew I wanted him."

"Payback is hell, huh?" To me, he says, "Last year, Mom worked out a trade with Adam to get Ellison when they both knew I wanted him. I didn't even like Smith initially, but I have to say my revenge move is working out quite nicely."

Gigi rolls her eyes like a teenager. "There's a lot of time left. I wouldn't be acting so cocky if I were you."

They continue talking about their fantasy football league while I zone out. I don't even understand how the real game works, let alone the fantasy version. I watch Gigi, trying to find any hint of her knowing about me and Brad, but I don't see it. She's acting exactly like she always does. So is Brad. He's much better at this than me. I wanted to run away and avoid her, but watching the two of them makes me realize what a huge mistake that would've been. She would've known something was up.

Just then, the door opens and slams shut. Brittany rushes around the corner with Adam strolling in behind her. My stomach drops. This is going to totally blow our cover. He wouldn't come over here if we just left his house a few minutes ago.

"Come on," Brittany says, grabbing my arm and pulling me up from the chair. "We need to talk. Oh, hi, Mrs. Campbell," she says when she sees Gigi standing at the counter.

"Hey, Mrs. C," Adam says, sitting down next to Brad. "Long time, no see, man," he continues while giving Brad a fist bump.

"Weren't you guys just together?" Gigi asks. My heart stops.

"Yeah," he says casually. "I kicked him and Hailey out because I had homework, but then Brittany called and said she needed a ride over here. You know me—I can't resist a damsel in distress."

Gigi smiles and says, "Can you stay for dinner?"

That's the last I hear because Brittany drags me around the corner and into the living room.

I can't believe how easily both Brad and Adam are able to come up with excuses on the fly. I'd be stuttering and blushing and totally giving myself away, but they acted perfectly natural and Gigi didn't suspect a thing. It makes me wonder if they have a lot of practice lying to their parents. It doesn't seem like them, but they're awfully good at it.

"What happened?" Brittany whispers.

"Let's go to the basement," I suggest, wanting to put as much space between me and Gigi as possible.

When we settle ourselves onto the sofa downstairs, she asks me again, "So?"

"What?" I ask slowly, now a little worried Adam might have told her something about Brad's text.

"You and your mom," she says, drawing her eyebrows together. "Unless there's something else?"

What is wrong with me? She didn't suspect anything until I started acting suspicious.

"No, nothing else," I reply, shaking my head. "The visit just has me on edge."

"What happened?"

"We got into a fight and she smacked my face and I elbowed her in the nose."

Brittany's eyes grow wide. "Holy shit. What'd DSS do?"

"Separated us."

"Are they going to make you see her again?"

"No," I say, shaking my head. "Well, hopefully not. She'll need to pass a bunch of drug screenings, which I doubt she can do."

"Good."

I nod. "Sherry's goal is to prevent any more visits before I age out."

"When's your birthday?"

"Middle of March."

"That's not too far away."

I nod again and then it dawns on me: *It's really not that far away.*

I've finally gotten into a good situation, and everything will change again in a few months. "Um . . . what exactly happens when I age out?" I ask, as unexpected dread starts to creep in.

"You'll get an apartment or go to a group home."

"I don't have money for an apartment."

"DSS will help. That's what LINKS is for—to make sure none of us"—she uses air quotes—"'falls through the cracks.'"

The fact that I'm expected to be on my own in five months is frightening. More than frightening. It's terrifying. I suppose I should have realized it was coming, but the timing never really clicked. I'll still have school, plus I'll need a job to pay for an apartment. And I have no car to get anywhere. Suddenly, the Brad issue seems juvenile when I'll soon have real-world adult problems to deal with.

"What's wrong?" Brittany asks.

"I'm—I'm scared. I'm not ready to be on my own."

"None of us ever are, but it'll be fine. My friends who have aged out are doing okay. It takes a while, but most of them get their act together. Plus, you have the Campbells," she says, rocking her shoulder into mine. "They're not going to let you starve."

I guess. But it's not like I expect them to invite me over for dinner all the time after I move out. Once I'm gone, their responsibility to me is over. "When's your birthday?" I ask.

"June. Hey, maybe we can be roommates," she says, her eyes lighting up.

That would make the whole situation better. At least we'd have each other to lean on as we try to hold down jobs and scrape up enough money for rent. "That would be good."

"We'll get a place downtown so we can walk to our jobs," she says, moving to the edge of the cushion. "Maybe we can be waitresses at Southern Prime. I heard they make a killing in tips. Plus, you get a free steak every time you work!"

I smile at her excitement. It's nice to see this from her perspective, since she's more of a glass-half-full kind of person while I usually feel like I'm staring at the bottom of an empty glass.

Before we can say anything else, the boys come barging down the stairs. "Who wants to play Ping-Pong?" Adam asks when he clears the bottom step.

Brittany hops up, beaming, and joins him at the table. As soon as she does, his mouth spreads into a massive grin, making me wonder what's going on between the two of them. Maybe it's not just me and Brad kissing in private.

Brad steps near me and lowers his hand to my shoulder. He squeezes it and then runs his fingers down my back. The whole thing didn't last more than a second, but my nerves shoot through the roof. I spin to the stairs, sure Gigi will be standing there, but it's empty. Then I focus on Brittany and Adam, worried they saw, but they're too preoccupied with each other to have noticed.

Finally, I look at Brad, who's standing innocently next to me. I have to give it to him—he's much smoother than I am.

"Does your mom know?" I whisper.

He shakes his head. "Not a clue."

"Adam?"

He shakes his head again. "Like I said—he won't ask questions. Brittany?"

Now it's my turn to shake my head.

"See, we're two slick secret agents living dual lives."

"You really think we can do it?" I ask.

"If today was a test, we aced it."

Huh. I guess we did. As nervous as I was, no one suspects anything.

"Well?" he asks. "Are you still thinking about it or have you made your decision?"

I'm about to automatically say what a bad idea it is, but then I catch myself. Is that just a gut reaction from the-glass-is-always-empty Hailey? I glance at Brittany and Adam, who are laughing together like they don't have a care in the world.

Is it wrong of me to want that? Probably. But do I deserve it after everything I've gone through? I'd like to think so.

I bite my lip and look into Brad's eyes.

I see the hope building the longer I take to answer.

The fact that I kissed Brad today probably means the decision was already made, even if I hadn't admitted it to myself. Maybe, sometimes, the most logical option isn't the best one. Maybe I need to tell my brain to go on a long vacation so I can follow my heart.

I slowly nod.

"Yeah?" he asks, his entire face lighting up.

"Yeah," I say with more confidence.

That's it.

It's done.

I have officially agreed to have a totally inappropriate and secret relationship with my foster brother.

What could possibly go wrong with that?

CHAPTER 20

"HAILEY, I GOT YOU SOMETHING AT THE STORE YESTERDAY," GIGI says when I come down to the kitchen on Friday morning.

Brad and I have been sneaking around for almost a week and so far, so good. Granted, there hasn't been much sneaking because we have school and he has football. The only alone time we really have on weekdays is the ten-minute drive to school, and we can't do anything in the car while he's driving. Tomorrow is Saturday, though. Everything can change tomorrow since we have the entire day together.

"I don't need anything," I say to Gigi, giving her a confused look as I wonder what she got for me.

Shortly after I was placed here, Gigi gave me a notepad and told me to write down when I ran out of shampoo or bodywash or anything else. It seemed silly at the time, but I'm grateful she did because it's much easier to write things on a piece of paper than to ask her directly. Then, once a week, always on Saturday afternoon, a bag magically appears in my bathroom with everything I need.

I still feel a little guilty when they spend money on me, but I always request the cheapest brand of anything and she usually gets it for me. Every now and again, she'll throw in a nicer version of what I asked for or an unexpected surprise like nail polish. I complain, but she just shushes me and tells me they were on sale.

The problem is there's nothing on my list right now, and it's Friday. What in the world did she get me?

"This is something Gil and I thought you needed." She reaches into a bag and pulls out a box. On the front of the box is a picture of a phone.

"What? No," I say, shaking my head. "I can't take that." It's too much. They're only supposed to pay for necessities. A phone is absolutely not necessary.

"We want you to have it. For emergencies. It's just a cheap disposable phone, but we'll feel safer knowing you have a way of getting in touch with us if something happens. I've already programmed in our numbers and Brad's."

She hands me the box, but I try to push it back to her.

"We won't take no for an answer," she says, forcing it into my hands. "If it makes you feel better, just hold on to it and only use it if you're in trouble."

I'm about to protest again, but Brad enters the kitchen. He takes one look at the box and says, "It's about time."

"Okay, I've gotta run. I'm already late," Gigi says, heading out the door and leaving me no choice but to accept it.

Brad and I both grab a quick breakfast for the road, then load into his car and head to school. In the car, I open the box, pull out the phone, and take a look at all the features. Besides talking to people, I can text, take pictures, and get online. This isn't just an emergency phone.

"Call me," Brad says, "so I'll have your number."

While I'm doing that, he says, "This will definitely make things easier."

"What do you mean?"

"We can text between classes, before practice, late at night when we're supposed to be in our rooms." He gives me a mischievous grin, and I get the sense he's not talking about innocent texts.

"It's for emergencies only."

"She only said that to make you feel better. She's not going to care if you use it regularly."

"I doubt she'd want me to use it for the kind of texts you're talking about."

He grins at me again. "They don't monitor my phone. I'm sure they won't monitor yours, so they'd never know."

"I am not sending or receiving sexy texts on a phone your parents bought for me." No way. Never gonna happen.

He laughs, then squeezes my knee.

We talk about other topics until he pulls into the lot at school. After climbing out of the car, we walk to the edge of the parking lot, where Adam and Abbie are waiting for us.

"Give them your phone so they can add their numbers."

"You got a phone?" Abbie asks. "Finally! It's like you've been living in the Dark Ages."

"It's only for emergencies," I say as I hand it to her. She adds her information, then passes it to Adam as we walk into school.

The day goes by like any other day until lunchtime. While I'm sitting at a table with Brittany and her friends, we hear a quiet buzzing sound. Brittany reaches into her bag, grabs her phone, but tosses it back in. "Not me," she says. Everyone else does the same, then looks at me.

"It's not me. I don't have a—" I stop myself. I do have a phone. But who would be calling me?

I pull my backpack onto my lap and search around inside. I have to open three pockets before I find where I stashed it. Flipping it open, I see I have a text. From Brad.

I'm sitting with you at lunch today.

My head snaps up, and I search his usual table. He's not there yet.

No, you can't, I type. He's told me this every day this week and I give him the same answer every time. Changing our lunchtime routine is about the least secretive way to have a secret relationship. You'd think a self-proclaimed James Bond would realize that.

Why not?

I roll my eyes. He knows why. Instead of explaining it to him for like the fifth time, I decide to go with something else. It will upset the delicate balance of this school.

What?

It's like when they introduced goats into the Galapagos and almost killed off all the giant tortoises.

What?

I glance up again and see that he's sitting at his usual spot now, staring at his phone.

I saw a special on TV last night, I type.

Am I the goat or the tortoise?

Goat.

He smiles as he types. I'd rather be the tortoise.

You can't be the tortoise. You're the invasive species trying to take over our niche in this corner of the cafeteria.

I'm so not following you.

You should've watched the special.

He laughs and shakes his head. The Panthers were playing.

This phone is for emergencies. I gotta go.

He looks up and meets my eyes for a moment before focusing back on his phone. So you don't want me to sit with you?

Nope.

That hurts.

Get used to it.

I stop my rapid-fire texting and look up to take a bite of my hamburger, only to find five pairs of eyes staring at me.

"You're smiling like a madwoman," Brittany says. "When did you get a phone and who are you texting?"

"This morning," I reply. "Gigi gave it to me."

"Whoa." Her eyes grow wide. "That's huge."

"It's just for emergencies."

She shakes her head. "That means they see you sticking around for a while. If they considered you a short-timer, they wouldn't have gotten you a phone."

I take another bite as her words sink in. Is there more behind the phone? Is it some symbolic gesture of them accepting me into their family? I didn't see it that way, but Brittany makes a good point. If so, then this *is* huge. I feel like I was just chosen first in a game of dodgeball or something, only that never happened and this is way more important than a stupid game.

"Who are you texting?" she asks again.

"Just a friend," I say, trying to hide my smile.

She automatically looks to Brad's table, where he's typing on his phone. "Uh-huh," she says, turning back around and stuffing a carrot stick into her mouth.

The phone buzzes again. I look down at the display. Want to meet behind the gym after school?

Why?

I want to see you before practice.

Why?

I miss you.

I'll see you tonight.

That's too long.

I can't miss my bus.

It takes a moment before his next reply. I glance in his direction and see him whispering to Adam only moments before a new message appears. Adam will drive you home. He's got a meeting and will be leaving around 3. I told him you had to make up a test.

I take another bite and chew thoughtfully. It would be nice to have a little alone time with him. We haven't really had that since our kiss last Saturday. It's actually kind of ridiculous that we agreed to a secret relationship but have done nothing secretive in six days.

OK, I finally type.

:)

As soon as the final bell rings, I bolt out of class, make a quick stop at my locker, and then race toward the gym. I exit out the back door and find him already waiting there, casually leaning against the wall.

This spot is the perfect place to be alone. There are large recycling dumpsters on two sides of us, the brick wall of the gym on the third, and nothing but pine trees on the fourth.

"Nice place," I say, stepping beside him. "Very private."

"Exactly."

He grabs me by the waist and pulls me to him, his mouth moving toward my ear, then over my jaw. "I can't believe you called me a goat," he whispers before covering my lips with his own. His hands slide down and cup my butt.

"Goats are very cute," I whisper back, as I think about whether this is a good idea. Sure, it's private, but someone could walk by and see us. Unfortunately, the feeling of my body pressed against his makes rational thought difficult.

"This is a bad idea," I murmur, my hands sliding up his face and into his hair.

"I know."

"We should stop."

"In a minute."

His tongue darts into my mouth, surprising me. He must notice my reaction because he pulls away slightly and focuses his kissing on my lower lip instead.

I smile against his mouth. Brad's always so confident and sure of himself. It's cute to see him acting a little shy.

"Why are you smiling?" he asks.

"You're cute."

"Like a goat?"

I laugh. "A shy goat."

"What makes you think I'm shy?"

"Because I got like less than a second of tongue action."

He grins down at me. "That's because you seemed unsure. You're shy, not me."

"Reeeally?" I say, drawing out the word. I've done this hundreds of times. How many times has he done it? A few?

He nods a couple times, a half grin on his face revealing his dimple.

I grab onto his shirt and drag him back to me, letting my own tongue show him exactly how wrong he is. He responds immediately, deepening our kiss and making my knees go weak. He may not have much experience, but he knows what he's doing.

He really, really knows what he's doing.

"I take it back," I whisper when we come up for air.

"I'm not cute?" he asks.

I grin at him, but before I can say anything, a beeping sound comes from somewhere near my ear. Brad reaches to his wrist and pushes a button on his watch.

"One minute until I need to get dressed for practice," he whispers.

"You set an alarm?"

"I was worried I'd lose track of time with you."

I laugh at his answer. Always practical Brad.

We make the most of our last minute and then reluctantly say bye to each other. The good news is we found another safe place to be alone together. The bad news is the more we kiss, the more I want him, which is only going to make things harder.

I slowly walk to the parking lot, enjoying the giddy-light-headed-mushy feeling Brad brings out in me. I know I'm smiling uncontrollably, but I don't care. There's no one around to notice, and I want this feeling to last as long as possible.

"You might want to brush your hair," I hear from behind me in a familiar voice. I spin around to find Abbie there, wearing a grin. "It looks like you fell asleep on your desk."

My hand flies to my head, smoothing down the long strands. "Yeah . . . um . . . study hall . . ." I did fall asleep in study hall, but I'm sure that's not the reason my hair is a mess. It's much more likely Brad's fingers played a role.

She steps to my side. "I hate when that happens," she says with a smile. "How'd that test go?"

"Oh . . . fine."

"Good. Let us know if you ever need another ride home. We're always happy to help our friends." She smiles at me again, even larger this time, and I get the vague feeling there might be more to her words.

I swallow and nod, afraid to say anything else.

"Hey, do you want to study together for our geometry quiz? I didn't do so hot on the last one."

"Um, sure, but you'll probably want Brad there, since he tutors me. He's the only reason I'm passing that class."

She gives me a sideways glance. "He tutors? When did that start?"

"Right after I moved in. At least for me. I—I don't know if he tutors anyone else." Although I doubt it. With school and football and trying to make the most of our alone time, he wouldn't be able to fit it in.

"Jeez, when a guy's practically your second big brother, you'd think you'd know this kind of stuff. I've been killing myself in that class for months! He so owes me," she says, shaking her head but still grinning. Despite all their bickering, they really do care for each other, and for the first time ever, I kind of wish my half sister was still around, although I realize it's a completely selfish wish.

"He especially owes you after reading your diary," I point out. "That was really low."

"Right? I still need to get him back for that. You gotta let me know if you find any dirt on him, okay?"

"I'm not sure there is any dirt on him."

"That's the problem," she groans, linking her elbow through mine and leading me toward Adam's car.

A few minutes later, Adam meets us and then they drive me back to the Campbells, no one discussing further why I need a ride, although both of them offer to do it again anytime I want. It's almost like I gained not only a family with the Campbells, but an extended family with Adam and Abbie.

Maybe I don't need my half sister after all.

CHAPTER 21

A FEW WEEKS LATER, I STEP INTO THE KITCHEN TO FIND GIL
and Gigi putting on jackets.

"We're running errands. Want to come?" Gil says.

"No, thanks. I've got a little more homework to finish."

"Do you need anything other than what's on your list?" Gigi
asks, lowering her phone into her bag.

"Nope, that's all. Thanks," I reply, grabbing a glass out of the
cupboard.

"See you later," Gil says with a wave as they both head to the
garage.

I fill the glass with water and wonder where Brad is. On weekends, we usually study together after his morning workout, but I
haven't seen him since I woke up a couple of hours ago. I guess I
could've asked his parents, but I'm being especially cautious around
them. That generally means not even mentioning his name because
I seem unable to control my smile whenever I think of him.

I suppose I could call him, but I don't want to seem like the
overbearing girlfriend.

After I down the water, I put the glass in the dishwasher and then start to head upstairs, but the sound of the garage door opening causes me to pause. Either Gil and Gigi forgot something or Brad's home.

I linger on the bottom step and crane my neck to see around the doorway. I catch Brad's back as he shuts the door.

"Hey," he says when he rounds the corner.

"Hey."

"What are you doing?"

"Wondering if I should call you," I say.

"Yes. The answer is always yes," he replies with a smile.

"I didn't want to be annoying."

"You could never be annoying. So you missed me, huh?" he says with a smirk.

I try to come up with a sarcastic reply but completely fail. Instead, I settle for the truth. "Maybe a little."

Rather than respond, he wraps his arms around me and lowers his lips to mine.

"Your parents," I warn him, taking a step back.

"Gone. I saw them leave."

"Still. They could come back. What if they forgot something?"

"We'd hear the garage door open."

"What if they came in through the front?"

"We'd hear the front door open."

"What if they have video cameras around the house?"

"You really are paranoid," he says with a laugh. "Luckily, my plan was to leave anyway. Have you had lunch yet?"

"No."

"Do you have anything else to do?"

"Not really."

"Come on, then," he says, reaching for my hand and then leading me through the doorway, stopping only momentarily to grab my jacket from the closet.

I protest until it's clear we're going to the park. I guess it wouldn't be too unusual for siblings to be seen eating lunch together at a restaurant, but I'm worried someone would see right through our act. It's a small town where everyone knows everyone, so it could easily get back to Gil or Gigi.

A few minutes later, we end up at the park—our park—and it's quiet as usual. I get out of the car and start to head to the dock, but Brad stops at the trunk, where he grabs a plastic grocery bag.

"Lunch," he says, holding up the bag, when he joins me.

"That's sweet. Thank you."

We sit down at a picnic table, and then Brad starts pulling items out of the bag one by one. Crackers, cheeses, and deli meats end up sprawled in front of me.

"I got you a surprise," he says with a twinkle in his eye.

"This whole thing is a surprise."

Grinning, he says, "It gets better."

Then he hands me a little bottle of Sunny D and a coloring book with crayons. It's one of those pretty adult coloring books with geometric shapes—much nicer than anything my mom ever got me.

The corners of my eyes prickle, and I worry I'm going to cry in front of him. I'm not used to getting gifts for no reason. Actually, I'm not used to getting gifts at all. Plus, no one's ever done anything this thoughtful for me before. How did he even remember my story? It was late at homecoming when I told him, plus he had the whole Michelle thing on his mind.

"I was going to get you some flowers, but then I realized you couldn't take them home. For a moment, I thought about leaving them here, but knew you wouldn't like how"—he uses air quotes—" 'wasteful' that would be."

"You thought right," I reply, thumbing through the book. Flowers are nice, but they would be a waste in our situation, since I could only enjoy them for the hour we were here. This is a hundred times better. "Thank you," I say, closing the cover and smiling at him. "This was really sweet." Leaning across the table, I kiss his cheek, but he catches my lips with his own and turns it into something much more.

These are the moments I look forward to every day. The stolen kisses and touches when no one else is around. In the car when we're at an empty intersection. Behind the gym at school. In an empty theater during a matinee showing of an awful movie.

Some days, we only manage to hold hands on the way to school, but other days, like today, we get much more.

His tongue slips between my lips and I feel that familiar twinge of guilt winding its way through my body for doing something I know we shouldn't be doing, but I've learned to live with it. The pure thrill I get from our . . . whatever it is we have . . . has a way of pushing the guilt to the back of my mind. At least while we're kissing. When I'm alone, I sometimes persuade myself we should stop sneaking around, but the moment his lips land on mine again, that thought flies right out of my head.

I never imagined someone like him would have any interest in someone like me, but he does. It's crazy and stupid and dangerous, but I'm loving what we have, even if it's a little messed up and a lot inappropriate.

We eventually separate and dive into the food. Once we're stuffed, I open the book and beginning coloring a spiral design. Brad's sitting on the opposite side of the table, so he starts on the top while I take the bottom.

"Does this bring back good memories of your mom?" he asks.

"Yes and no." It's good in that I'm reminded of a time when we got along, but bad in that anytime I think of her now, I remember our last meeting.

"What was the worst part of living with her?" he asks.

I pause, my turquoise crayon poised above the page as I stare at the black lines of the swirl. I wasn't expecting our conversation to go there, although I'm sure he has lots of questions about my past. It's not like I go around offering details all the time.

Lowering my crayon, I focus on the page in front of me, carefully following the curve with a turquoise line. "That's a hard question to answer," I say.

"You don't have to tell me if you don't want," he replies.

I shake my head. "It's not that." Well, not entirely. It's still embarrassing to give him glimpses into my world, but he knows it wasn't all rainbows and unicorns. "There are really two different kinds of bad with her. There's the physical stuff like being hungry. There were times when she forgot to pay the electric bill, so the little food we had spoiled, but I still ate it. You knew it was going to make you throw up, but you didn't care because your stomach already hurt so bad."

"God," Brad says, blowing out a breath. "Aren't there supposed to be programs to make sure kids have food? How did that even happen?"

I shrug. "It was usually in the summer, when I didn't get meals at school. When I was young, my mom had WIC, and later on, she got food stamps, but there's a whole underground where she could trade them for cigarettes or beer."

"Classy," Brad says with an edge in his voice. "Starve your kid for cigarettes."

His comment causes my lips to curl up. I should probably be mad at him, but what he says is true. It's not like I haven't had the same thought hundreds of times. It's actually kind of reassuring to know he's on my side.

"Then there's the whole emotional thing," I say, filling a spiral with color. "She'd let me down over and over again, but I kept trying. It was actually kind of pathetic."

"Pathetic how?" he asks without looking up.

"Like, why did I care? Why did I want her to love me so much? Why did I try over and over again? Apparently, I'm a glutton for punishment."

"You're not a glutton for punishment. You're an extremely selfless person, even when people don't deserve it." He reaches across the table and squeezes my hand. "You gave her lots of chances to be a mom, and she never stepped up."

He's right. I gave her more chances than she deserved. I look up, meeting his gorgeous eyes, and see a strange mixture I can't quite place, although there seems to be a fair amount of compassion with at least a dash of pity. Maybe two dashes. That's my cue to shut up about my past.

"Sorry my life is kind of messed up," I say, switching my turquoise crayon for salmon.

"Why are you apologizing?"

I shrug. "I don't know. You and your parents are so squeaky clean. . . ."

"You think I'm squeaky clean?"

"I *know* you're squeaky clean."

"I could be hiding something monumental from you."

"Like what?" I ask with a smile.

"I could be the mastermind behind a for-profit underground homework exchange network."

"You're not."

"I could have a police record."

"You don't."

"I could be in the witness protection program for turning state's evidence about horrible crimes."

"I don't even know what that means, but, no, you aren't. Tell me one honest thing no one else knows about you."

"A bad thing or a good thing?"

"Either."

He taps his crayon on the paper, leaving orange dots around the outside of the design while he thinks. After a few moments, he says, "I want to go to Duke next year."

I give him a confused look. "That doesn't seem so earth-shattering. Why haven't you told anyone?"

"Have you met my dad?"

I laugh at his seriousness. "Still, Duke's a great school. I'd think he'd be happy."

Brad shakes his head. "My grandpa went to Wake. My mom went to Wake. My dad went to Wake. Even two of my uncles went to Wake. I *have* to go to Wake Forest. I'm the last hope for my entire generation of Campbells."

"Seriously?"

He nods. "I have five cousins, but two of them joined the military, one went to Princeton, one got a Fulbright to Cambridge, and one went to some technical school. I'm the last hope. Believe me, I've heard that plenty over the last two years."

"It's not like you're saving the world. It's just a school. Who cares if there's a missing Campbell generation there?"

"Exactly! Maybe you need to have a talk with my parents."

A loud flock of geese fly overhead, drawing our eyes upward. We watch them clear the pond and then disappear beyond the forest, which is becoming dotted with oranges and reds as fall sets in. "Why Duke?" I ask.

He shrugs. "It's a good school like Wake Forest, but it'd be exciting to live on a campus I haven't visited hundreds of times with Mom and Dad. It'd be a new adventure. A completely new start. It'd be . . . my school."

"What do you think your dad would say if you told him?"

He shakes his head. "He wouldn't want to hear it. The only correct answer is Wake." He pauses. "I just . . . I just wish Dad would lay off me for once and let me make a major decision for myself. I don't get why he trusts me most of the time but thinks I'm unable to make the big decisions. It's frustrating."

"I bet it's because he loves you and thinks he's helping."

He blows out a long breath. "I know," he says. "I know he's

not trying to be difficult. He truly believes this would be the perfect opportunity for me. Maybe he's right. It's not like I've gotten an offer from anywhere other than Wake and EGU. Since I'm not going to EGU, Wake may be my only option unless we win the state championship."

"Could that happen?"

"Maybe. It's looking good to get into the semifinals, but any further will be tough."

"Well, if no other schools work out, Wake Forest isn't a bad only option to have."

"Nope," he says, returning to the picture in front of him. "It could be much worse. So, where do you want to go to school?"

"You're assuming I'm going to college."

"Of course you're going to college. What else would you do?"

"Get a job."

"Where?"

"I don't know. Walmart?"

"You did not just say that."

"Why? What's wrong with Walmart?" I ask, laying down my crayon and staring at him.

"Nothing's wrong with Walmart," he replies, staring back. "It's an acceptable place to buy low-cost housewares or even have a summer job. It is not, however, a place to have a long-term career."

"We can't all be headed to Ivy League colleges with our pick of careers, you know."

"Wake isn't Ivy League."

I roll my eyes. "You know what I mean. Walmart is a good option for me."

"It just seems like it'd be a waste of your potential. I could see you as a social worker or a nurse. Maybe an elementary-school teacher. I don't know, something where you'd help people."

"I'm not looking for a career. Just a job. I'll need money to live. A job at Walmart seems the quickest and easiest way to do that."

"So, money's the problem? You're afraid you can't afford college?"

I shrug. "Not necessarily. If I could get into a state school, I'd get free tuition."

"Why?"

"Because I'm in foster care. We get a few special perks. It's the price of . . . putting up with what we have to put up with."

"Definitely not worth it," he says, shaking his head. "But at least it's something. Have you started looking at schools?"

"No. I'm not sure I'd be accepted anywhere."

"What's your GPA?"

"Two-point-eightish."

"You could get in somewhere, especially if you got it above three this year."

"Maybe. We'll see."

"You are applying to college even if I have to hold your hand while you fill out the paperwork."

I smile at his words and sit up a little straighter. "Thanks." I'm sure he doesn't realize it, but he's only the second person—after Sherry—who has ever believed in me. I'm still not convinced I could get into college, but Brad's confidence makes me a little more optimistic.

While I finish coloring in the small piece of white left in the design, Brad stands and comes around to my side of the table. He straddles the bench, facing me, and his arms circle my waist.

Lowering the crayon and closing the book, I turn to face him. He's wearing a dangerous grin, so I reflexively look around the park to make sure we're alone. We are.

"Thanks for the fun date," I say, propping my left leg on the bench.

"Sorry it couldn't be somewhere more interesting."

"I like this place," I say with a smile. "It's ours. Where we first kissed. Our first date."

"Where we first did some serious making out?"

I raise my eyebrows. The most we've done so far is kiss. Granted, we've had some intense kissing sessions over the last few weeks, but that's been the extent of it.

"Strictly PG-rated, of course," he says, "just in case some un-suspecting kid comes by to play on the swings."

"That would be embarrassing."

"There's always my car," he suggests.

I'm not sure how much privacy his car would provide in the middle of the parking lot on a sunny afternoon. I bite my lip as I consider the idea.

"Or in the woods," he continues.

I glance at the trees across the water. That wouldn't be bad, but we'd have to walk like half a mile around the pond to reach the woods. I shake my head.

"Our basement? Mom and Dad won't be back until close to dinnertime."

"No way. I'm not making out in your parents' house. That's too dangerous."

He looks around us as though there's someplace right here that's even more private, but unless we want to make out in the bathroom, there's not.

"Okay, your car," I say, standing and taking his hand.

"Yeah?" His face lights up, making it clear he didn't expect me to agree. He must not have any idea the effect he has on me.

"Yeah, but you have to move it to the corner spot and back in so we can see if anyone is coming."

"You realize no one has ever come by all the times we've been here, right?"

"That could easily change."

After climbing into the car and changing parking spots, he lifts the parking brake and turns off the ignition.

"So," he says, sliding his seat back.

"So," I reply, taking one last look around us. The coast is clear. I climb over the console and into his lap, my arms hanging loosely around his neck.

"Okay," Brad says, taking a deep breath. "This is a nice way to spend the afternoon."

I laugh and then bite my lip. I wonder what he was thinking when he suggested some serious making out. And what I'm willing to do. No sex. Not yet. Even though I'd love to see how different—better—it'd be with Brad compared to Chase, that'd be pushing the limits of our inappropriate relationship a little too far. Not that he's thinking about going there, I'm sure. He's a virgin.

There are lots of other things we can do, though. "So, what did you have in mind?" I ask.

He smiles. "I'm not sure. I didn't think you'd actually take me up on the offer."

"Well, I have," I reply with a grin.

"Yes, you have."

I move one leg so I'm straddling him with my knees next to his hips.

He gulps. "I should mention I don't have any condoms, so this will have to stop short of . . . that."

"That?" I ask with a laugh. "You made fun of me for not being able to say virgin, and you can't say 'sex' all of a sudden?"

He smiles. "I can say 'sex'; I'm just not a fan of the word. It's kind of . . . impersonal."

"So, what do you prefer?"

"I'm not sure. 'Making love' is kind of corny, and I don't want to use a certain curse word for it because that makes it seem trashy."

"Getting jiggy with it?" I suggest.

He wrinkles his nose.

"Hanky-panky?"

"That sounds like something out of a country-western song."

"Intercourse?"

"That makes me feel like I'm back in sex ed."

"Get busy?"

"You truly are gifted in the vocabulary world," he notes, grabbing my butt and rearranging me on his lap. He peels off my jacket, then slides his hands under my shirt.

"You're on lookout," I say, as I kiss the side of his neck.

He nods, but doesn't say anything as his hands glide up my back.

"Sleep together? Home run?" I whisper, getting back to our conversation.

"Okay, stop. You're scaring me," he says with a laugh. His hands still. "Let's use something all our own."

"Like what?"

He purses his lips and appears deep in thought for a few moments before saying, "Playing chess."

I laugh at his suggestion. "You can't be serious. That's totally random."

"I am serious. Random is perfect. We could talk about it when others are around, and no one will know."

"But what if one of us wanted to play actual chess?"

"Do you play?"

"No, I don't even know how."

"Me neither," he says, smiling.

"You're serious?"

"Sure."

I laugh again and shake my head. Playing chess it is. I honestly don't care what we call it, especially since it's not going to happen for a while still.

"Of course, if you wanted to . . . play chess today, I could make a run to the store," he says, nuzzling my neck.

I glance at his pink cheeks and smile. "As tempting as that sounds, I think I'd like to wait."

"Are you sure? I can be there and back in five minutes flat." He gives me his goofy smirk, making it clear he's joking. Well, mostly joking. I'm not sure what he'd do if I gave him the okay.

I playfully nudge his shoulder. "Not gonna happen today. Sorry."

He laughs and says, "It was worth a shot."

Did I really just tell him no? I never said no to Chase, even when I *really* didn't want to do it. Now I want to do it, but I tell Brad no? It's strange, but I feel a weird sense of pride. Like I just aced a geometry test. Of course, that would take a ton of work, and this was just one word. It's kind of ridiculous I'd be proud of myself for something so simple, but I am.

I reach under his shirt, finally getting a taste of the abs he's teased me with for weeks. I consider pulling his shirt over his head, but then worry what someone would think about a shirtless guy in a car if they happened to walk by.

Instead, I lower my lips to his, as his hands begin roaming around my back again, slowly working their way lower.

Zₐₐt . . . ₐₐt . . . ₐₐt . . .

"You've got to be kidding me," he groans.

I grab his phone from the console and peer at the name while handing it to him.

Michelle.

"That can definitely wait," he says, silencing it, then tossing it onto the seat next to us.

"Why is she calling you?" I realize I sound like a jealous girlfriend, but the words escaped my mouth before I could stop them.

"I have no idea."

"Maybe you should've answered?"

"No way." His lips find my neck, and I try to get back into it, but the phone begins vibrating again. It's distracting. It's like Michelle is sitting in the seat watching us. And judging us. Or judging *me* at least.

"Have you told her you're not interested yet?" I ask, glaring at the vibrating phone-slash-invisible Michelle next to us.

"More or less," he says, reaching over and silencing it again.

"Is it more or less?" I ask, snapping my head back to him.

He rolls his neck and drops his hands. "Way to ruin the mood, Hailey."

"I think Michelle already did that."

"She's nobody to me. You realize that, right?" he says, reaching for my hand.

I pull it away as I reply. "Then you would've told her weeks ago and she'd be leaving you alone right now."

I crawl back over the console, move his phone to the dashboard, and slump in the passenger seat. I don't know why I'm treating him like this. I believe him when he says he doesn't like her, but why can't he stop her from acting the way she does?

"First fight, too," he says, as the phone starts vibrating again. "This place really is ours." He frowns as he starts up the car and heads back to his house.

CHAPTER 22

A SOFT TAP ON THE DOOR INTERRUPTS MY GEOMETRY homework. I've been up in my room ever since Brad and I returned from the park. He offered to tutor me when we got back, but I said I wanted to be alone. Now I've been working on geometry for two hours already, and I'm still not done. If he had helped me, it would've taken less than an hour.

Why do I let Michelle get to me? Why can't I just ignore everything she does? I believe Brad and trust Brad, but it still annoys me to no end that she thinks she can call him and text with him and sit next to him at lunch every day while I'm on the opposite side of the cafeteria.

The tapping continues. "Come in." I expect Brad, but Brittany strolls through the door.

"What's going on?" she asks, hands on hips.

"What are you doing here?"

"Michelle invited me over for movie night."

"Michelle? This isn't her house."

"She said she talked to Brad about it."

I roll my eyes. He probably called her back after I stormed off to my room.

"So, what's going on?" Brittany asks again. "Brad sent me up here. He said he didn't know if you were coming down or not."

"Is Michelle there?"

"Yeah."

I flop back on my bed.

Brittany joins me, sitting on the edge of the mattress. "Did something happen with her?"

I sigh because I want to tell her, but I can't without revealing our secret. "No, not really. Just more of the same," I say.

"She's just jealous of how much time you get to spend with Brad. She wishes she could live in the bedroom down the hall from him."

I groan, rolling on my side to face her. "She's just really annoying, you know?"

"Yeah, I know, but if you stay up here, she wins."

I sit up and lean against the headboard. She's right. What do I gain by being up here? Nothing. What does she gain? An entire evening sitting next to Brad without me around. "You're right," I say, my mind made up. There's no way I'm letting her share a blanket with him or snuggle next to him during a movie.

"Are you and Brad okay?" Brittany asks.

I bite my lip. "Why?"

"He seemed worried. Like you might not be talking to him or something."

I shrug. "I just wish he'd do a better job of putting her in her place."

"To be fair, I'm not sure her attitude would change just because Brad tells her she's being a bitch to you."

She's right again, I realize, as the annoyance is replaced by the sickening gnawing I get in my stomach whenever I do something wrong. I shouldn't take my irritation at Michelle out on him. He doesn't deserve it. He's done nothing but go out of his way to make me feel special. I can't blame him for the way she acts.

"Come on," Brittany says, pulling my up from the bed.

We both head to the basement, where I plan to secretly apologize to Brad as soon as I can. Unfortunately, the moment I step into the room, my blood boils.

Brad's in my usual spot with Michelle right next to him.

Like *right* next to him.

He nudges Michelle and says, "Scoot over," while he tries to clear some space for me.

Instead, I take the spot next to Abbie in the middle of the sofa. I try to stare straight ahead, but out of the corner of my eye, I catch the ear-to-ear smile that appears on Michelle's face when I sit two people down from Brad.

Brittany settles near Adam, who raises his chin in greeting and then focuses back on the movie.

We sit like that for about twenty minutes. Brittany, Adam, and Abbie joke and laugh like always. Michelle keeps trying to talk to Brad, but he gives her only one- or two-word answers. I sit there fuming.

Suddenly, Brad gets up, walks to the kitchenette, and grabs a

Gatorade. He chugs it, standing next to the counter. When our eyes meet, he motions with his head for me to join him.

I narrow my eyes at him instead.

He blows out a silent breath and clenches his jaw.

Michelle says, "What are you doing? You're missing the movie."

He replies, "I'm not feeling well. Good night." Then he turns and heads upstairs while we all stare at his retreating figure until it's gone.

"I should check on him," Michelle says, jumping up. I have to resist the urge to tackle her right there in the basement. Why should she check on him? How about Adam, his best friend? Or me, his foster sister?

"Oh my God," Abbie says, looking at me after Michelle is gone. "Just tell her you and Brad are a thing already so she'll back off."

My stomach drops. "We're not a *thing*."

"Uh-huh, riiiight," Abbie says, rolling her eyes.

"We're not," I lie again, my eyes moving between her, Brittany, and Adam. They all give me polite smiles like you give a toddler who's trying to tell a story, but you only understand every third word.

"What? We're not!" I say more forcefully as my cheeks heat up.

Adam holds up his hands. "Whatever you say." Then he focuses back on the movie.

Brittany and Abbie continue to smile at me.

"We're not, okay? Because that would be wrong. Really, really wrong."

"Yeah, okay, whatever," Abbie says with a wave of her hands.

"Just tell her, so their complicated stuff can be over. I'm tired of it already. I shouldn't have to take sides between them."

Before anyone can say anything else, Michelle, with red eyes, stomps down the staircase. "I'm leaving," she announces when she reaches the bottom. She grabs her bag and spins around, crashing into Brad, who followed her down. She glares at him before stepping to his side and up the steps.

I hate to admit it, but seeing her obviously upset is about as exciting as that one time I got an A- on a geometry quiz. Brad must have finally told her he wasn't interested.

"I should go with her," Abbie says, racing up the steps.

I glance back to Brad, who's standing in the stairwell, his arms braced against the doorframe above his head, his face tense.

"You okay?" I ask, finding it odd how the tables have turned the last few minutes. I feel on top of the world now that Michelle's been set straight, and he looks like he wants to punch something.

He nods in silence, his jaw tight.

"Let's get out of here," Adam says to Brittany, standing and pulling her by the hand. When they walk past Brad, he says, "Call me later."

Brittany waves and then winks at me, which I ignore. Then, just like that, we're alone.

"You seem upset," I say.

"Sometimes she drives me crazy."

"Join the club."

He surprises me by smiling, most of the traces of his anger disappearing. After sitting next to me on the sofa, he rests his hand on my knee and says, "The good news is she absolutely knows where I stand."

My eyes grow wide. "She can't know about us," I whisper. "The others already suspect something, but at least I kind of trust them. I have absolutely zero faith in her. She'll tell someone. I'll get kicked out." I'm sure she'd love it if that happened. Then she'd have Brad all to herself.

He shakes his head. "I didn't tell her about us. I just told her I absolutely was not interested in her and never would be."

His words make me grin uncontrollably. She needed to hear that months ago. "How'd she take it?"

"Not great," he says with a laugh. "But you don't need to worry about her anymore." He puts his arm around my back and nuzzles my neck.

I kiss his cheek and scoot away before he can take things any further. "Sorry I was acting like a jealous girlfriend."

"It was actually kind of hot. I didn't realize you cared so much," he says with a smirk.

"It's just seemed like she felt as though she had a claim on you. It was annoying."

"No claim," he replies, shaking his head.

"Good. And Abbie will be happy."

"Why's that?"

"She said she was sick of taking sides between you two, so your complicated stuff needed to end."

His eyebrows arch up. "Abbie said that? What else did she have to say?"

"Nothing."

He sits back and watches me, almost like he's waiting for me to say more.

"What?" I ask, suddenly self-conscious.

He shakes his head. "Nothing. You good?"

I nod.

"Really?"

I nod again, but slower. Was the complicated stuff simply that she liked him and he didn't return the feelings, or was there more?

I bite my lip. "Actually . . ."

"Yeah."

"Was there more to the Michelle situation?"

"What do you mean?"

"Why was it complicated?"

"It wasn't complicated to me."

I roll my eyes. "Why did Michelle and Abbie think it was complicated?"

"Because she agreed to something and then changed her mind, but didn't bother mentioning it to me."

"What'd she agree to?"

"Sex with no strings attached."

My mouth drops open. "With you?"

"Yeah."

I poke my finger into his chest. "You lied to me! You said you were a virgin."

All this time, I trusted him. Everything he said, I believed. I never doubted him for a second, but he lied to me during one of our very first conversations. Has he continued lying? I know he lies to his family like it's nothing, but me? If he's been doing that, he's no better than Chase.

"I never said that," he replies. "You couldn't even ask the question because you couldn't say the word 'virgin.'"

Okay, that may be true. And I know how he likes to push boundaries, always looking at semantics to get away with whatever he wants. "But you made me believe you were."

"No. I told you to ask me the question, but you refused. I honestly had no idea what assumption you made."

"I felt like I could trust you," I say, pointing my finger at him again, my voice rising. "Have you been fooling around with her all this time? Is that why she wasn't taking a hint?"

He lets out a long breath and pushes my accusing finger down. "First of all," he says, "you *can* trust me. I don't lie to you. I'll never lie to you."

My eyes stay narrowed, but I let out a breath, some of my anger escaping with it.

"Secondly, no, I haven't been fooling around with her. This happened at the beginning of the school year. A week or two before I even met you."

Thank God. I know we don't officially have a relationship, but the thought of him messing around with Michelle while we're . . . doing our secret thing makes me sick to my stomach.

Suddenly, uplifting music blares from the TV. The movie is still on, and the young guy finally realized his mistake and is running through the airport to find the love of his life. It's kind of funny such an optimistic part of the movie would hit right now, in the middle of our argument.

"Plus," Brad says, ignoring the movie, "I actually had a reason. It wasn't like this was some drunken hook-up. We talked about it, and each wanted to practice with someone we knew and trusted. I know how ridiculous that sounds, but I'm the freaking quarterback.

People expect me to have experience. I didn't want to finally find a girl I like and be horrible in bed."

"And you thought one time was all you needed to be good in bed?" I ask, laughing as my anger fades away as quickly as it appeared. There's really nothing for me to be mad about. He technically didn't lie to me, and he only slept with Michelle once, before I was even in the picture. I can't be upset over that, even though the thought of him with *her* makes my skin crawl.

"Well, I could probably use some more practice," he says with a wicked grin, and then scoops me up and pulls me onto his lap. "You in?"

I roll my eyes.

"Let me be perfectly clear," he says, putting a finger under my chin and tilting my face up toward him. "I do not like Michelle. I have never liked her as more than a friend. I never will. It's you." He kisses my temple.

I hug him, then snuggle into his chest. "I'm sorry about the way I acted today."

"It's okay," he says, hugging me again. "I should've had this talk with Michelle weeks ago. It was my bad, not yours."

I kiss his cheek, and then I'm tempted to do more. It'd be nice to pick up our make-out session where it left off, but we're in his house with his parents right upstairs.

With a sigh, I scoot back to the corner of the sofa to put some space between us. He frowns, but picks up my feet and lays them on his lap. While the movie continues, he absently rubs them as I start to doze off.

"Ahem!"

My eyes snap open.

Gil is standing in front of the sofa. The sofa where I'm lying with my feet still on Brad's lap, while his head drapes over the back cushion, his mouth hanging open.

My feet scamper away from Brad, waking him in the process. "W-what's wrong?" he asks, his face contorted in confusion, his eyes still cloudy with sleep.

"Where is everyone else?" Gil asks.

I can tell as soon as Gil's voice registers with Brad because he snaps to attention, sitting up straight and fully waking in a fraction of a second. "Michelle drama," he says. "Then everyone went home."

I pull my legs to my chest and stare at the wall, afraid to see Gil's face. Why were we so stupid? If my feet were only a few inches away, Gil would have nothing to be suspicious about. Are a few inches going to be what gets me kicked out? What sends me to some new foster home? What sends me to a new school to start all over again?

"Did you need something?" Brad asks with a yawn. I can't tell if it's a real yawn or he's trying to pretend to be nonchalant about this.

"What's going on?" Gil asks.

"What do you mean?"

He frowns. "You two seemed awfully close when I came down here."

"Really? How so?" Brad looks between me and Gil with drawn brows, as though he hasn't a clue what Gil is talking about.

"You were holding Hailey's legs."

"That's weird. I didn't even notice. Did you notice, Hailey?"

I gulp against the sandpaper now lining my throat.

Without waiting for an answer, Brad continues, "She must have stretched out after we fell asleep."

Gil asks, "Can I talk to you for a second, Brad?"

"Sure, Dad." He stands and they move to the hallway, where I can hear hushed whispers, but no actual words. It doesn't last long. In less than a couple of minutes, Brad returns and Gil heads upstairs without saying anything else to me.

Brad lowers himself next to me, a sly smile on his face.

"What?" I ask, my heart pounding against my ribs. "Is it over? Is he calling Sherry?"

"No," he says, shaking his head. "He's more worried than suspicious."

"What did he say?"

"He told me how we need to be very careful around you. He said—and I'm quoting now—you're 'in a fragile emotional place and close personal contact could create the potential for displaced affection and blurring of appropriate boundaries' and then something about eroding the trust you so desperately need and then more blah, blah, blah."

"What does all that mean?"

"He's worried you're going to confuse friendship with a sexual relationship and end up hurt."

"Oh. Wow. Okay." I don't know what to make of his words, although they don't leave a good taste in my mouth. "So, he thinks I'm chasing after you?"

"I wouldn't say that. I think he thinks you're in a difficult spot and are looking for someone to be close to. He's fine if that's me as long as I'm"—he mimics Gil's voice—" 'extra vigilant in setting boundaries.' "

I scrunch my forehead as I try to understand. "He's worried I'm going to try something with you?"

"Funny, right? If I didn't risk losing you, I would've loved to tell him I'm the one trying to persuade you to play chess."

"Oh my God," I groan, burying my face in my hands. "How can I face him tomorrow morning when he thinks I'm trying to jump your bones?!" Brad laughs, and I peek at him between two fingers. "I'm serious, you know."

"I know, I know," he says, rubbing my leg. "I wouldn't worry about it, though. He's a psychiatrist. He sees crazy shit all the time. This is nothing for him."

"We need to be more careful," I say, my voice firm.

"Agreed."

"We got sloppy."

"Yes."

"No more snuggling at home. It can only happen at the park from now on."

"Or in my car."

"If your car is at the park."

"Okay," he says, grabbing my hand. "You should probably head up to your room. I'm sure he's sitting in his office, covertly keeping tabs on us. I'll be up in about ten minutes if you want a good-night kiss."

"Because that wouldn't be a terrible idea at all."

He leans over and gives me a quick, but not-at-all-innocent kiss on the mouth.

"Boundaries," I warn him with a wag of my finger as I walk away. Even though we ended up laughing about this, we do need to be more careful. Gil could have definitely come to a different conclusion. What would have happened if he had and I was headed back to DSS tonight? I'd probably never see Brad again. I'd probably never get another placement even a fraction as good as this one.

We cannot let that happen.

CHAPTER 23

"HOW WAS THERAPY?" GIGI ASKS WHEN I CLIMB INTO HER SUV
a couple of weeks later.

"Good."

I've been visiting a therapist ever since Gil found me and Brad
in the basement. He thought it would help me work through my
"trust" issues and come to some sort of happy place with my mom.
I think he's expecting a "Kumbaya" moment. Like that would *ever*
happen. I've wasted way too many tears and too much energy on
her already. The kid shouldn't be expected to make things right. If
she can't do it, I'm not, either.

But I still go to therapy. I'm just relieved Gil never suspected
the truth between me and Brad. If I need to go to therapy to keep
playing along, that's what I'll do. It's really a small price to pay.

"Oh, before I forget—do you want to go to the game in Raleigh on Saturday with us or with your friends?" Gigi asks, looking
in her side-view mirror for an opening in traffic.

It's the regional finals for Brad. If they win, they'll be in the

championship game. I'm sure Brad not only sees the championship, but also his path to Duke since the recruiter said he had to see
how Brad finished the season. He's got a lot riding on these next
two games, but you'd never know it by looking at him. He's calm,
cool, and collected, just like always.

The outcome of the game doesn't mean anything to me because
either way, he's leaving Pinehurst. Whether he moves to Winston-
Salem or Durham, there's a good chance it will be the last I'll see
of him. I'd prefer it if he'd stay right here, but there's nothing in
this town for him. It's a bad situation—his happiness versus my
happiness. It'd be nice if there were an ending to make everyone
happy, but that's not life.

You'd think I'd be an expert on disappointment by now and
completely unfazed by it, but I'm not. It still stings. Maybe even
more than it used to. I guess that's my prize for finding people I
can count on—more pain when we eventually go our separate ways.

I say, "I'll probably go to the game with you and just meet up
with my friends there."

"Okay." She pulls away from the curb, turns off her signal, and
says, "Do you mind if we stay in Raleigh for a few hours after the
game? I'd like to do some Christmas shopping." She pauses. "Actually, why don't you invite Brittany? Then the two of you can
hang out at the mall while Gil and I shop."

"Sure, sounds like fun."

She changes lanes and then asks, "So, how's school going?"

"Fine. I got a B-plus on my last geometry test."

"That's wonderful. Your grades continue to go up and up. You
could probably get into college if you wanted."

I slowly turn my head to watch her. She's never talked to me about college before, and I wonder if Brad mentioned it to her.

"You think?" I ask cautiously.

"Yes. Do you want to go?"

"I'm not sure." It's the truth. I've been thinking about it more and more since Brad and I talked. Part of me has always dreamed of going, but another part of me assumes that's all it is—a dream.

She pauses while braking for a turning car in front of her, then asks, "What's your hesitation?"

I shrug. "It just seems like a lot. What if . . . I can't handle it?" This is the first time I've ever put my fear into words. Chase told me over and over again I couldn't do it. What if I try and only prove him right?

"You're scared you'll fail?"

"Maybe . . . yes."

We stop at a light, and she turns to face me. "You should never make important decisions based on fear. Isn't it better to try and fail than not to try at all? At least then you could say you gave it your best shot. Not that I think you'd fail. You're doing well in school now."

"I guess." Of course, there's also the issue of all the changes that will hit with my birthday. I probably need to make sure I have a place to live and food to eat before I start thinking about luxuries like college. "It's just . . . I've got a lot of changes coming up," I say with a shrug.

"Because you'll age out of foster care?"

I nod. "I'm not sure what I'm going to do."

"What do you *want* to do?"

"Honestly?"

She glances over at me. "Yes, honestly."

Staring out the window, I watch the people walking from one store to another at the strip mall. It's not easy to tell her what I want because I know it's asking too much of them. They've already given me more than I ever imagined and I'm going to ask for even more? How selfish does that make me?

Gigi reaches over and pats my knee.

With a sigh, I say, "I want to stay with you until graduation, but I know it's greedy of me."

"Oh, honey," she says, squeezing my shoulder, "we just assumed you'd stay here through at least graduation, if not the summer."

Her one little sentence starts to lift an elephant-sized weight off my chest. Would they actually allow me to stay? "Really?" I ask. "You'd do that for me?"

"Yes, of course."

"I'll pick up more chores, and I don't need an allowance," I say quickly, before she can change her mind.

An angry honk sounds behind us, drawing Gigi's attention back to the road. The light's green, and the whole line of traffic is waiting on us. "Don't worry about that," she says, turning left.

"I don't want to be a freeloader when DSS stops paying."

"You won't be a freeloader. We never planned on keeping the checks anyway. We've been saving all the money and will give it to you when you turn eighteen, so you'll have something to help you get started."

My jaw falls to the ground. Why would they do that? It's

beyond generous. The money is supposed to cover all my expenses. "You don't have to do that."

"Hailey, we never did this for the money. We did this because we want to help you. We want you to go to college, but if you choose not to, you can stay here as long as you need to find a job and save up enough money to get a car and a place of your own."

I stare out the window in shock. I'm just some random girl thrown into their home, but they're treating me like family. It's almost like they're my real parents. Well, normal real parents, not my real, real parents.

The fear that's been gnawing on my insides for the last few weeks starts to fade. I won't be spending my eighteenth birthday in a homeless shelter somewhere. And I'll actually have enough money for a deposit on an apartment whenever I need it. This may not seem like much to Gigi, but it changes everything for me. The corners of my eyes start stinging, and I fight back happy tears.

"Do you mind if we stop at the store?" Gigi asks. "I need to pick up a few last-minute things for Thanksgiving tomorrow."

I shake my head because I don't trust my voice. I might actually be able to make all this work and go to college. Me. College. It's . . . unbelievable, really. How many times did Chase tell me it wouldn't happen? How many times did my mom tell me I wouldn't even finish high school? Enough to make me believe it. But they could both be wrong. I could actually do it. If I can just get my GPA up a little, my application might have a fighting chance.

I pinch myself. The small red mark makes it clear I'm wide awake. Everything is completely real, yet as unbelievable as the craziest dreams I've ever had.

CHAPTER 24

THREE DAYS LATER, IT'S BRAD'S BIG DAY. AFTER SHOWERING, I head downstairs to eat a quick breakfast before we leave for the semifinal game. I grab some cereal from the pantry and pour it into a bowl.

As I'm adding milk, Gigi enters, talking on her phone.

I ignore her conversation about some big client coming into her store today and think about the game. During Thanksgiving, Brad's uncle asked him how he thought they'd do, and Brad seemed very confident. It'd be nice if the win could come as easily as Brad said it would.

"Good morning, Hailey," Gigi says, laying her phone on the counter when she's finished.

"Good morning."

"Is Brad up?"

I shrug. "I haven't seen him yet."

She walks into the living room and looks up at the landing. "Bradley!" she yells.

"Yes?" he asks, coming down the stairs into the kitchen.

"Oh, sorry," Gigi replies. "I thought you overslept."

"No chance of that." He looks at me and smiles. "Good morning."

I smile back and focus on my cereal as he puts four waffles in the toaster before grabbing a bottle of Gatorade and a Clif Bar.

After downing half the Gatorade in a couple of gulps, he sits next to me and tears open the bar as he waits for his waffles.

"Are you nervous?" I ask.

"Nah," he says, nudging my leg with his own under the table. He leaves it pressed up against me. I glance at Gigi, but she's focused on adding sugar and cream to her coffee.

"I don't get nervous," he continues.

Gigi snorts from the other side of the room.

"I think your mom disagrees."

"Brad used to get so nervous before games we'd have to take a bucket in the car. He'd throw up once or twice on the way there!"

He makes a face at her back. "I haven't done that in years."

"No, instead, you have your pregame ritual."

"There's nothing wrong with a good-luck charm."

I turn to see him better and tuck my foot underneath me on the chair. "What is your good-luck charm?"

"Have you ever noticed how he paces in the end zone before a game?" Gigi asks, stepping to the refrigerator.

"Yes . . ."

"Mom!" Brad yells, glaring at her back.

She glances over her shoulder and smiles at him. "You said there's nothing wrong with a good-luck charm."

"What exactly do you do in the end zone?" I ask.

"Nothing."

"Are you blushing?"

"No."

"Yes, you are." He's adorable when he blushes. I wish I could see it more often, but he's hardly ever embarrassed, unlike me.

He rolls his eyes and takes a bite of his bar.

"Now I've really got to know what you do."

"No, you don't."

"What is it, Gigi?"

She laughs and points a spoon at the two of us. "Tell her, Brad. It's cute. She'll like it."

"Fine. I talk to the ball, okay?" he says, holding his hands out in front of himself, like he just surrendered in a war.

"You talk to the ball?"

"Yeah. It's like a pep talk."

"For the ball?"

"Yeah."

"Does it listen to you?" I try to keep a straight face but totally fail.

"Very funny."

"I'd love to hear what you say."

"No, you wouldn't."

"I would, too," Gigi adds, grabbing a container of yogurt from the fridge. "Do you tell it to keep a tight spiral?"

"Or to stay nice and inflated throughout the whole game?" I ask.

"Or to home in on your receiver's hands like a ballistic missile?"

"I've had enough," he says, pushing his chair back just as the waffle pops up. He gives my shoulder a quick squeeze while Gigi reaches back into the fridge for something else. "I'll be looking for you in the stands," he whispers.

I smile and say, "Good luck."

✳ ✳ ✳

"Ooh, let's go in here," Michelle says, leading us into a store that has cute but no doubt superexpensive clothes in the window.

Brittany and I sat with her, Abbie, Adam, and one of Adam's friends at the game. The win didn't come as easily as Brad thought it would, but they hung in there and got a last-minute touchdown, sealing the deal. The Patriots are now in the championship game next week. Brad is one win away from his dream of Duke.

When the game ended, Abbie found out about our plans to go to the mall, and they all decided to join us. Adam and his friend disappeared into a video-game store the minute we got here. I don't mind spending time with Abbie, but Michelle's already getting on my nerves. She insists on going into all the expensive stores and turns up her nose anytime Brittany or I suggest one that has stuff we could actually afford.

I flip the tag on the first thing I see in the current store and my suspicions are confirmed. I will not be buying anything from here. Brittany and I lean against the wall near the entrance, waiting for Abbie and Michelle to finish.

"Maybe we should just ditch them," Brittany suggests.

"That'd be rude."

"They invited themselves along! And we go in three stores Michelle wants for every one we want."

"If it were just Michelle, I'd have ditched her an hour ago, but it's not fair to Abbie."

Brittany scrunches up her face, but agrees.

After a few minutes, she stands up straight and steps into the doorway, something in the mall obviously catching her attention. "Hey . . . is that . . . ," she asks, pointing to a bench not too far from us, "your ex?"

Her words make my heart momentarily stop, but then I realize there's no way. What would he be doing in a random mall in a city an hour from home at the exact same time as me? It's impossible. I join her by the door, now curious about the Chase look-alike.

He's facing away from us, so it's hard to tell anything.

"Wait until he turns around," Brittany says. "I swear it's him."

It only takes a minute for him to face us, and my heart to stop for real. It *is* him.

Crap, crap, crap.

I slink back inside the store and hide behind a mannequin. There is no way I'm leaving until he's gone.

Brittany joins me but positions herself so she can see him through the window if she leans far enough to the right.

"Did he see me?" I ask.

"I don't think so. He's still talking to that other guy."

"Okay, good," I reply, biting my nail, thinking about the odds of running into him here. They have to be like a thousand to one. Is he following me? It didn't seem like it. It looked like he was in the middle of a deal out there, but this is way outside his normal territory. Maybe he's thinking about branching out. Not that it matters to me. The only thing I care about is avoiding him the rest of our time at the mall. Maybe I should find Gigi and ask for the car keys. I could hang out in her SUV and listen to music for a few hours. That wouldn't be so bad.

"Ready?" Abbie asks, stepping next to us with another bag slung over her shoulder.

"Not really," I reply, continuing to gnaw on my thumbnail.

"What's wrong?"

"Her ex," Brittany says, pointing out the window.

Both Michelle and Abbie look toward the bench.

"Oh yeah. I remember him from that one time at Brad's. What's his name? Chad?" Michelle asks.

"Chase."

"Was it a bad breakup or something?"

"Yeah," I reply. I'm not getting into any details about me and Chase with Michelle. Luckily, she doesn't push me for more information.

"We can't just hide in here," Abbie says, tapping her fingers on a clothing rack. "What if the three of us surround you? We'll block you from his view."

"Or we could wait until he leaves," I suggest.

"We have no idea how long that could take," Michelle complains.

"Actually, he's leaving right now," Brittany says.

I sneak a peek around us, and relief washes over me when I see she's correct. He's almost out of sight already.

We exit the store and go in the opposite direction of him, but I can't stop glancing over my shoulder every couple of minutes, afraid he's sneaking up on me.

"I want to go in here," Brittany says when we reach a place that looks more like my kind of store, especially if they have a clearance rack. Michelle wrinkles her nose and says she'll wait outside for us. I expect Abbie to stay with her, but she rolls her eyes and joins us, making me like her even a little bit more.

I spend a few minutes constantly checking through the window for Chase, but then realize how ridiculous I'm being. There's no way he'd come into a store like this. I'm safe in here. Out in the mall is a different story, but at least for now, I'm safe.

"You should try this on," Abbie says, holding up a pink-and-white summer dress in front of me.

"How much is it?" I automatically ask.

She checks the tag. "Originally forty dollars, but it's seventy-five percent off."

"That is a good deal," I say, fingering the soft fabric.

"Here," she says, shoving it into my hands. I take it, then check the sale rack where she got the dress and find another dress, a pair of jeans, and two shirts to try on. Brittany finds a few things, too, and we head to the dressing rooms. Abbie takes a seat, offering to watch our jackets and bags.

Ten minutes later, I'm yanking off the jeans when I hear Michelle's whiny voice again. "What's taking so long?" she asks.

"We're almost done," Brittany replies from the dressing area next to me. I hear the scrape of metal as she pushes the curtain aside. "It's not like we haven't waited on you a gazillion times today," she says under her breath.

I smile and pull one of the dresses over my head. It's really cute. I step outside to get a second opinion and find Michelle sitting in the chair that was holding my jacket. I wouldn't mind except my jacket is now lying in the middle of the floor where anyone could step on it or trip over it.

I grab it and shove it in the corner, fighting the urge to give Michelle a dirty look as I model for Abbie. "What do you think? Should I get it?"

"Definitely."

After we pay, I immediately become cautious again, but the others seem to have forgotten about Chase lurking around the mall. They're all chatting as we exit the store, while my eyes scan the people walking by.

Luckily, I don't see him. I step next to Brittany and take a deep breath. I need to relax.

"Hales."

Or not.

It's the familiar voice I was hoping never to hear again, coming from right behind me.

I try to ignore it and keep walking, but his bony fingers land on my shoulder.

"Hales," he says louder, drawing attention from the other girls now, too.

I turn around to face him. "Chase," I say, trying to keep my voice steady.

"Where's your boyfriend?" he says with a sneer. "I thought he never let you out of his sight."

I swallow against the lump in my throat. "He's not my boyfriend."

"Ain't no reason for him to act like he does unless you're fucking him."

"I'm not," I say, trying to step away from him, but he squeezes my shoulder.

"You're looking good," he says, his eyes roaming up and down my body, but stopping at my chest. I cross my arms self-consciously and take a step back.

He takes a step forward, still holding on to me.

"Please," I beg, my heart beating like a drum. "Leave me alone. I haven't done anything to you."

Just then, a large-framed man appears behind Chase. "Is there a problem here?" he asks, using his elbow to nudge Chase's hand from my shoulder and putting himself between us. He makes a clear path for me, so I take it without a second thought. "Thanks," I whisper before rushing to a nearby bathroom in record time.

I lock the door of my stall and lean against it, letting out a long breath as I get my racing heart under control. God, that was scary. Chase has never made me feel like that before. Liked a caged animal.

I take another deep breath and dry my sweaty palms on my jeans. I found a new place to live, new friends, a new sort-of boyfriend, but I'll never be able to escape my past. It's always going to be there, just waiting to creep back in and steal me away from everything good when I least expect it.

That's the part Sherry and Brad don't understand. It's easy enough to tell me to move on from my past, but I can't stop things like this from happening. I'm powerless against Chase. My mom. My shoulders droop. If they want to ruin my life, they'll eventually find a way. Maybe not today. Maybe not next week. Maybe not until I move away from the Campbells, but they'll find a way.

I see Brittany's shoes under the door to my stall. "You can come out," she says. "He's not coming in here."

I slowly unlock the door and come face-to-face with the mirror. What I see brings tears to my eyes.

Scared, helpless Hailey.

It's the old me.

One run-in with Chase and I'm right back where I was months ago. How can he do that to me? How can I let him do that to me? A tear rolls down my cheek and onto the edge of the sink.

Michelle and Abbie join us. "He's gone," Michelle says. "That guy spooked him."

I wipe my cheek.

"I'm strong, right?" I ask Brittany.

She wraps me in her arms. "You are the most kickass, badass, rock-star, superhero foster kid I know. He needs to get the fuck out of your way because you've got plans and there's no room for his extra baggage on the Hailey freight train. If he doesn't, you'll smash his useless ass into a million pieces."

I smile.

One last glimpse in the mirror tells me all I need to know. I do have this. She's right. I might need a little pepper spray to help, but I can deal with Chase and my mom. I will not be helpless Hailey ever again. I refuse to do it.

I straighten my shoulders and take a deep breath. Brittany hugs me again, smiling at me in the mirror.

"I just texted Adam and told him we're ready to go. Do y'all want a ride home?" Abbie asks, catching our eyes in the mirror.

"Let me see how much longer Gil and Gigi are going to be," I say, fishing my phone out of my bag.

Gigi texts back that they'll be here at least another hour, so Brittany and I take Abbie up on her offer. Even though nothing ended up happening with Chase and I'm feeling better about myself, he did kind of ruin our fun shopping trip. Plus, it'd be nice to get back to Pinehurst and see Brad before his parents return. We've hardly talked at all today.

I'm a little nervous to step into the mall again, but Adam and his friend meet us at the bathroom and walk with us all the way out to his car. If Chase is still around, he doesn't show himself.

"So, are you going to the game in Charlotte next Saturday?" Abbie asks when we're just about home.

"Yeah," I reply with a nod. It's the championship game—it's not like Gil and Gigi would ever miss that. Gil could be on death's doorstep, and he'd still have the nurses wheel his hospital bed into the stadium.

"What about you, Brittany?" she asks.

"I'm not sure. I'd need a ride."

"Why don't y'all come with us?" Abbie says. "Michelle and I got a hotel room in the same hotel as the team. You can stay with us. It will be fun!"

"I'm sure Gil and Gigi wouldn't let me," I say, shaking my head. I can't imagine spending an entire night with Michelle.

"They won't care. Just ask them!"

"It *would* be fun," Brittany says, rocking her shoulder into mine.

I give her a look, then say, "Maybe," as I study the pine trees passing by. There's no way I'm asking them.

Brittany is dropped off first, and then it's my turn.

"Thanks for the ride," I say with a wave to Adam as I step out of the car. I'm about to shut the door when Michelle's legs hit the ground.

"I have something to tell Brad," she says, joining me outside the car.

I glance inside to Adam, who shrugs his shoulders and gives me a sympathetic look. I roll my eyes, blow out a long breath, and then walk up the path to the doorway, completely ignoring her behind me.

When I reach the porch, I push the lever on the doorknob to let myself inside, but it's locked.

Reaching into my jacket pocket, I find it's empty. I try the other one and then both pockets of my jeans, but all I find is my phone. "Crap," I mumble, trying the door again and then hitting the doorbell. "This day just gets better and better," I say under my breath.

Michelle steps up next to me as Adam pulls out of the driveway. "What's wrong?" she asks.

"I lost my key."

"I can let you in. I always water Mrs. Campbell's plants when they go on vacation." She reaches into her bag and pulls out a key chain with five or six keys and then unlocks the door.

I step inside and punch in my four-digit security code for the alarm, while she waits on me.

"Well, thanks," I say when I'm done, shifting my weight from one foot to the other. "I don't think Brad's here."

She continues standing next to me. It's like she wants me to invite her to stay, but I've had more than enough Michelle for one day.

"Yep, you bet," she says, checking her phone. "You're right. He's at dinner with the team."

My jaw clenches at her response. Are they still texting each other? How often does that happen?

"I guess you can talk to him at school," I say, and hold the door open a little wider. She finally takes the hint and climbs down the steps before crossing the lawn toward her house.

After slamming the door, I fall against it and groan. Then I grab my phone.

Why are you still texting her? I type to Brad.

Who?

Michelle?

I haven't texted her in weeks.

You told her you were at dinner with the team.

No.

ARE you at dinner with the team?

Yeah, but I didn't tell her that. Maybe someone else did?

That makes no sense. Why would she make it seem like she was texting with him if she wasn't? I groan when I realize the answer— to get under my skin. Ugh. That's exactly what she did, too.

Sorry, I type. And congrats on the win, BTW.

Thanks. Are you home?

Yeah.

Mom and Dad there?

Not yet. I came back with Adam. They'll probably be here in another hour or so.

I'll be there in ten minutes.

I smile at my phone as I take off my shoes and jacket. When I'm done, I reply, Good. I was hoping we could spend a little time together.

Yeah? What'd you have in mind?

We still haven't played chess. I want to, but . . . it just hasn't felt right. Well, being with him always feels right—very right—but I start to feel guilty when things go too far. Like I'm testing an invisible boundary and one time I'll push it beyond its limits and everything that's finally good in my life will come crashing down.

Not chess, but maybe . . . checkers? I type.

His response comes in not even two seconds later. I'm in.

Do you know what checkers entails? I don't even know what it entails since I typed it on a whim, so there's no way he could.

Nope.

And you're still in.

Yep.

I smile and shake my head. You should really ask for more details before you agree to something. I could totally take advantage of you.

And that would be bad how?

You're okay with being taken advantage of?

By you during checkers and chess? Hell yeah.

I laugh at his response. Good to know.

Excited for checkers. Driving now. See you soon.

Not even a minute later, the phone rings.

"Hello?" I answer, expecting Brad.

"Please, please, let's go to Charlotte with Abbie." It's Brittany's fast-paced, excited voice.

"You're forgetting that Michelle will be there, too."

"Don't worry about her. I'll keep her bitchy attitude in check."

"You can go."

"I already asked my foster mom. She said only if you're going and the Campbells are staying in the same hotel."

I groan.

"Come on, Hailey. It'll be fun. I promise."

I groan again, but finally say, "I'll ask." Brittany's done a lot for me. If she wants to go, it's the least I can do.

A high-pitched squeal pierces my eardrum. When she's done, I add, "Don't get your hopes up, though. Gil and Gigi might be planning on driving home that night. If they are, I'll have to go with them."

She squeals again and then hangs up.

Brittany's right—it would be fun with just Abbie. The problem is Michelle. Stupid, stupid Michelle. If she weren't around, things would be so much easier. I'll probably never understand what any of them see in her, although maybe every group of friends has that one annoying person they all just deal with. Like Brad always says, congruency is boring. Maybe you need a little Michelle in your circle to keep things interesting.

CHAPTER 25

ONE MINUTE LEFT AND WE'RE DOWN BY FOUR POINTS. I DON'T
see any way the Patriots can pull off the win now. My heart breaks
for the whole team, but especially Brad and his dream of Duke.
He's worked so hard, but it all comes down to a few seconds. A few
measly seconds can reverse eighteen years of dedication.

"Come on, Pats!" Brittany yells from beside me, bouncing up
and down.

The stands are painted in green and yellow—from clothes to
signs to foam fingers—and it seems like our entire school must be
here. The sound is deafening.

They get ready for another play. I hold my breath as Brad draws
back his arm, but instead of throwing it, he frantically searches for
his teammates. Two players from the other team rush toward him,
and I cringe, anticipating the impact. Fortunately, he tosses the ball
just in time and those players change course. Unfortunately, Brad's
teammate drops the ball.

They try again two more times, but it's the same result.

There are only fifteen seconds left now, and they still have a quarter of the field to go. There's no way. Abbie must agree because I see her wipe her eyes, already resigned to the loss.

I watch Brad in the huddle. Even though I can't see his face, I can tell he's yelling. His entire body is wound up with energy. He doesn't think it's over.

They line up again, and Brittany grabs my hand. I grab Abbie's, and she grabs Michelle's. We squeeze and watch the final play of the game. Brad gets the ball, steps to the side, and a big guy runs right at him. "No!" I yell. The worst part of these games is watching him get tossed around.

Brad must see the big guy because he changes direction, only to have someone else come after him. "Throw the ball!" I yell. Anything to prevent him from getting tackled.

But he doesn't throw the ball.

He spins around, just out of the grasp of the guy who dove at him, and then he runs. He never runs. What is he doing? There are two guys from the other team in front of him. He rushes past one of them, who grabs his waist, but he shakes free and keeps running.

Oh my God!

Brittany starts pulling on my hand. "Go, Brad!" she yells. "Go! Go! Go!"

He's so close now, but there's still one player in his way. The player lunges at Brad's knees and I tense, hiding my eyes in my shoulder. I can't watch.

The deafening crowd becomes eerily silent.

"What happened?" I ask, glancing at Brittany, still unable to look at the field. "Is Brad okay?"

Brittany's jaw is practically touching the ground and her eyes are as big as full moons. "What?" I ask again, tugging on her arm.

"He just freaking hurdled that guy!" she yells. "We're waiting on the ref. . . . Touchdown!" The crowd erupts in cheers and starts storming the field. We're caught up in the wave and couldn't resist if we wanted to. It's like we're on a magic carpet with a mind of its own as we're carried down the steps and onto the field.

Once we're on the grass, the crowd spreads out more. "Let's find Brad!" I yell.

The four of us continue holding hands and search through the green uniforms, flying confetti, pom-poms, and crazy fans. Then, between two cheerleaders, I see him. His helmet is off, and he's gripping another player's hand in one of those man hugs, but his eyes are scanning the crowd.

"This way," I say, leading the girls in his direction.

It's clear when he spots us because he drops the other guy's hand, pats him on the shoulder, and then heads directly for us. For me.

"Congratulations!" I yell when we get close.

I've never seen such sheer excitement on his face. He drops his helmet and rushes at me, grabbing me by the waist when he reaches me and spinning me around.

"I'm so proud of you," I yell in his ear.

Just then, another player thrusts the trophy into his hands. He leans down and says, "Meet me in the lobby of the hotel?"

I nod and step aside so he can enjoy this moment with his team. From a distance, we watch him hold the trophy overhead and scream while cameras flash and coolers of Gatorade are dumped over the players.

I can't even imagine what he must be feeling right now. All his work for years *has* paid off. He's getting exactly what he wants. He can go to Duke.

There's that small, annoying part of me that feels sad about him moving away, but I push it aside. Tonight is about Brad. Only Brad.

* * * *

"Hey! It's the MVP!" someone yells as Brad enters the lobby. Everyone from the game has moved here, lingering outside and in the lobby, and on the ninth floor where the players are staying.

My room, with Michelle, Abbie, and Brittany, is on the fourth floor. I still can't believe Gigi agreed. They were planning on driving home after the game, but when I mentioned Abbie's idea, she thought it sounded great and quickly booked a room for her and Gil in the same hotel.

I'm not sure where Michelle and Abbie are right now, but Brittany, Adam, and I have been hanging out in the lobby, waiting for the team to arrive.

Brad, freshly showered and looking as good as ever in jeans and a gray T-shirt, walks through the crowd, getting slaps on the back, high fives, and fist bumps as he passes everyone.

"Good game, dude!" Adam says, standing and giving him a quick, one-armed hug when he reaches us.

Brad gives me and Brittany hugs, too, and then says, "Party's upstairs. Let's go."

We follow him to the elevator and then take it to the ninth floor. As soon as we exit, we realize the lobby was tame compared with this. People pour from one room to another, many of them carrying red plastic cups as music blares every time a door opens.

"This way," Brad says, leading us down the hallway to a specific room.

The security lock is flipped onto the doorframe with the door resting on top of it so we can easily enter. Brad clutches my hand and leads me inside, and we weave our way through all the people. We try to find a place to sit, but it takes forever to move a few feet because everyone wants to congratulate him.

Suddenly, a piercing whistle sounds in the hallway, followed by a deep, booming voice. I can't quite make out the words with all the music, though.

"What's that?" I ask.

"Coach," Brad says, turning around. "Come on." We backtrack until we're in the hallway again, which is noticeably emptier than it was a few moments ago. The football coach stands at the end with his hands on his hips.

He yells, "Get your asses downstairs right now so you don't end up in jail." The regular students dip into the rooms away from the coach, but the football players come out, hanging their heads, and following his instructions.

One of the guys walks past him carrying a red cup. The coach grabs the cup, sniffs it, then smacks him on the shoulder. "No booze, Sharif. Thanks to some generous parents," he says to the other players in the hallway, "we have a nice ballroom downstairs where you can party. No alcohol. No drugs. Let's be safe tonight."

The players start working their way downstairs, but the rooms are still crawling with people.

"Campbell," the coach says, raising his chin toward Brad, "you and Alvarez clear this place out. Pronto."

Brad nods. "Yes, sir." He turns to me. "I'll just be a minute. Do you want to wait downstairs?"

"I'll wait by the elevator." I don't tell him this, but I want to see him in action. From the first day we met, I've been impressed by the way he draws everyone in. They all love him. I know why I love—like, I mean like—definitely like because I can't be thinking love—him, but it's fascinating watching him interact with people who don't know him as well. He's a natural leader. It's impressive, but also . . . sexy.

Way too sexy.

God, I'm practically drooling.

"Ready?" Brad asks after the last group boards the elevator.

I nod. "That was pretty hot," I say, reaching for his hand since we're alone.

"What? Getting everyone to leave?"

"Yes. And your performance during the game. You are especially . . ."

He raises an eyebrow.

"Sexy tonight."

Just then, the elevator dings and the doors open. We enter. As soon as the doors close, his mouth is on mine and his hands grip my butt. "You, too," he whispers against my mouth. My hands roam down his chest, and I think about going farther, but luckily, I find some shred of self-control. We have like a minute on the elevator, maybe two if we're lucky. We need to keep this quick and innocent.

Brad draws me nearer, his body pressed against me, leaving no doubt he's being honest about finding me sexy as well, and quickly getting out of the realm of innocent.

My body is torn between doing what's right and what feels

right. I run my hands along his butt. It feels very right, but the gnawing in my gut tells me it's definitely not right. Not here. Not now. With a deep breath, I take half a step away from him.

He reaches into his pocket and removes a plastic card. "Do you know what this is?"

"A key."

"A key to my empty room. Carlos decided to bunk with some friends."

"Oh."

"It's yours, if you want it. You can stay all night."

"An all-night chess tournament," I murmur. This could be the best opportunity we'll ever have. I'd be crazy to pass this up, right? It's almost like a sign we were meant to do this tonight.

"Only if you want to," he says. "Do you?"

Of course I do. It's just a matter of how bad of an idea it is. How much do I risk losing?

Only my placement. Which is basically my entire life.

But that's only if they found out. Could Sherry find out? She's like three hours from here. There's no way she'd know. Gil and Gigi are the bigger problem.

"I don't want your parents to kick me out," I say.

"They'll never know. Even if they did, I'd make sure they wouldn't kick you out."

"Promise?"

"Yes."

It's a terrible idea. I know it is, but I want to do it. I want him. I've wanted him for months, and this is the best opportunity we'll ever have.

I bite my lip and nod.

Brad's brows shoot up at my answer. He definitely wasn't expecting it. "Do you think Brittany will cover for you?"

I nod again.

Handing me the key, he says, "Room 904. In case we're separated."

The elevator stops moving, and Brad steps away, smoothing the front of his shirt and pants. I do the same and take another deep breath.

As soon as we exit, we can tell where the party is by the deep bass and our rowdy classmates.

"Party," he says, motioning to the ballroom, "or chess," he adds, looking back at the elevator we just exited.

"Chess can wait," I say. "We should go to the party. People are here to celebrate you."

"No, they're here to celebrate the win."

"Which is largely due to you."

His lips spread into a massive ear-to-ear grin, making it clear how much he's enjoying this. "Okay," he says, leading me to the ballroom. "Let's stay for a little while."

As soon as we step inside, we see Brittany and Adam, tearing it up on the dance floor. I still don't understand how they're not a couple. They're perfect for each other.

"This way," I say, grabbing Brad's hand and taking him in their direction. They wave to welcome us, and then Brad surprises me by encircling my waist with his arms as he starts swaying his hips. It's not like Brittany and Adam, but it's a lot more than we did at homecoming.

I consider putting a little more space between us, but no

one's paying any attention. Plus, plenty of classmates who are only friends are dancing exactly like this—just look at Adam and Brittany.

Over the next three hours, we dance, eat pizza, talk, and laugh. It's awesome. Amazing. The best night of my life.

The trophy sits on a table at the front of the room and throughout the night, different groups go up and try to get the most outrageous photo with it. My favorite, though, is one of just Brad holding it overhead. He looks so triumphant. I love that look on him.

Well past one in the morning, we decide to call it a night. Brad heads up first while I talk to Brittany.

"What's up?" she asks, wiping sweat from her brow.

I motion for her to step farther into the corner with me, away from some of our classmates. "I need a favor."

"Sure. What?"

"Um . . ." I pause, not exactly sure how to put this. I run a few scenarios through my mind, but quickly realize I need to be up front with her.

"So, Brad and I . . ."

She raises an eyebrow.

"Are . . . um . . . kind of . . . uh . . . like . . . dating . . . secretly."

"No shit," she replies, rolling her eyes.

My stomach starts churning at her words. If she knows, who else does? "Are we that obvious?"

She rocks her shoulder into me. "Don't worry. It's only obvious to your best friends. I've actually been impressed by the act you've got going, especially at school."

I gulp. "Does Michelle know?"

She shakes her head. "She's way too self-centered to put two and two together."

I nod, happy to get a little good news. "So, he . . . uh . . . invited me to stay in his room tonight."

Her eyes grow wide, and her jaw drops.

"So . . . um . . . do you think you could cover for me? Tell Abbie and Michelle I'm staying in the Campbells' room? And if the Campbells happen to call or stop by, come up with some excuse for where I am?"

She nods. "I've got your back. Have fun tonight," she says with a wicked smile.

On my way into the lobby and then the elevator, my feet move a little quicker and I feel a little lighter as I realize how lucky I am to have Brittany. Foster care takes a lot from you—your parents, your school, your friends, your home—but, at least in my case, it also gives a lot. Like a best friend who I'd trust with my life.

When I get to room 904, I unlock the door and enter in record time, not wanting anyone to see me. Brad is sitting in bed in athletic shorts, no shirt, watching TV, and looking really . . . sleepy.

I can't help but laugh. I don't know what I was expecting, but I guess I thought it would be more romance and less middle-aged married couple.

"What are you laughing about?" he asks, turning off the TV.

I wave my hands, motioning to the entire room. "This. You're usually a little more . . ."

"Southern gentleman?"

"Yeah."

"Sorry. I thought about getting flowers, but the nearest twenty-four-hour grocery store is ten miles away. I did, however," he says, reaching to the nightstand next to him, "get you chocolate." He holds out a Snickers bar.

I walk to the bed and take it from him. "Nothing says romance like Snickers."

"That's what I was thinking. It's chocolate. Peanuts. Caramel. I pity the guy who has never given his girl a Snickers."

I sit down next to him and unwrap the candy bar. After nibbling a piece off, I hold it out to him. He takes a gargantuan bite, leaving me with less than half left.

"What the heck?" I ask with a laugh, holding it up.

He reaches into the drawer next to him and pulls out three more. "Sorry, I'm really hungry. It was a tough game."

I take another dainty bite and then give him the rest of it to eat. While he's chewing, I climb over him, into the middle of the bed, and sit with my back against the plush headboard, like he's doing.

"So, when do you think you'll hear from Duke?" I ask, unwrapping the second Snickers.

His face breaks into a huge grin. "Already got a message from the recruiter."

"You're in?"

"If I want it."

"You do, right?"

He nods again, but his grin falters. Not much, but enough to make me wonder. "Have you talked to your parents?" I ask.

"I saw them briefly after the game, but I didn't tell them about Duke. Have you talked to them?"

"I checked in with them when I got back to the hotel, like they asked. That's all."

"Was that their only rule for tonight?"

"No, I also had to stay in the hotel all night and not drink or do drugs."

"They didn't mention sex?"

"No."

"Really?"

I nod. "I guess they figured there wasn't much risk of it tonight."

"Is that why you're so willing to play chess all of a sudden?"

I smile. I hadn't considered that, but I guess it could play a role. With a shrug, I say, "Maybe," although I think the bigger reason is my crumbling self-control.

"Well, you really won't be breaking any of their rules, so you don't have to worry about getting kicked out."

"Except the unspoken rule of not hooking up with your foster brother."

"Unspoken doesn't count. If they expect you to follow a rule, they need to tell you."

Of course he would say that, being Mr. Semantics and all. "You're always a stickler for the finer points of rules. Maybe you should be a lawyer instead of a psychiatrist." I hand him the candy bar, and he takes a more normal-sized bite.

"Do you have anything I can wear for pajamas?" I ask. "I left all my clothes in my real room."

He slides out of bed and rummages through a large duffel bag. After only a few seconds, he shakes his head. "Nope. Nothing. You'll have to go full-blown commando."

"Only if you do," I say, joking.

Except he reaches down, hooking his thumbs into his shorts.

"Wait!" I say, raising my hands. "I've got caramel stuck in my teeth, confetti stuck in my hair, and sweat covering every part of me. I need to get cleaned up before we do the whole naked thing for the first time."

He holds his hand out toward the bathroom. "By all means. I'll just be waiting here for the naked chess to commence."

I go into the bathroom and start with a quick shower. I plan on using the fruity sample-sized shampoo and conditioner, but I'll have to use the entire bottle of conditioner to get the tangles out of my hair. Why do they make these bottles so small? Would it kill them to give you at least two uses out of each one?

I wrap a towel around me and lean out the door. "Hey, Brad?"

"Yes?"

"Are you going to need any conditioner in the morning?"

"What's conditioner?"

"For your hair."

He gives me a blank stare.

"To get the tangles out."

He smiles. "I don't think I've ever had a tangle."

"Really?"

He laughs. "Really. Why are you asking me this?"

"Can I use the whole thing?" I ask, holding up the bottle for him to see.

"Knock yourself out."

I climb back into the shower. When I'm done, I try running my fingers through my wet hair, but I really need a brush to get it looking more manageable.

"Hey, Brad?" I ask, leaning through the door again.

"Yes?"

"Do you have a brush?"

"No."

"A comb?"

"I don't know. Look through my bag."

I poke through the mesh pocket area but don't see one. There's another pocket, one that's zipped and not see-through. I unzip it and move things around with my fingertip as though the less I disturb them, the less snoopy I'm being. Luckily, I find a comb resting against the back of the pouch.

After combing my hair, I decide to focus on my teeth. Brad has both toothpaste and mouthwash sitting on the edge of the sink.

"Hey, Brad?" I ask, leaning back into the room again.

"Yes?"

"Can I use some of your toothpaste and mouthwash?"

"Yes. My toothbrush is in there, too."

I wrinkle my nose. "I'm not using your toothbrush."

"Why not?"

"That's disgusting."

He laughs at me. "You think my mouth is disgusting? After all the times you've kissed me?"

"No, but . . . toothbrushes are personal. Like your dad said, we need boundaries."

"Got it. Swapping spit and other stuff okay; swapping tooth-brushes not okay."

"Yes," I say with a nod. "That's a deal breaker for me. If you ever use my toothbrush, I'll have to go all ninja-Hailey on you."

"I'd like to see that."

I smile and retreat to the bathroom, where I put a little tooth-paste on my finger and scrub the best I can. While scrubbing, I get a peek of a green foil wrapper sticking out of Brad's bag. I move closer to get a better look and see a mountain of them inside the pouch.

"Hey, Brad?" I ask, leaning out the door again, this time with a mouth full of toothpaste.

"Yeah?"

"Why do you have like twenty condoms in here? Do you have plans I should know about?"

"Nope. That's my full supply. I thought it was less likely Mom would look in there than under my sink or in my nightstand."

"So, there's not a line of girls outside waiting to come in here?"

"Very funny."

I lean back in and spit into the sink.

"Hey, Hailey?"

"Yeah," I reply, looking at myself in the mirror.

"Are you nervous?"

I pause. Am I? Why would I be nervous? I've done this before; it's not like it's my first time. "Why?" I ask.

"You're talking an awful lot for such a quiet person."

He's right. I'm never this chatty. God, I am nervous. It's only been a couple months. It's not like I'll have forgotten everything. Plus, he's only done it once. He's probably doesn't have superhigh expectations.

Of course, all my experience is with Chase. Brad is nothing like him.

"Are you nervous?" I ask.

"A little."

"Really?"

"Yeah. Things are going well. I don't want to ruin it."

I step out of the bathroom in my towel. "Are you naked yet?"

He throws back the blanket to show me his athletic shorts. Then he picks up a T-shirt lying on the bed and tosses it to me. "Maybe we should wait."

I grab the shirt out of the air, then hold it against my chest. "We may never have this perfect of an opportunity again."

"You forget we'll be in college with college dorm rooms in no time."

"You'll be in Durham, and I'll be who-knows-where."

"You'll come visit me."

I walk around the bed and sit down next to him. "If I'm lucky enough to get into college, I probably won't have a car."

"Then I'll visit you."

"You'll be playing football. Are you really going to have time for that?"

He shakes his head.

I stand and pad back to the bathroom, where I rinse my mouth and change into his extra-large T-shirt, which hangs to my knees. Then I crawl into bed next to him, wrapping my arms around his chest as he stares at the ceiling.

I suddenly feel bad for bringing us down tonight. This had been an awesome day until three minutes ago. I know we need to talk about next year, but not right now. Tonight, we should just enjoy the time we have alone.

"I'm sorry," I say, laying light kisses on his neck, determined to salvage what's left of the night. "Let's have fun. I'm in the mood for some serious making out."

"Checkers?"

I nod. "Naked checkers."

With that, he flips off the light, and we finally get to enjoy each other without the constant worry of someone finding us and kicking me out.

CHAPTER 26

WITH A GOOD STRETCH OF MY LEGS AND A YAWN, I OPEN MY eyes. Sunlight streams in from the window, basking the room in a warm orange glow and making me wonder how late it is.

"Good morning," Brad says from beside me. I turn my head. He's lying on his side, watching me.

"Good morning. How long have you been up?"

"About half an hour."

"Have you been sitting there, staring at me the whole time?"

"Would it be creepy or sweet if I said yes?"

"Creepy."

"Then, no. Definitely not."

I laugh and pull his arm around my waist. The last thing I remember before falling asleep was being curled up against him, completely surrounded by his warmth with his heart beating against my back. There was a sense of safety and calm I've never felt before. It was like I had finally found where I belong.

"What were you really doing?" I ask, snuggling into his chest.

He tilts his head toward the phone lying on the nightstand. "Reading about the game . . . and watching you."

I smile at his words. It doesn't seem nearly as creepy if he was also doing something else. "What'd they say about the game?"

"We made an incredible comeback and won against impossible odds because of the underappreciated but extraordinary talent of a certain player."

"A certain quarterback?"

He smiles.

"Feel free to gloat. You deserve it."

Tightening his arm around my waist, he pulls me even closer. "I'd prefer a replay of last night," he whispers, his mouth at my neck.

We didn't play chess last night, but what we did was a thousand times better than anything I ever did with Chase. "What time is it?"

"Nine. The bus isn't leaving until ten thirty. I'm supposed to have breakfast with the team at nine thirty, but I can skip it."

"I need to meet your parents at ten in the lobby."

His hands roam under his way-too-big shirt I'm wearing, lifting it up over my butt and making my skin prickle with goose bumps. "Do you need to get ready?" he asks, his lips moving closer and closer to my own.

"Yes," I reply, draping my leg over his hip. He hooks his fingers in the crook of my knee and draws me even closer.

"But I can probably wait a few minutes," I say. Tilting my head, I take in his face. His beautiful face with mussed-up hair, stubble on his chin, and those vibrant blue eyes. "You're really hot," I note, running a finger along his jaw.

"I—"

A knock at the door interrupts us.

"It's probably one of the guys. Let me get rid of him," Brad says, unwinding himself from me and standing.

As he goes to the door, I lift the blanket over my head.

I hear the lock click and then the creak of a hinge as Brad must open the door.

"Dad," he says in a high voice that's not his. My body immediately stiffens, and I hike the blanket even higher. What is he doing here?

"Hey, Brad. I went out and collected all the local papers this morning. Thought you might like a hard copy of the articles on the game."

"Oh, thanks. That's really nice."

"You coming down to breakfast?"

"I'm not hungry. I think I'll relax here until the bus leaves."

"You're not hungry? Are you sick?"

"No," Brad says with a laugh. "Still tired, I guess."

"Sorry. Did I wake you and Carlos? I ran into Michelle downstairs, and she said you were up."

"What?" Brad asks. "I haven't seen Michelle since last night."

"She was leaving as I was coming in. She said you were up and would love to have the papers."

I can't see Brad, but I imagine him rolling his eyes. "Thanks," he says, and I hear some rustling, "but I was asleep."

"Oh, sorry," Gil says, "I'll get out of your w—whose shoes are those?"

Oh my God. I left my pink sneakers by the bathroom door. No, no, no. I'm such an idiot!

"Daaad," Brad says, drawing out the word. "I *really* would like to be alone."

"Oh," Gil says. After a pause, he adds, "Right, right. Sure. Okay." There's another pause and then he says, "Yes, okay. I'll be going. Just . . . just remember what we've talked about. Do you need . . ."

"*Dad*," Brad says again. "I'm good. I'll see you at home."

Finally, the door slams shut.

"Oh my God!" I yell, throwing the blanket from me and bolting up in bed. "He knows!"

Brad shakes his head. "He knows there's a girl here, but he doesn't know it's you."

"Yes, he does. Oh my God." I cover my face with my hands. "It's over. This is all over. This is as bad as it gets. And it's all Michelle's fault. She must've figured it out!"

"I can think of many ways it could've been worse."

I shake my head and jump off the bed, collecting my clothes from last night and making a beeline for the bathroom. While I'm yanking on my jeans, Brad eyes me from the doorway, his arms gripping the top of the doorframe. I'm freaking out inside, and he's as relaxed as he was five minutes ago.

I turn around and put on my bra under his shirt. "He has to know those are my shoes."

"He's not very observant. Now if it were Mom, that'd be a different story."

"They're bright pink! He has to know."

"You give him too much credit."

I whip his shirt over my head and throw on my sweatshirt from yesterday. When I turn around, he's still standing there, smiling.

"What are you smiling about?"

"How you're being so modest today."

"What?" I squeeze past him, pick up my shoes, and then sit on the bed to lace them up.

"You realize that last night, I saw everything you just turned around to hide, right?"

I shoot him an annoyed look.

"What? It's cute," he says, strolling over to me and kissing the top of my head. "Don't freak out. We're fine."

I blow out a long breath. "I hope so. I need to get back to my room."

He nods, gives me a better kiss on the lips, and then I open the door a crack, make sure the coast is clear, and run for the stairwell. I don't run. Ever. So the fifty-foot sprint leaves me breathless. Once on the steps, I slow down and catch my breath. I can't believe what just happened and how Brad is being so nonchalant about the whole thing. So much for this being the perfect opportunity for us to be together.

When I get to the fourth floor, I open the door and turn right to reach my room. Unfortunately, Gil and Gigi are standing at the door not even five rooms from where I am. I spin around without thinking and crash my shoulder into the wall.

Stifling the scream that wants to come out, I try to sneak back to the stairwell.

"Hailey?" It's Gigi's voice.

I turn back around and wave. "Oh, hey. Good morning."

"What are you doing?"

Brittany sticks her head into the hallway. "Hey, how was the fitness room?" she asks.

"Oh," I mumble, looking at my feet and shuffling in their direction. I'm glad she's covering for me, but I seem physically unable to flat-out lie to their faces. "I didn't make it there. I don't know where it is."

"Do you want to grab breakfast with us?" Gigi asks.

I bite my lip. Which answer is less suspicious?

"Sure," I reply.

"Great," Gigi says, turning around and heading in the direction of the elevator.

"How was the party last night?" Gil asks.

"It was fun."

We continue chatting all the way down to the restaurant, Gil and Gigi as friendly as always, while I try to hide my inner freak-out.

When we're seated, I unfold my napkin and try to lay it on my lap with shaky fingers, but it falls to the floor instead.

Gil, who was in the process of sitting down, says, "I'll get that for you." He leans over. Rather than grabbing my napkin and standing up, he pauses, his eyes focused on the napkin partially draped over my foot.

My foot with the stupid pink shoe.

I curl my legs and try to hide them under the chair.

He sits down without my napkin and looks at me, his eyebrows drawn and his mouth in a hard line.

"Were you really looking for the fitness room this morning?" he asks.

I gulp and search for water. My mouth feels like a desert. There are three glasses of orange juice at the end of the table, so I stretch and grab the closest one. I take a long gulp and then a deep breath.

"Well?" he asks.

Gigi says, "What are you doing, Gil? You're scaring the poor girl."

He raises his hand. "This is important."

"Hailey?"

I shake my head.

"Where were you?"

I take another gulp of juice. Then another. I keep doing it until the glass is empty, then I reach for another one, but Gil stops my hand with his own. "Please answer me, Hailey."

"Gil—" Gigi tries again, but he raises his hand once more.

"I—I was in . . . in . . . Can I please have more juice?" I squeak.

He hands me a glass. I down it in three gulps and then stare at the tabletop as I whisper, "Brad's room."

Gil leans back in his chair.

"What happened? Did you have a fight with the girls this morning?" Gigi asks me.

Oh my God. She's giving me an easy out. I say yes and all this is brushed behind us.

I start to nod, but I can't do it. My head won't listen to me and it shakes instead.

"Did you need to get something from him this morning?" Gigi asks.

The shaking continues.

"Did you have a question for him?" she asks, genuine concern making the faint wrinkles around her eyes more noticeable.

The shaking continues.

"Did you stay with him the entire night?" Gil asks.

At least my head stops shaking.

"Why would you sleep in Brad's room?" Gigi asks, but immediately realizes the answer to her own question. "Oh," she says, her mouth holding the round shape way longer than needed.

"Come on," Gil says with a sigh as he pushes back his chair. "Let's see what Brad has to say."

A couple minutes later, we're back in his room. He's showered and changed when he answers the door.

"What's . . . up?" he asks after opening the door. His pause makes it clear he realizes something big went down.

"What's going on with you and Hailey?" Gil asks, pushing the door wider and leading us all inside. Gigi and Gil sit on Carlos's still-made bed, while Brad and I stand in the middle of the room.

"What do you mean?" Brad asks, glancing between them and me, probably trying to figure out how much they know.

I whisper, "I told them I stayed the night."

He continues studying my face, and I get the impression he's thinking about how he can manipulate the situation.

"Sit. Both of you," Gil says, motioning to the bed we snuggled in only a little while ago. Brad lowers himself across from Gigi, while I take a spot a couple of feet away.

Brad looks at me again, so I whisper, "They also know it's not because I got in a fight with my friends or needed anything from you."

He nods and looks at his parents. There's another long pause before he says, "I like her, okay. She likes me." He shrugs. "That's the way it is."

I glare at him. I realize I'm unable to lie to them, but I also wouldn't just volunteer *that* information. There's a happy middle ground he could've gone for. Instead, he's admitting everything we've hidden for months, as though it's no big deal. But it's a *huge* deal. There was a reason we kept it hidden.

Gigi pulls her hand to her mouth while Gil stares at Brad.

Then Brad grabs my hand and stares back. I try to jerk it away, but he squeezes it tighter. "We like each other. We're together."

"You most certainly are not," Gil says calmly.

"We most certainly are."

I try yanking my hand away again, and this time he lets it fall.

"Bradley, that's enough," Gil says, gently placing his hands on his knees and glaring at his son. His voice is quiet and calm, but his glare speaks volumes. If he looked at me like that, I'd be in tears, but Brad just tenses his jaw and stares back.

It's as if the two of them are in some silent tug-of-war, but it's a perfectly even match and the rope doesn't move at all. It just sits there still as can be while the two of them flex their muscles and try to get the upper hand.

I've never seen Brad act like this, and it's making me even more nervous. I thought Gil and Gigi finding out was as bad as it could get, but Brad might single-handedly make it even worse with the way he's acting.

"Honey," Gigi says as she looks at Brad, her face taut. "We didn't raise you to treat us like this."

"No, you raised me to do whatever you say," Brad says, finally breaking the stare so he can look at his mom. "It's not just this. It's college, too. Dad wants to control every aspect of my life. I'm tired of it."

Crap, crap, crap. All his built-up anger is coming out in one fell swoop, and I'm stuck in it. It's like a tornado has blown through town and I'm caught in the middle, spinning around wildly. If Brad doesn't shut up, we might leave insurmountable wreckage in our wake.

"Those are two entirely different issues," Gil says, his voice still calm. "One is based on DSS regulations and the other is what I think is best for you long term. Where do you want to go to school? EGU?"

Gil still doesn't know about the Duke offer. He thinks Brad's only options are EGU and Wake Forest.

"Maybe," he replies.

I know it's a lie, and I can tell he's just trying to start something with his dad. He's going to do anything he can to turn this into an all-out war.

"You can't be serious," Gils says.

"Why not?"

"Wake is ranked in the top thirty colleges in the country; EGU doesn't even make the top two thousand."

"I'm sure plenty of EGU graduates have stellar careers. They even have a medical school."

I want to run out of the room, but I can't stop staring at Brad. It's like when you see a car accident. You know you should look away, but you can't stop watching the carnage, which gets worse and worse the closer you get. In this case, it's getting worse and worse the more Brad talks.

But Gil doesn't even flinch, despite the anger that I'm sure is brewing under the surface. "You might as well take it easy next semester then. No reason to be valedictorian if you're just going to EGU. Hell, you don't even need to be in the top ten."

"That's what I was thinking. I could switch out of my AP classes to take something more fun. Art. Choir. Drama. Auto mechanics. That sounds like a full schedule for next semester."

"Almost," Gil says, nodding. Then, he holds his chin between his thumb and finger as if deep in thought before adding, "You need to include underwater basket weaving to really round out your experience."

Brad's clenched jaw twitches, and then the side of his mouth inches upward slightly, like he's trying hard not to smile. "Is that a thing?"

"It might be at EGU."

Brad's mouth twitches again and then he states, "I'm going to Duke." Any hint of a smile is now long gone.

"What?" Gigi whispers.

"I am. They made me an offer last night. And Hailey and I are dating, whether you like it or not."

I bury my face in my hands. "Actually," I whisper, dropping my hands, ready to try to salvage anything I can, "I'm going to disagree with Brad here. Sorry," I say, glancing at him. Looking back at Gigi, I continue, "I apologize for what I . . . we did, although I didn't technically break any of your rules. I still understand it was wrong, and I'm sorry. I promise I'll stay away from him. I can't lose this placement. I need you. All of you." My eyes sting, and I have to wipe at them to keep any tears from falling.

"That is a very mature approach," Gil says.

"What the hell?" Brad asks, turning his anger to me briefly before focusing on Gil again. "I'm eighteen; she's only a few months from eighteen. If we want to date, we should be able to date."

"DSS would disagree with you," Gil states.

"They don't need to know."

"They need to know if one of their adolescents is having a sexual relationship with another adolescent in the same foster home."

My face has never been hotter, and I have to stare at the carpet, unable to meet anyone's eyes as they talk about me like I'm not sitting right here.

"Okay, fine," Brad says. "But, we're not having sex."

I peek up to find Gil narrowing his eyes again and Gigi rubbing her face before saying, "You expect us to believe she stayed here all night and nothing happened?"

"Not sex. And she hasn't broken any of your rules," Brad points out. "We've never had sex—not at home, not here. She checked in with you when she got to the hotel, just like you asked. She didn't leave the hotel last night; she just changed rooms. And she didn't drink or use drugs."

"A sexual relationship is not just sex," Gil says.

"Then you and DSS should be more specific."

"Please," I whisper, pleading with Brad. "Don't make this worse than it already is."

"What exactly do you want?" Gil asks Brad, completely ignoring me. "You want us to bless a relationship between our son and his foster *sister*? You know this is supposed to be a safe place for her."

"It is a safe place."

"Until you break up, making her question everything we've done."

"That won't happen."

"You're right it won't, because you two will not have this type of relationship."

"Gil," Gigi says, resting her hand on his arm. "Let's take a moment and think about this. I talked to Sherry yesterday, and she went on and on about how well Hailey's doing. Maybe this is . . . isn't as bad as it seems."

"How long has this been going on?" Gil asks, alternating his gaze between me and Brad.

"A couple of months," Brad answers.

"Months?" Gils asks, his eyes growing wide. "You've been sneaking around for months? You didn't notice?" he asks, turning his focus to Gigi. "You notice everything."

She bites her lip and shrugs. "I—I, no. I thought they had developed a very close friendship."

"We have," Brad says.

Gigi gives us a strained smile and then says, "Let's all take a little time to calm down. We can talk about this more when we get home. And we might need to add Sherry to the discussion."

My heart drops. I know what will happen if Sherry's involved.

The only option for me to try to keep what I have is to give up Brad. I can live without fooling around. I can't live without the Campbells. They're essential to me like air, food, and water. If I lose them, life as I know it is over.

Gigi meets Gil's eyes. He offers her a barely noticeable nod, but the clenched fists in his lap and his tense jaw give away how uneasy this whole conversation has made him.

Brad blows out a breath, stares at me, and shakes his head. I see disappointment in his eyes. He knows the decision I've already made.

CHAPTER 27

THE THREE-HOUR RIDE BACK TO THE CAMPBELLS' HOUSE IS awful. Not because Gil and Gigi yell at me or anything. I just can't stop thinking about how Brad and I are over. And how hard it will be to go back to being simply friends.

I chew on my thumbnail and look out the window as peach farms and then golf courses start flying by. We're almost back.

Brad taps my foot with his, causing me to turn and meet his eyes. He was supposed to ride on the bus with the team, but he changed his mind after everything happened.

"Sorry," he mouths.

I give him the same response I've given him the last four times he's done this—a shrug. It's not like it's his fault.

We pull into the garage, and I head to the back of the SUV to get my bag while Gil unlocks the door. Slinging my backpack over my shoulder, I climb the steps inside.

"In the car!" Gil yells, charging back into the garage and practically knocking me over.

"What?"

"In the car. Now!"

He's not making any sense, but his urgency gets me moving. Brad and Gigi do the same and then he backs the car up, tires squealing, and peels out of the driveway.

"What's wrong?" Gigi asks, gripping the dashboard.

"Call 911. Someone broke into our home. It's trashed."

"What?" Gig and Brad ask at the same time. They live in Pinehurst. It's the safest city in North Carolina. Homes don't get robbed here. They just don't.

Unless . . . criminal ex-boyfriends of foster kids show up.

No, no, no. It can't be Chase. He wouldn't do this, would he? I mean, it's one thing to steal a TV, but to trash an entire house? He's never done anything so horrible before. I have to believe it wasn't him. It couldn't have been him.

Gil says, "I don't know if they're still in there, but we're going to a neighbor's until the police check it out."

"Trashed?" Gigi asks, her voice cracking. "The artwork?"

"I don't know. I didn't get that far."

"Please not the Meier," she cries, her hands trembling as she dials her phone. The Meier is a family heirloom. Brad said it's been passed down generation to generation within her family for more than one hundred years. If it's gone, she'll be devastated.

I swallow against the lump in my throat and stare out the window. It can't be Chase.

"You okay?" Brad whispers.

I nod but don't say anything as my eyes well up. If Chase did this, I'll never be able to forgive myself for bringing him to them. Two tears fall down my cheek and land on the windowsill.

"It's going to be okay," he says, patting my knee.

The next four hours are awful. The cops come to make sure it's safe. Then it's our turn to inspect the damage while they further investigate what happened. The detective walks through the house with Gil and Brad, writing down everything of value that's been stolen, including the Meier.

Gigi crumpled to the floor once she saw her gallery. Most of the paintings are either destroyed or gone.

"DeRubeis original, valued at forty-five hundred earlier this year," Gil says, taking charge.

I sit next to Gigi and chew on my nails. I haven't seen any broken windows, which gives me a sliver of hope Chase might not be involved. He's definitely not smart enough to get through their security system, so he'd have had to muscle his way in some other way.

The detective makes a note as Gil continues. "Warhol original," he says with a sigh.

"Value?" the detective asks.

"Five hundred two years ago."

"Five hundred dollars?"

Gil looks at him like he's crazy. "Five hundred thousand dollars."

The detective drops his pen. I slump against the wall and stifle a cry. *Please, please don't be Chase*, I silently beg.

"Fuck," Brad says, kicking a closet door.

"We have insurance on it," Gil says to no one in particular. "The most important piece is the Meier. If you can only get one piece back, please make sure it's that one."

The detective blows out a long breath, and then shakes his head before picking up his pen. "We'll do our best."

"Mr. Campbell," one of the policemen says, joining us upstairs.
"Yes."

"There's no sign of forced entry anywhere. Whoever did this knew how to get in."

I raise my head at his words. It was a professional. It couldn't be Chase.

"That's impossible," Gil says. "No one has the security codes but us."

"Can you call your security company? Get the records of when people entered and exited over the weekend?"

Gil agrees and then rushes downstairs to his office. The detective stands awkwardly in the hallway until Brad offers to take him to his room.

I continue gnawing on my nails.

After a few minutes, they exit, Brad's jaw clenched and the veins in his neck throbbing. Then they go into my room. I stand to join them but run into Brad as he's leaving. "Don't go in there," he says.

I push through anyway.

The dresser's overturned, the bed's been flipped upside down, and my clothes are strewn everywhere. The worst part, though, is the words *Fucking bitch* in red spray paint in at least twenty places, including the carpet and ceiling.

I close my eyes as the tears start to fall. It *was* Chase. Who else would call me that? I don't know how he did it, but he did. I hate him. No, hate's not strong enough. I hate my mom. Chase . . . Chase, I loathe with every fiber of my being, with every ounce of me I ever gave to him.

Brad wraps his arms around me, but it does nothing to soothe

the river of contempt coursing through me. How will I ever make it up to the Campbells? I sniff and wipe at my face. I won't be able to. There's no way. I'll never be able to fix what Chase has done.

My shoulders shake, and Brad squeezes me tighter.

The detective excuses himself, and Brad leads me back to the landing, where Gigi is. We sit down next to her, and Brad puts an arm around each of us as we sob.

Just then, Gil turns the corner and starts up the stairs. He sees us and stops. His jaw is tight and pulsating as he clenches his teeth. "They broke in at three a.m. this morning and then again about an hour before we got home."

"How?" Brad asks.

Gil's nostrils flare. "They used Hailey's security code."

"What?" I ask, my sobs ending as my head snaps up. "That's impossible. I've never told anyone my code. I swear!"

"The detective also found this note by the front door," he says, waving a piece of notebook paper enclosed in a plastic bag.

"What's it say?" Brad asks, standing.

Gil holds it in front of his face and reads the words. " 'Thanks, Hailey. I'll find you once things calm down, Chase.' "

I bolt up and sprint down the stairs. "No!" I yell. "I never gave the code to him. I'm not lying. I swear!"

I pull the paper from Gil's hands and study the words. It's not from Chase. The writing is way too nice. What in the world is going on?

"I'm calling DSS," Gil says, before turning around.

"No!" I shout. "There's got to be some other explanation. I never gave anyone my code."

He looks over his shoulder. "We don't have a choice." He stalks away, and I realize my entire life is about to crumble.

"I didn't give him my code," I whimper. I turn around and see Brad staring at me. "I didn't do it. I promise. You have to believe me."

"I—I," he whispers, falling back to the step and hanging his head. "I don't understand." He shakes his head.

My mouth trembles, and my eyes well up again. "You promised you'd never let them kick me out," I say, smearing tears over my cheek as I try to wipe them away. How many times did he tell me that?

He meets my eyes, and I see something I've never seen in him before. Defeat. He's given up on me. The one person I trusted more than anyone has given up on me.

Suddenly, all the anger I've harbored against Chase and my mom seems minor.

"I believed you," I say with shaking shoulders. "I believed you, Brad! You're no better than anyone else!" I yell as I shove him in the chest and then escape outside into the cold, dark night.

I sit on the steps, wrapping my arms around myself as I wait for the white sedan with the yellow license plate.

This—cold, dark, and alone—was always my future. I let them convince me I could have more, be more, but it was never going to happen. This is it.

This is my life.

CHAPTER 28

I HUG BRITTANY TIGHTER. AFTER THE LAST WEEK, I NEEDED TO see her. Out of everyone I know, she's the most likely to understand what I'm going through.

We're sitting on the sofa in the commons area of my group home. I don't know if Sherry couldn't find another foster family for me or thought this would be better, but I'm now living with twenty other sixteen- and seventeen-year-olds who have no family and are just waiting until we're adults and on our own. It's not horrible. Between here and my new school, we get three meals a day, and I have a warm bed to sleep in, but it's not like being with a family.

Brittany hugs me again, then holds me at arm's length. "What's going on?"

"I don't know," I say. "I mean, it must have been Chase. It had to be. I . . . I just want to kill him. You should have seen their house. It was . . ." I take a deep breath and fight back the tears that threaten to fall. I'm surprised my cheeks aren't raw from all the crying I've been doing lately.

"It's not your fault," Brittany says, putting her arm around me.

"It wasn't. It really wasn't. My mom wanted me to help Chase. To get him inside. But I refused. I never gave them the security code. I swear. I would never do anything to hurt the Campbells."

"I believe you."

"And that note wasn't from him. The handwriting was way too nice. Plus, he calls me Hales, not Hailey."

Brittany's quiet for a moment. "Did you give the security code to anyone? Maybe he was working with someone else."

"No. I wouldn't do that. I would never do that."

"Then how'd they get it?"

"I don't know."

"Did you have it written down anywhere?"

"No."

She falls against the back of the sofa and sighs. "This doesn't make any sense."

"I know."

"Who gave you the code?"

"Gigi."

"Any chance she had it written down somewhere?"

"I don't know."

"Have you talked to Brad?"

"No, I can't. He looked so . . . disappointed." He keeps e-mailing me, saying he wants to talk, that he blames Chase, not me, but I don't respond. I don't know what to say. Unless Chase and all their stuff are found, he'll always think I played a role, even if I didn't. That's what hurts the most. He honestly thinks I'd do something like this to them.

"Bummer," Brittany says.

I fall back next to her. "I know this is what my life should be like," I say, motioning to the cinder-block walls around me and the tiny Christmas tree. "It's just I got a taste of something better and . . . it was addictive. Loving parents. Loving . . . whatever Brad was to me. Once you have it, it's hard to lose, you know?"

"Yeah, I know."

"I almost wish I had never met them. If I had come straight here, I wouldn't know any better. And they'd still have all their stuff."

"Don't say that."

"It's true."

"Have you talked to your mom or Chase?"

"I tried calling them, but both numbers have been disconnected."

Brittany hugs me again. "This sucks."

I nod and then sigh. It really does.

* * * *

Two weeks later, I'm sitting on my bed, tapping a pencil on my geometry book as I stare out the window at the cold, gray afternoon that looks just like I feel. Without Brad's help, I'm really struggling with geometry at my new school. It doesn't help that they're ahead of where I was at Pinecrest, so I've had to learn a month's worth of stuff in only a couple of weeks. And to really top things off, we have a test tomorrow. It's our last day before Christmas vacation, and the teacher is giving us a test. Who does that?

I sigh and then decide to take a break.

"Want a snack?" I ask one of my roommates, who's reading in the bunk above me.

She replies, "I'm good. Thanks, though."

I slide off my bed and head for the kitchen, where I find an apple. I start to wander back to my room when the door to the computer room catches my eye.

I shouldn't go in there.

I walk past it but slow down. It's like my feet have a mind of their own. I pause, biting my lip before glancing at the clock on the wall. It's been a whole thirty minutes since I last checked. Not that long. Still . . . maybe our geometry teacher decided to cancel the test and I can stop killing myself trying to cram all the information into my brain between now and tomorrow. Yeah. That's the only reason I want to check my e-mail.

If I keep telling myself that, maybe I'll believe it.

I turn and rush into the tiny room, happy to find one of the three computers empty. The two other guys in the room barely glance at me as I slide into the chair. I sign in to my e-mail and bite my nail as I wait for my messages to load.

I have like fifty messages from Brad, ten in the last day. They're all kind of the same—apologizing for the way he acted the night of the robbery and asking me to call him. Never in any of them does he say he believes it wasn't me.

Just then, a new message appears. From Brad.

My fingers snap to the mouse to open it.

Are you even getting these? Where are you? I'm worried, okay? Sherry says you're fine, but it'd be nice to have a little confirmation. Would it kill you to send a few words letting me know you're not lying dead in a ditch somewhere?

I automatically hit reply and type I'm fine. I can't persuade myself to hit the send button, though. I tap my finger on the mouse and stare at the two words. I haven't said anything to him since Gil kicked me out. But despite feeling like a stray dog they kicked to the curb, I'm still holding on to the messages. I check my stupid e-mail every chance I get, and my heart skips a beat the moment I see a new message from Brad or Gigi. Gil doesn't write, not that I'm surprised.

What is wrong with me? I walked away from my mom and Chase without ever looking back, but I hold on to these messages like they're a big ol' glass of sweet tea in the Sahara. It's ridiculous. I should just block both of them. They kicked me out of their home; I should kick them out of my in-box and my life.

I move the mouse until the cursor is over the block-sender button. I lightly tap the button, but, again, can't push it all the way down.

"Are any of you almost done?" Tom, another foster kid, asks, sticking his head into the computer room. "I've got to finish something for school."

"Yeah, I'm logging off right now," I reply quickly before clicking send. I guess Brad deserves to at least know I'm okay.

* * * *

Four days later, Christmas music fills the hall outside my room.

"What time is it?" Christina, one of my roommates, groans. "Like five a.m.?"

I glance at the clock. "Nine," I say, pulling my blanket up to my chin and rolling to face the wall. One of the nice things about the three girls I share this room with is we're all late risers. The same can't be said for the girls across the hall. They remind me of the

Campbells—up at the crack of dawn and getting more done before I wake up than I get done the entire day.

Christina jumps out of bed, throws open the door, and yells, "Turn that shit down! Some of us are still sleeping!"

I hear parts of a snide comment but can't make out the whole thing. The music does quiet, though, and my roommate crawls back into bed.

I spend the next twenty minutes dreading having to get up, but I'm on dish duty this morning, which means I need to be in the kitchen by nine thirty. Plus my stomach is growling, so I should get there a little early in order to snag some breakfast.

I tiptoe out of the room and then join a bunch of others in the kitchen for bacon and eggs. Afterward, two guys and I clean all the dishes and then head out to the commons area, where more and more people are starting to gather. I'm surprised to see our small tree with gifts underneath.

"Where'd all that come from?" I ask the guy next to me.

"Generous strangers. Ever seen those trees at the mall with little tags filled with names?"

"Yeah," I respond.

"Well, this is the result," he says, spreading his hands to where it looks like Santa just dumped his entire sleigh.

Eventually, everyone gathers in the room and the director, Kathryn, starts to hand out presents. I end up with five boxes with the same wrapping paper and a card in front of me, and I wonder who my very generous stranger was.

I start with the biggest box and am stunned when I push the tissue paper aside and find it stuffed with a bunch of things—pajamas, three T-shirts, and a new backpack, which I desperately need. It's kind of a weird feeling to get such a nice gift from someone you don't even know. It almost feels like acing a test by cheating. You're happy but feel guilty at the same time.

"Oooh, nice," says Sara, the girl sitting next to me. "Look what I got!" She holds up what looks like a toolbox, but it's filled with every kind of makeup imaginable. It's way more than I'd ever want or need, but she won't leave her room without looking flawless, so it's the perfect gift for her.

I move on to another box, slipping my finger under the tape, when the tag catches my eye. This one isn't from a stranger. It's from Gil and Gigi. How in the world did they get this here? Sherry told me they don't know where I am. Plus, why would they get me something after kicking me out?

"Um, Kathryn?" I ask, holding up the box. "Where'd this come from?"

She smiles. "One of the social workers brought some things by yesterday."

Oh. I guess that makes sense. I continue opening the box, but more slowly now. I'm not sure how I feel about them getting me something after everything that happened. It's nice of them, of course, but I'm trying to put distance between us, not accept gifts from them.

Inside is a really cute outfit—dark jeans and a bright pink shirt with sparkles.

"That's pretty," Sara says, touching the fabric. "I might need to borrow that sometime," she adds, rocking her shoulder into me.

I smile at her and try to ignore the emotions bubbling up inside of me. It's not a good feeling. If the last gift made me feel like I aced a test by cheating, this one makes me feel like I aced an entire class by cheating. On the surface, it seems wonderful, but underneath, I'll always know the truth about them. And I'll always think about what they did when I wear the outfit.

The next box is from the Campbells, too. A hundred-dollar gift card. Now I feel like I got into an Ivy League college by cheating. I can't spend their money now. There's no way.

I slip the gift card into the makeup toolbox and hope Sara will find a good use for it.

With a sigh, I check the tags of the final two boxes. The sigh turns into a groan when I read the name. Brad.

He got me the blue fleece I admired during one of our first trips to the mall and a T-shirt with the words DUKE FOOTBALL. He also attached a note:

> *I decided on Duke. Dad freaked, but I stood my ground.*
> *He's coming around. Hopefully I can give you a tour of*
> *the campus sometime. Please call or write. Miss you—*
> *Brad*

I drop the note back into the box and stare at the T-shirt. I so did not expect him to go to Duke after what happened with me. I figured he learned his lesson and would let his dad dictate everything from college to career to marriage. Even kids. If Gil says one baby is the perfect number, then it must be the perfect number.

I smile, imagining Brad standing up to him again, like he did in the hotel, except this time, he seems to have won. Did Gil scream or just give Brad that silent look that says a million things all at once? Did Gigi say anything? How did Brad spin it?

Crap.

What am I doing?

I don't care how the conversation went. They kicked me out. They didn't want me as part of their lives anymore, so I shouldn't care what happened when he told his parents.

I focus back on the pile of things around me. All that's left is the card, and I can't imagine who it's from. I tear it open and quickly read the cover before checking inside. As soon as I do, a five-dollar Dollar Tree gift card falls out and then I see the name of the sender. No freaking way.

> *Heard you got kicked out of your latest place. Guess we're not so different after all. Hope the group home isn't as horrible as I've heard. Keep up your grades. Maybe you really can graduate. Mom*

I stare at the card, my jaw practically touching the ground. I'm shocked she even thought of me, let alone spent money on me.

I reread the note and feel a lump in my throat, especially with the last sentence. She never paid much attention to my life, but every now and again she would take interest in school and ask me if I was failing. I always thought she was putting me down, like she expected me to fail, but maybe, in her own weird, twisted way, that was her being proud?

I drop the card and lean back on my elbows as I watch everyone else show off their presents. A year ago, I never would've been able to predict this was what my Christmas would look like. Even a month ago, I wouldn't have been able to predict it, although my vision then would've been much more *Leave It to Beaver*, Campbell style. This isn't . . . bad. It's better than what it would've been like with my mom, but it's not like it would've been with the Campbells, even with Kathryn passing out hot chocolate and Christmas cookies.

The good news is I still have a best friend, and she and her foster mom are picking me up in about thirty minutes so I can spend the rest of the day with them. I realize Christmas is supposed to be a time for family, but maybe that was never meant to be my life.

Maybe I'm not meant to ever have a family.

CHAPTER 29

"THANKS FOR THE RIDE," I SAY TO ADAM, WHO'S STARING AT the prison in front of us. I'm sure he's never been here before. Neither have I until today. I don't even want to be here now, but Chase is inside and I need to talk to him.

It took over a month, but the cops finally found him in Georgia with his cousin Dwight. A few pieces of artwork were found in Dwight's garage, but not the really valuable ones or Gigi's Meier. I feel like I have to at least try to find out what Chase did with those. I owe that to the Campbells after bringing him into their lives, even if I didn't help him get inside their front door.

"Do you want me to go with you?" Brittany asks from in front of me.

I shake my head. He'll be even less likely to tell me anything if he has an audience.

"I'll be quick," I say, reaching for the door handle.

"Be careful, okay?" Adam says, glancing over his shoulder at me.

I nod and then push the door wider, but it slams into something.

Looking through the window, I see a man standing there with his back to me.

"I'm so sorry," I say, climbing out.

The man stills, and I get a sinking feeling in my stomach when I notice the back of his head and his broad shoulders. His very familiar broad shoulders.

"Hailey," he says, turning around to face me.

"Brad." I gulp. "W-what are you doing here?" I ask, although I'm pretty sure I know the answer.

"Hoping to see you."

Yep, Adam the backstabber. I glare through the window, but he and Brittany are talking and not paying a bit of attention to us.

"Why didn't you call?" he asks. "Or send more e-mails? 'I'm fine' wasn't exactly enough to ease my mind, you know."

My jaw clenches at his words. His family kicked me out, yet I'm supposed to feel bad about not calling?

"I don't blame you," he says, reaching for my hands.

I let them lie limply in his. "But you think I helped him," I say pointedly. That's what it comes down to—either Brad trusts me or he doesn't.

"I—I don't know." He sighs. "Did he threaten you? Or us?"

I shake my head as every muscle in my body tenses. He doesn't trust me. After everything we've been through, he still doesn't trust me.

"I just want to understand."

"There's nothing to understand. I didn't help him," I say, ripping my hands from his.

"Hailey, I don't blame you." He tries reaching for me again. I take a step back.

"But you think I did it," I say, narrowing my eyes at him. "I didn't help him!" I yell at the top of my lungs. I clench my fists at my sides as my heart pounds in my ears. "I thought you were better than them, but you're not. You're worse. You made me fall for you and then act like this." I jam my finger into his chest. "I would never help Chase. Ever."

My shoulders shake with anger. His face is pale; his mouth hangs open. The eyes I used to stare into forever are wide and only make my blood run hotter now. Without saying another word, I turn toward the prison so I don't have to see the one person in the world who has hurt me the most.

* * * *

"Babe," Chase says thirty minutes after I finally get cleared to see him. He presses his palm against the glass like he wants to connect with me. As if I'd want anything to do with him.

"How'd you get in their house?" I ask.

"I've got my ways," he says, sitting back and struggling with the phone between his shoulder and ear. He reaches up with his cuffed hands and adjusts it.

"Who helped you?"

"Nobody."

"Someone gave you my security code. Who was it?"

When I mention the word *code*, there's a slight change in his cocky attitude. His lips form a thin line, he blinks twice, and he stares at me like a deer caught in headlights. Then, as quickly as it happened, it disappears.

"How you like all your new friends?" he asks, staring at his dirty fingers.

"What?"

He starts digging the dirt out from under his nails. "You thought you could just waltz into their fancy life like you belong? You ain't never gonna belong in that life. They ain't your real friends. They ain't gonna let you pretend to be one of them."

My heart momentarily stops in my chest. "Did one of them help you?" I ask slowly.

He smiles and slouches back in his chair again.

"Who? Which one?" I ask, leaning forward. "Michelle?" Oh my God. The nice handwriting. It has to be hers!

He shrugs.

"The blond?"

He shrugs again.

It's her. It has to be her. Oh my freaking God. Michelle framed me? She's even crazier than I thought. How has she fooled all her friends for so long? It has to be because she's beautiful and rich and has perfect grades. Nobody would even think twice about trusting her. Me, on the other hand . . .

My heart pounds in my chest as I think about what Michelle did, but then starts to slow as I realize what this means. I can prove to the Campbells it wasn't me. I don't plan on ever seeing them again, but at least my reputation can be salvaged. At least they'll know what a big mistake they made.

"Thank you," I whisper to Chase. This is the most helpful he's been in a very long time.

I'm about to lower the phone when I realize I haven't even talked to him about the main reason I came here. "Where are the paintings?" I ask.

"What paintings?"

"All of them, but especially the big blurry one of a garden."

"I don't know what you're talking 'bout," he says

"They need that one back. It's not worth anything," I say, holding his eyes. "You'll get nothing for it, but it has sentimental value to them. Please give it back to them."

"I already told you—I don't know nothing 'bout no paintings."

I roll my eyes and shake my head. The Campbells need to get the Meier back.

"If you tell me, I'll try to help you," I say, my stomach churning at the thought of making a deal with the devil.

"I don't need your help."

"Really? Michelle's going to give you up the minute they arrest her. She wouldn't even last a minute in juvie."

His hands still, and he stares at me, providing further proof it was Michelle.

"If they get everything back, I'll try to convince the Campbells not to press charges." Maybe. Or maybe not. It's not like I'm actually talking to them anymore.

"Everything?"

"Yes."

He scratches his cheek and then says, "I can't get everything back."

"How much can you get?"

He stares at a spot on the wall behind my head while answering, "I'm not sure. I need to make a call."

"I'd do it quickly if I were you."

He nods, and then I hang up the phone and leave without another word.

CHAPTER 30

"WELL?" BRITTANY ASKS WHEN I SLIDE INTO THE CAR.

"Do you mind stopping at the police station on the way back to the group home?" I ask Adam.

"Noooo," he says, drawing the word out. "Care to tell us why?"

"No offense," I say, buckling my seat belt, "but your friend Michelle has serious issues."

"Michelle?" Adam and Brittany say at the same time.

"What's going on?" Brittany continues, turning completely around in her seat to face me.

I explain what I found out, and they both stare at me like I'm delusional or something.

"So, police station?" I ask, motioning to Adam to start up the car.

He holds up his hands. "Before you do anything, let's think through this. Chase has a lot to gain by pinning everything on someone else."

"You think he lied to me?"

"I'm not saying that, but how would Michelle have your code? Did you give it to her?"

I shake my head.

"Plus, there's still the issue of getting inside. Someone used a key."

"I'm sure he used her key."

"Whose key?" Adam asks.

"Michelle's key."

"Michelle doesn't have a key."

"Sure, she does."

"No, she doesn't."

"Yes, she does," I insist. "I lost mine a while back, and she let me inside with hers."

Adam shakes his head. "Brad would never give her a key. I don't even have a key. Give me a sec," he says, pulling his phone out of his pocket. He types something, then sets it on the dashboard before focusing back on me.

"What happened after she let you in?" Brittany asks.

"She . . ." And suddenly it all makes sense. "She stood there and watched me enter my code."

"No way," Brittany says. Then, as if a lightbulb just went off in her head, she yells, "The mall!"

Adam and I stare at her.

"When we were at the mall with her," Brittany continues, "I came out of the dressing room and saw her messing with your coat. She said it fell and stuff came out of your pocket. She was putting it all back."

"My key . . ." That was the day I noticed my key was missing.

"Yeah."

"That would explain it," Adam says, glancing at his phone. "Because Brad said his family never gave her a key."

"So, police station?" I ask again. It's not like I doubted Michelle was guilty, but it's nice to understand how she did it.

Adam still hesitates. "Are you sure you want to get the police involved? Maybe we should tell the Campbells first."

I shake my head. "I'm not talking to them."

He taps the steering wheel with his fingertips. "You really want to do this to her?"

After what she's done to me? Absolutely. I nod, so he starts up the car without another word.

Five minutes later, we're in a small, gray room at the Carthage police station. There's nothing in the room but a table, three chairs, and a wall-length mirror. It's cold and intimidating, probably exactly what they were going for.

"What happened between you and Brad today?" Brittany asks, as we wait for someone to join us.

"He didn't believe me, and I stormed off," I reply, staring at the chipped tabletop.

"Don't you want to talk to him about Michelle?"

I shake my head. He needed to trust me even without knowing what really happened. It's too late now.

Just then, the door opens and a tall man with gray hair, a gray beard, khaki pants, and a black button-down shirt enters. He smiles and sits across from me.

"You have information about a crime?"

"Yes." I nod, my throat going dry. I've never been in a police station or talked to a cop before. Even though he's acting friendly, it's a little unsettling, which is ridiculous, since I didn't do anything wrong.

"Which crime?"

"The burglary of the Campbells' house in Pinehurst."

He takes a notepad and a pen out of his pocket, then lays them on the table. "What do you know?"

"I think Michelle Adler is responsible."

"I see," the guy says, writing in his notepad. When he's done, he leans forward on his elbows. He tents his fingers and taps them back and forth a few times before continuing. "Why do you think that?"

"Chase Miller, who was already arrested, indicated she might have helped. Plus, I used to live there, and I think she stole my key and had access to my security code."

"Anything else?"

I shake my head.

"Okay. I'll relay this information to the proper authorities. Can I get your name and number in case I have any questions?"

"My name is Hailey Brown, but I don't have a phone anymore." I left it at the Campbells' when they kicked me out, and I don't know the number for the group home.

"Address?"

"I'm not sure. I'm in a group home in Sanford. I don't know what the address is."

He eyes me suspiciously, and I get a sinking feeling in my gut. He's going to think I was involved, too. Everyone thinks I'm involved.

"How can I reach you?" he asks.

"I . . . I guess you can call DSS. My social worker is Sherry Billows. She'll know where I am."

He nods and then leads us out of the room and the station. As we're walking to Adam's car, I whisper, "He thinks I helped them. Why does everyone think I'd do something like this?"

Brittany lowers her arm on my shoulders and squeezes. "Because you're a foster kid."

* * * *

As soon as I'm back at the group home, I rush to the computer room.

After fighting with Brad at the prison, I know exactly what I need to do. I open my e-mail and barely glance at the ten new messages from Brad before checking the box to select every last one in my in-box and deleting them all. Then I go to settings and block both his and Gigi's e-mail addresses.

That's it. It's done.

I'm officially moving on from the Campbells. They'll realize I wasn't involved when Michelle is arrested. And if Chase tells me where any of the artwork is, I'll just relay that to the cops, too.

Rather than feeling like a weight's been lifted from my shoulders, it's like I've got a fifty-pound backpack on. I want to spring up and skip back to my room, happy that I'm moving forward like I did with Chase and my mom, but I'm rooted to this spot. Even if I wanted to, my legs can't lift the extra weight.

I end up sitting there for more than an hour, kind of searching celebrity gossip websites and kind of trying not to think of the Campbells and what I just did. It's so . . . permanent. Even though

I wasn't talking to them before, it was reassuring to see a new message every time I logged in. I felt . . . loved.

Crap.

How could Brad make me feel loved after *everything* he's done the last few weeks? Did I just make the biggest mistake of my life?

* * * *

"There you are," Sherry says, stepping into my room a few days later. "Ready for panel night?"

I make a face. I so don't want to do this, but Brittany pleaded with me to go since her foster mom is making her go.

"Come on," she says, tugging on my hand and pulling me up from my spot. "It's not so bad. Plus, you get pizza and brownies."

Twenty minutes later, we pull into the parking lot of DSS, and then Sherry leads me though the back doors. The room is already crawling with people, most of whom I don't recognize. I see Brittany in the corner talking to another foster kid, so I head over there.

"You made it!" Brittany says, hugging me. "I was worried you were going to flake on me."

"I wanted to, but Sherry wouldn't let me. So, any tips for getting through this?" I ask, motioning to the room quickly filling with soon-to-be foster parents. This is their final class before they're eligible for their licenses.

"Yep. Tip number one: Never let them inside your head. After all the training they've gone through, they already feel sorry for us. Don't give them any more reasons to . . ."

"Pity us?" I offer.

"Yes!" both Brittany and the other foster kid say at the same time.

I nod. I totally get that. "What's tip number two?"

"There is no tip number two."

"That's it? Just one tip?"

She smiles. "That's all you need to know."

While we're grabbing pizza and soda, I glance at the door and my heart sinks to my stomach, immediately eliminating my hunger. Gil and Gigi walk through, all smiles as they shake hands with other parents. At least Brad's not with them.

I take a long sip of Coke and then follow Brittany to a table at the front of the room. I pick at my crust, still not interested in eating.

And then Brad strolls through the door.

Crap, crap, crap.

His eyes survey the room until they land on me. He starts to walk in my direction, so I push my chair back and stand, ready to race out of the room.

"Thanks, everyone, for joining us tonight," Joelle, Brittany's social worker, says. I stop and sit back down as Brad takes a chair next to Brittany. After everyone is seated, she continues, "On our panel tonight we have two foster families and three teens in foster care. We'd like this to be an informal session, so please feel free to ask questions of either the social workers or our panel. This is your chance to get real-world answers to your burning questions."

She then introduces us and opens the floor to the foster parents-in-training.

"What do the children in your care call you or what do you call your foster parents?" a woman in the front row asks.

"Mom," Brittany answers. "I've been with her for almost three years, so she seems like Mom to me."

I glance down the table at Ms. Gonzalez. She smiles at Brittany and adds, "We decide together. I've been called Mom, Grandma, Aunty, Betty. It really depends on the situation."

"How do your foster kids and biological kids get along?" a man in the back asks.

Brittany turns to me and smirks. I kick her under the table.

"Brad and Hailey, would you like to take this one?" Joelle asks. Sherry nudges Joelle with her elbow and shakes her head, but it's too late. Everyone is looking between the two of us, separated only by Brittany.

Brad clears his throat. "Um . . . well . . . ," he says, unusually flustered. "It was a little weird initially, although part of that could've been because I've always been an only child. We quickly got into a routine and became friends. Good friends. Great friends, actually." He leans back in his chair and looks at me. "More than friends, really. Do you have anything to add, Hailey?"

"Nope," I reply. *Don't let them inside your head.*

"What do you do for punishment?" someone in the middle asks.

Gil raises his hand, indicating he'd like to answer. "I think that really depends on the age of your placement. Obviously, what works for toddlers won't work with teenagers. Our experience is with a teen, and we treated her like we do our biological son. She lost her allowance for a few days when she didn't follow one of our rules."

"But," Gigi says, "we also made a very big mistake. We had some bad things happen and reacted emotionally in the moment by terminating the placement. It was the wrong thing to do, and we've regretted it for weeks. I—I worry we've irreparably damaged our relationship. And as much as these kids need you, I think you'll find that you need them, too. I—I . . ." She takes a deep breath before finishing, "I wish we could have a do-over."

Brittany finds my hand under the table and squeezes. I feel about a million pairs of eyes on me, so I focus on a piece of fuzz on my shirt.

Don't let them inside your head.

My stupid eyes betray me, and a couple tears drip down my cheeks.

"This is for the teens," someone asks. "What's the worst part of being in foster care?"

"Constantly moving around," the other foster kid says. "I've been in five homes and three different schools over the last year."

"Aging out," Brittany says. "Other kids have parents around for most of their lives. We only get them until we're eighteen, and then we're all on our own."

Everyone looks at me, waiting to hear my answer. I still feel wetness on my cheeks, so I wipe it away while I think about my response. I know what the worst part is, but do I want to share that? "I . . . I guess it'd be feeling something for your foster family. Then it hurts even more when they bail on you. Because everyone bails on us sooner or later."

A few women in the audience draw their hands to their mouths, and I realize I've said too much. I let them inside my head.

"Maybe you need to give them a second chance," Gil says from down the table. "Foster parents aren't perfect. Sometimes we need second chances as much as the children do."

"And maybe you shouldn't ignore all the attempts we make to

apologize," Brad adds. "We fucked up, we know we fucked up, but you won't even give us the chance to tell you that."

Jaws drop open at Brad's words, but my lips reluctantly lift a little. He did mess up. And so did his parents.

"Okay," Joelle says with a clap of her hands. "Let's take a quick break. We've made some improvements to our children's play-room. I'll give you a tour."

She ushers everyone out except me, Sherry, and the Campbells.

"All righty," Sherry says, looking between the four of us, "it's time for y'all to talk. Gil?"

He meets my eyes and says, "We're really sorry for the way we behaved, Hailey. It was a terrible situation. We were incredibly stressed and jumped to conclusions. We never would have treated Brad that way, and we shouldn't have treated you any differently."

"We should've believed you," Brad says, angling his body toward me. "If you said you didn't help Chase, then you didn't help Chase. I should've believed you. That's the bottom line. You never gave me a reason not to, yet the moment you needed me the most, I let you down. I hate myself for what I did."

"Easy for you to say now that you know it wasn't me," I say, tracing the edge of the table with my thumb.

Confusion is written across all their faces. "What do you mean?" Gigi asks.

"Now that you know Michelle let Chase in."

"What?" they all ask at once.

"She stole my key and watched me enter the code so she could take it to him. I told the cops. Hasn't she been arrested yet?"

"Um, no," Brad says. "You're serious?"

"Yeah. Chase basically said it was her. And everything else lined up perfectly. Adam and Brittany know—they didn't tell you?"

"No. Adam mentioned something might come out soon but never told me that important piece of information."

Just then, Ms. Gonzalez, Brittany's foster mom, comes through the door. "Sorry to interrupt, but can I talk to Hailey for a moment?"

I nod and stand, happy to get away from the Campbells. When I reach her, she says, "Brittany just told me everything that happened. I'm sorry. I had no idea that was why you're in the group home. If you'd like, you're more than welcome to stay with us. I'm licensed for two placements and Jonas moved in with family last week, so I have the space. We'd love for you to join us."

"Really?" I ask, stunned.

"Wait," Brad says, standing. "Mom, Dad, do something."

"Well," Gil says slowly, "we were hoping you'd reconsider coming back to stay with us."

My eyes shift between Ms. Gonzalez, the Campbells, and Sherry. They're all waiting. "Um . . . I'm not sure."

Brittany's head bobs up and down behind Ms. Gonzalez as she jumps to see what's going on. When she catches my eye, she points at herself and mouths, "Pick us!"

"Well?" Sherry asks.

"Well," I start. After a long swallow, I continue, "I appreciate the apology, but I don't think I'm ready to live with the Campbells again. What happened really hurt me, and I think it might take me a while to get over it."

Brad's face falls, Gil nods, and Gigi gives me a sad smile.

"So I guess I'd like to be placed with Ms. Gonzalez."

"Yes!" Brittany yells from the hallway. "Sorry, Brad!" she adds, peeking around Ms. Gonzalez's shoulder.

Sherry nods. "Okay, I'll get all the paperwork straightened out."

We all take our seats again as the rest of the people return, although Brad ends up next to me this time.

"Is this it, then?" Brad whispers, sliding his foot up against mine. I glance down at the contact. It's like all the times we tried to pretend nothing was going on between us. What I didn't expect is the little tingle that runs up my leg, just like it always used to.

I bite my lip because I don't know what to think. My body obviously still likes him, but that's not enough. Do I forgive him? Do I believe he'd never let me down again? Unfortunately, I don't know the answer to those questions. "I'm not sure," I say.

"At least that's not a no," he replies, squeezing my knee. "I'm not giving up on us. I'll keep fighting until you tell me to get lost."

* * * *

And fighting is exactly what he does. Since I'm staying with Brittany, I'm back at the same school as Brad. While he was always nice to me at school, he's been really going out of his way for six weeks now. He sits with me at lunch and brings little bags of sour-cream-and-chive potato chips, my favorite, at least twice a week. He's in my creative-writing classroom the period before me and leaves special surprises taped to the underside of the desk, like a box of Sno-Caps or a photo of the two of us or some memento of our time together that I can't believe he still has, like our tickets to homecoming or the receipt from the Mexican restaurant where we admitted we liked each other.

All this week, I've been finding notes in my locker between every single class. They all contain something he likes about me. My strength. My resilience. My compassion. My smile. That my second toe is longer than my first. I have no idea why he likes that or why he even noticed it in the first place, although I suspect it's because he's running out of things to write after four and a half days of notes.

It's all very sweet and very Brad. If I didn't have the whole robbery thing still weighing on me, I'd be a melted pile of mush. But I do, and that doubt still sits there in the back of my mind, sneaking in and slapping my wrist whenever I have the urge to hold his hand or run my fingers through his hair.

Smiling, I fold the current note about how he likes my strange fascination with goats and stuff it into my pocket. Brad's not the only one going out of his way to be nice. Gigi and I have dinner at least once a week. It was awkward the first couple of times, but we're getting back to our old selves. Things are still a little tense with Gil, but he's trying, too. We've met at a coffee shop twice but struggled to find things to talk about each time.

I close my locker and start to head for the cafeteria when Brittany rushes toward me. "Hey!" she says, out of breath. "Did you get any valentines?"

I scrunch up my face. It's the first Valentine's Day in years when I don't have a boyfriend. Not that Chase ever did anything even remotely romantic, but it still felt nice to have him around on the special day. "No. You?"

She sticks out her tongue and shakes her head. "It's a stupid, sappy holiday anyway."

"You did not come all the way over here just to ask me about valentines, did you?" Her last class is on the other side of the school, so we usually just meet in the cafeteria for lunch.

"No. Did you confirm that your electronic transcript was sent with your college applications?" she asks.

I shake my head. "I just assumed they were. Why?"

"Adam told me a horror story about the school messing up and suggested I check with the office. Want to come with me?"

"Okay, sure."

Fifteen minutes later, and after the office assistant gave us both very dirty looks for questioning their systems, we're finally on our way to lunch. At least the transcripts were sent. I still don't know if I'll get in, but I'd hate to be rejected over a technical error. If they don't want me for me, fine. I can accept that as long as everything was submitted and I was actually considered.

"I really hope you end up at NC Central," she says as we turn the corner.

"Me, too," I reply, scanning the people in the hallway. Usually, this late into lunch, the corridor would be clear, but there are big guys lining both sides. And they're all looking at us.

"Um, do you notice anything strange?" I ask as I slow down.

"Nope," she says, continuing to lead me forward.

When we reach the first guy, he pulls his hand out from behind his back and shows me a gold rose. "For a new beginning," he says, handing it to me.

I give him a confused look and say, "You want me to take this?"

He laughs and nods, holding it a little closer to me. I cautiously take it from his hand like it might be one of those trick flowers that squirts me with water. It doesn't.

After taking two more steps, another guy, one I recognize as someone from the football team, steps up to me holding a yellow rose. "For friendship," he says.

I take that one just as cautiously as the first, and then I'm met by yet another guy. "For the impossible," he says, giving me a rose that matches the color of Brad's eyes.

This continues all the way down the hall. By the end, my arms are overflowing with at least twenty different roses in a rainbow of colors. For beauty. For happiness. For forgiveness. With every rose comes a different message. Since I don't know most of these guys, I'm sure they're not the real messengers. I search the hallway, looking for him, but he's nowhere to be found.

"Are you in on this?" I ask Brittany.

"I don't know what you're talking about," she answers with a smile, steering me around the corner.

And there he is, looking as gorgeous as ever in khakis, a button-down shirt, and even a tie. He's also holding the most humongous bouquet of red roses I've ever seen.

He takes slow steps toward me. "For love?" he whispers with raised eyebrows. "Hailey, will you be my valentine?"

I have to bite my lip to stop from smiling way too big. "This is a little over the top," I reply, stepping right in front of him.

"I fucked up really big. The apology needed to be epic."

"This is pretty epic."

"So you forgive me?"

I don't know exactly when it happened, probably because it was a gradual thing, but my anger and resentment have faded. It just seems unfair to hold one thing, even if it was a really bad thing, as more important than hundreds of good things. Plus, the good things continue day after day, tipping the scale even more.

I nod and stop biting my lip so he can see my smile. It suddenly feels like the old us.

He moves the bouquet to one hand and wraps the other around my waist, pulling me close. Lowering his mouth to my ear, he whispers, "Does this also mean you want to be my girlfriend? Like official, we're-not-hiding-it-from-anyone girlfriend?"

His breath tickles my ear and reminds me of our night in the hotel before everything fell apart. Despite our secret relationship, life seemed much easier back then.

When I don't answer, he continues, "I can't promise I'll never mess up again, but I can promise it won't be like that. From now on, I'll always be on your side. It'll be you and me against the world."

"You make us sound like superheroes," I say with a small laugh.

"Well, you do have some pretty amazing superpowers."

I give him a sideways glance.

"What? I'm serious," he replies. "You single-handedly took me from having zero interest in a girlfriend to becoming a bumbling fool laying his heart on the line in front of the entire student body despite a very high risk of rejection and complete and utter humiliation."

I glance around. He's right. Hundreds of eyes peer out at us through the windows and open doors of the cafeteria.

"It would be pretty humiliating if I threw all these flowers in your face and stalked out of here."

"Yes," he says, nodding, "but you're worth the risk."

"Because my second toe is longer than my first?"

He laughs. "It's one of the many cute things about you. Along with your eyes," he says, gently kissing my temple. "And your nose," he says, tapping it with his finger and then sliding that finger down to my mouth. "And especially your lips."

His eyes move from my eyes to my lips and back. I feel like it's our first kiss all over again. He's asking my permission without saying the words. And what I do next has the power to change everything.

If I turn my head, it's over. Maybe we stay friends until the end of school, but then we'll go our separate ways. Five years from now, the memories of him will fade to only a vague feeling of happiness and longing with a few key moments like this spotlighting him in the highlight reel of my life.

Or I can take a giant leap of faith with him. One kiss can change everything in my life once more.

He shifts from one leg to the other as he stares deep into my eyes, waiting for my decision.

I swallow and lick my suddenly dry lips.

I don't want him to make a guest appearance in my highlight reel. I want him to be my sidekick. My costar. The guy who cheers me on when things go well and cheers me up when they don't. The guy who tells me when I'm being an idiot and the one who pushes me to be more. I want him by my side for all of it.

And that's when it truly dawns on me—despite everything we've gone through and all the pain he's caused me, I still want him in my life. Because he's given me just as much, if not more, happiness and strength to believe in myself.

My fingers wind through his hair and pull his face closer. With zero hesitation, my lips land on his, and I kiss him like the world is about to be hit by a giant meteor. I feel him smiling under my lips as he pulls me even closer. "I love you, Hailey," he whispers.

From somewhere not too far away, I hear a familiar squeal and then feel Brittany wrap her arms around my back, squeezing me until it hurts. I laugh and turn toward her just as Adam and Abbie join us. Then Gigi, who must have been hiding out among the students, waiting to see what my answer would be, steps beside us.

"I love you, too," I mouth to Brad as the others fall into us, forming a massive group hug in the middle of the hallway.

I've finally found what I've always been searching for. What I've always needed.

For better or worse, these people are who I need.

They are my family.

EPILOGUE

"LAST ONE," GIL SAYS, BALANCING A BOX IN HIS ARMS AS HE lowers the back door of his SUV.

I sling a bag over my shoulder, and Gigi extends the handle of a rolling suitcase. It's the end of August, and I'm officially moving into my college dorm. College. How crazy is that? I pinched myself about a hundred times on the drive here, convinced the last year was just a really long dream and I was bound to wake up any minute.

Of course, if this were all a dream, I could've done without the Chase and Michelle drama. Luckily, we've had no more of that. Chase told me where the Meier was, but that was all. I was grateful the Campbells got that painting back, but it wasn't enough for me to ask them not to press charges. So he was convicted of felony larceny and sentenced to almost three years in prison.

The good news is the cops also found the Warhol. Apparently, Chase's cousin took it to a pawn shop and the dealer thought the whole thing was suspicious, so she alerted the police.

Gil and Gigi decided not to press charges against Michelle after she bawled her eyes out when they confronted her. She said Chase was only supposed to steal a TV or two. When she stopped by after the fact to leave the note, she was appalled by all the damage and instantly regretted what she had done. Of course, she didn't regret it enough to come clean. Regardless, Gil and Gigi talked to her mom about getting her into therapy. I have no idea if she's going, because she stopped hanging out with us. No one but Abbie was disappointed, although even Abbie's relationship with her went downhill. By the end of school, I rarely saw them together.

"There he is," Gigi says, tilting her head to the far end of the parking lot. There, far from any other cars, is Brad's black BMW. The door flies open, and then he sprints over to us.

He gives me a quick kiss before saying, "Sorry I'm late. Practice went long."

His red face and practice clothes make it clear he got here as quickly as he could. "Looks like it was a tough practice," I say, wiping his sweaty bangs from his eyes.

"Yeah, but good. We're coming together as a team." Brad's been living at Duke for about a month now. They require football players to get there early so they can have some hard-core practice before school and the season start.

It was difficult being away from him, but my two jobs helped make the time pass faster. Ms. Gonzalez let both me and Brittany stay with her throughout the summer, but we insisted on paying some of the bills, because it was obvious she struggled without the DSS checks.

And, luckily, Brad and I still got to see each other on weekends. Either he came back to Pinehurst or Gigi drove me to Durham, where I stayed with him in his on-campus apartment.

"Did you make dinner reservations?" Gil asks.

Brad replies, "Yeah. Vin Rouge at seven. It's a French place."

"My favorite," Gigi says with a smile.

"Really? I had no idea." He grins and then gives her and his dad a hug. After he takes the suitcase from Gigi, we head up to my room, where we pile our things next to a few other boxes.

"Should we start unpacking?" Brad asks.

"Actually, there's a campus tour in a few minutes. I thought it might help me learn my way around."

"Let's go," he says, holding open the door.

Fifteen minutes later, after saying bye to Gil and Gigi, who headed back to their hotel, Brad and I are at the student union, waiting for the tour to start. On the wall are oversized metallic letters for the name of the school: NCCU. NC Central. My school.

"Can you take my picture?" I ask, handing Brad my phone. I stand in front of the letters with a ridiculous grin and two thumbs-up.

"You're such a goofball," he says with a laugh, shaking his head and giving me back my phone after snapping a picture.

"Sherry will appreciate it."

While I'm sending it to her, he checks his phone. "You're not the only goofball," he says, turning it so I can see. There's a picture of Brittany and Adam standing next to Rameses, the Carolina mascot, and hamming it up.

"But they're just"—I use air quotes—" 'friends.' " I can't stop my eye roll. Those two might as well be a couple. They spent practically every free moment of the summer together, and with them going to the same college, it looks like that will continue indefinitely. "You really need to have a talk with Adam."

"I have. Multiple times."

"Brittany told me they made a pact to get married if they were both still single at thirty."

"Well, there you go. She finally got him to commit."

"For like twelve years from now!"

He shrugs. "That's better than nothing, right?"

"I'm glad you didn't pull an Adam with me."

He laughs. "I think it was more likely you were going to pull an Adam with me. You made me wait two months!"

"You needed time to realize your mistake."

"It took me less than five minutes to realize my mistake after you left. I should've chased after you that night."

I smile and shake my head. As painful as it was, the time apart was good for me.

"Anyway," Brad says, "Brittany and Adam are coming to dinner. Maybe you can bring it up then."

I can't believe how everything came together. We're at three different colleges, but they're only fifteen minutes apart from one another. I was accepted at another school—one in the western part of the state—but knowing Brad, Brittany, and Adam would be close to me here made my decision easy. While I'd like to think I can take on the entire world by myself, other people definitely make it easier. I don't have to do everything on my own. I know Brittany and Adam will step up in a heartbeat like they did when

Gil kicked me out. And Brad will never turn his back on me again. I truly believe that.

He steps next to me and wraps his arm around my back, leaving his hand on my waist. With a squeeze, he says, "I'm so proud of you."

I smile up at him. "I'm proud of me, too."

"You should be. You're a college girl now." He squeezes my waist again and adds, "My college girl."

Those words cause the hair on my arms to stand up, my heart to beat wildly in my chest, and my lips to spread into a massive grin. I did it. Against all odds, I'm actually making something of my life. And, while I know my past will always be a part of me, I'm not going to let it define me. I can do whatever I want. Be whatever I want.

I've got this.

ACKNOWLEDGMENTS

First and foremost, I'd like to thank Sara Mack, not only for being my writing partner and one of my best friends but also for coming up with the title of *Love Me, Love Me Not*. She's saved me more than a few times when my creative spark has been completely extinguished. I also have to give a shout-out to her daughter Syd for being my go-to girl for everything teen related.

Next is Joelle, who manages my writing life behind the scenes. I would be lost without her!

Next is Kat, my very patient editor. Although I was initially skeptical of our differences, I'm thrilled with the give-and-take approach we both used to completely transform the story, and I can't imagine a better editor for this project.

Next are my parents for instilling in me a love of reading, and Glen, my husband, for all the support and many extra hours of childcare he's provided so I can fulfill my dream of becoming a published author.

Finally are my beta readers, Jenn, Melissa, and Stacy, and all the Swoon Readers who made this book a possibility. Thanks for all your support and feedback. This book exists because of you!